Gimme the
Familiars
by
Jessica Mehta

from
Musehick Publications

Musehick Publications
musehickpublications.com

Gimme the Familiars

Jessica Mehta

author of

Constellations of My Body
Savagery
Orygun
Secret-Telling Bones
The Wrong Kind of Indian
What Makes an Always The
Last Exotic Petting Zoo

ACKNOWLEDGEMENTS

Thank you to editor Britney McEntire, who took on a project wildly different than what she likely saw coming. For respecting my voice, my vision, and making these stories—many of them my stories—worlds better than they were when newborn and trembling with big, wet eyes.
Thank you to Diane Covington, member of the Sanpoil Band of Colville Confederated Tribes, for creating and offering such gorgeous cover art. Discover more of her beauty at www.ChargingBuzzardStudio.com. Thank you to Paul Grimsley of Musehick Publications for taking a chance on a manuscript that burst through boundaries. Not every publisher would be so daring (trust me, I know).
Thank you to my husband, Chintan. It is not easy being the partner of a writer (or so I have heard). But you stand by me, dogged.

DEDICATION
For Chintan, my last best chapter—and the hungriest wolf.

Gimme the Familiars
A hybrid short story collection/mythology re-imagining

*A note on this manuscript: *Gimme the Familiars* is a connected short story collection steeped in memoir. Each chapter begins with a "mini chapter" that's a re-telling of a Native American myth. As a Cherokee writer, I included mostly Cherokee myths which were first told to me as a child. However, all are completely re-imagined, original work, and placed in a modern setting. The mini chapters are connected closely to each of the matching chapters, with the animals in the myths correlating to the monsters, heroes, and forgotten everyones we know in in our daily lives.
(Ourselves included).

i.   The Buzzard of the Highways

He watched from his post on the evergreen top, that one good tree that was could carry his pride. The other branches, the weak ones of the pear trees and the hybrid apples, they shook and wailed under his hooked feet like scared things. Desperate things. The types of things he glanced over, flipped his top knot like they were so ridiculous in his presence, but they were. They couldn't help it, those struggling branches, and not even the Oregon moss gave them a coat thick enough to act tough. Not like the buzzard would have noticed anyway. Not like he cared.

The four-wheeled monsters, the two-wheeled ones, they whipped by fast along the asphalt, as fast as he could fly. But they were scooted along in the filth, and sometimes their bellies scraped the bumps. Pathetic little things. Sometimes they were just as useless as the prey he watched sprint across the yellow, dashed lines.

Buzzard tousled his top knot over his scapular, glorious atop the world. Death was beneath him, bits of snake pancaked from a worn-out wheel. An hour ago, he'd watched it happen and for just a moment—he swore it, just a slip of time—he'd thought about snatching the slithering miniature beast for himself. Then it wriggled of course, spilling over with life and energy. He hadn't even been hungry, wasn't even thinking of slipping scales and long, long bone between his beak today. Snake was tough, not his favorite. But the eyes he could imagine popping in his throat, juices sluicing quick into his belly. And the tongue, the tongue. He liked to think of it splitting all the way to its other end, filling him with ribbony pieces of pink that soaked into his hollow bones.

Just look at them down there, pitiful and shrieking at each other. Crow bounced around ridiculous, pecking between wing flutters of the Vultures. "You're pathetic," he called down from his perch, waiting between the highway horn blows to rain down his judgments.

"Says who?" Young Vulture asked, tiny entrails spraying from his beak. "The one who thinks he's too good for us, sitting fat like a God in his tree?"

"Disgusting," said Buzzard. "All of you, the lot of you. Eating deadness. Eating trash." Young Vulture fluffed himself, rolled his eyes as his elders shushed him. Crow, he never spoke to Buzzard, pretended like he couldn't hear. Stupid, Buzzard knew he heard all.

As dusk slid its slippery black fingers over the pines, Young Vulture played the afternoon over and over in his head. Idiot Buzzard, so prideful. So vain. Him and his stupid pile of hair-feathers balanced like a crown in the sky. "Why's he gotta do that?" he asked his elders, but they quieted him like always with no answers. And he was sick of it.

Young Vulture, he knew where Buzzard slept. Knew the tree where he buried down in the night, the one with the wires wrapped around it and the bed made of dried grass and decaying pine cones. And he knew Buzzard slept well, slept hard, stomach full and heavy with the dying animals he'd snatched that day, their blood keeping him warm 'til morning.

He waited until the nests in his own tower were quiet all around him, nothing but the dream-induced fluffing and quivers in the purple sky. Grabbing the old knife from the storage branch, the rusty one that still held sharpness, he tucked it into his claw and delighted in its weight. He'd never touched it before, though he'd loved it the minute his brother had carried it home. "What are you, a magpie?" his mother had laughed. He'd always adored the shiniest things. Only then, with the slicer cradled like a scared rat below him, did he leave the roost, hop in silence from the commune before taking a wobbly flight into the deep.

Buzzard's nest wasn't far, and Young Vulture knew he'd be back before anyone would miss him. *I thought I'd seen a mouse. Today's carrion made me feel ill.* He ran over the excuses, rolled them across his tongue to make them taste natural in case any elders saw him come back and required an excuse. Something believable.

He'd never seen Buzzard's nest up close. The smell was different, the acid from the pines making it softer and warmer than his own. And he slept different than Young Vulture's elders, not curled up nearly as tightly. He slept alone, could spread out and let his feathers fall like grace across the branches. Now, in this moment, he looked almost peaceful.

His top knot, it really was beautiful, thick and grand. Young Vulture didn't really get the point of such a vanity, but like everyone else he admired it. Not that he'd ever tell Buzzard that (nobody did), but it was Fact. His own head was clean and bald, not a single feather to be found. It's what made him ugly.

The snip was over fast, but the memory burned into his brain. The sound the top knot made when the knife flashed through it. How it felt so much lighter than he'd imagined clutched in his talons. Buzzard didn't even move and now—now—now, now, now ...

Buzzard was ugly, too.

Fear gripped Young Vulture on the brief flight back, even as the river beneath him glistened like the shiniest of all greatness. And the top knot grew heavier, heavier in his grip, so heavy he couldn't keep hold. So he let go, let all that beauty get wrapped up in the winds and scattered like droppings to the earth below. The knife, too, the evidence of his badness.

Young Vulture slept late, a rarity for him. Like the rest of his family, he was often up early, eager to see what treats had been broken, beaten and splayed open like a gift on the black flattops below. Why didn't anyone wake him? Why was everyone lined up like dutiful soldiers on the big wire?

"What time—" he began to ask his mother as he settled next to her, his eyes still full of sleep.

"Shh," she said, motioning to the earth.

What seemed like miles below, Buzzard was hunched, looking bald and naked, amongst the empty cans and discarded sandwich wrappers. In his feet, a smashed squirrel's head lolled backwards. Young Vulture could smell the wheel-death of the big-tailed animal from way up here.

"Is he ... why's he eating carrion?" he asked his mother. She shrugged, eyes embarrassed for the poor thing, and nudged her son back to the nest.

Chapter One

Sex starts small, I learned that young. I was four, and (like most inching towards Kindergarten), I don't remember much. I remember this—standing on the autumn leaves while my father built a little house for me in the backyard. Years later, it would be home to the big pool pump even after the water had dried up and the lining got cracked. I remember finger painting with my mother on the rickety metal card table in the living room, her screaming at me to be happy and enjoy myself. I hated finger painting, it made me feel dirty. I remember the eyes of the Indian woman in the hallway painting, how they'd watch me no matter which way I walked, and how she'd only do it when nobody else was looking.

And I remember the time in the bathtub.

Our water came from the well, and I hated the taste. Like metal gone bad. Sometimes it had a rusty color, and I didn't want to bathe in it, but my mom didn't believe in showers. Demanded that baths were relaxing and, like her, I was only allowed to soak. But I'd throw a fit when the water was too brown, so she'd squirt in half a bottle of blue food coloring to bury my silence. "It's like a lagoon! A tropical paradise. Hawaii," she'd crow, even though she'd never been anywhere beaches were warm. She'd only seen the sands of Oregon, and we called them coasts here. And once, once, I'd been told we'd seen the blinding white sands of Florida, but I wasn't sure that was true. She said I was still in diapers and didn't remember, and the people in the pictures looked like they were in a play. My mom looked too young, my dad didn't have his moustache, and the baby they held had nothing of me in it. Those blue eyes in the photos had long turned to Cherokee green.

And sometimes not even the blue food coloring satisfied me. I swear, I could still see the grains of the filth. The well's underbelly would sneak in through the pipes, deposit a dusting of what I was sure were crushed insects along the porcelain floor. I wouldn't get in. "Jesus Christ, Justine," my mom would say, and then glub-glub half a cup of dish soap in the tub. It covered the secrets up, but I could still feel the broken bugs on my too-thick thighs and flat butt. I just knew enough not to complain anymore.

I'd stay in the bathroom for an hour. It didn't matter that the water went cold or that every last bubble popped. I didn't care that the dish soap dried up my skin so much that it began to pain, or that I could feel the slime of it seeping into my pores. That my hair, no matter how many times I dunked it, never really got truly clean in the soupy well water. I was told that *this* was Relaxing Time and it was the *only* time my mother left me alone. When I was ready to get out, I had to call her. She hated the thought of leaving soap to line and sit in the tub, so I'd have to stand as the water drained and she hosed down each piece of the liner, inch by inch. Once the escaping water reached my feet that looked just like hers, she'd start to hose me down, too. The well, it was running dry, and by then the water from the hose was always almost-cool at best. Usually, it had gone cold. And she'd have me spin, turn, hold up my hair to spray down my slippery neck. At four, I'd already learned fast to hate this process. It was like being one of those hanged, headless, skinless animals at the slaughterhouse down the street. Hooked and waiting for the butchery to be done while my insides, my private areas, were on display.

We had one bathroom in the entire house, and so I wasn't allowed to lock the door. My mom, in the summer, would always be in the yard, covering our one, long acre in discount perennials. Tending to the marijuana that she planted along with the tomato plants because they looked kind of alike. Pulling up weeds, yelling at my dad to mow the grass, swatting away the latest animal she had acquired, shrieking at it to behave against its instinct and act like she thought it should. Goats, turkeys, ponies, and rabbits. Sometimes, her or my dad would come into the bathroom, pull down their pants to defecate or stream yellow into the chipped bowl. I could only see the flanks of their thighs when this happened, the toilet was on the other side of the bathtub wall with the sawed-off spout. My mom's white-white jiggly side-butt or my dad's milk chocolate cream with the sparse black hairs. It always shocked me, how much lighter his Indian skin was on the parts where the sun couldn't reach. To me, he was Hershey brown, a color that must have run out of me in birth.

Sometimes they'd say something to me, most times they didn't. Especially not my dad—I don't think he knew what to say. But this time, when I was squarely Four, I was well-armed. I was always swimming in toys, always used, always garage sale finds he would bring to me in soft, worn-out boxes from his Saturday hunts. My favorite was a plastic alligator squirt gun. My mom hated that, that I often went to the boy toys instead of the cutesy stuff she liked. She hated that I hated *Sesame Street* and picked *He-Man* or *Thundercats* when I had a choice. She hated that I didn't like dresses, preferred the black t-shirts with monsters on them. Werewolves, vampires and Frankensteins.

Just a month ago, my mom had painted big, fat blue raindrops everywhere on the bathroom walls. I had to help, and it was obvious which were mine and which were hers. Mine were fast, hurried. I didn't want to be doing it. She did that, stuff like that. Our house was the weird one, but I was just now figuring out to be embarrassed. Embarrassment is something that comes in random bursts, like a growth. I guess it has to be that way, doesn't it? Otherwise babies would be way too embarrassed with their poop and vomit and nipple sucking to ever get big. Embarrassment was coming in buckets to me that summer, like it had gotten lazy and was playing catch up.

It had only been a couple of weeks since the last big embarrassment. My mom, determined that I would know everything about sex since she had known nothing, had blasted words like *penis* and *vagina* at me since before I could remember. *Intercourse, sex, orgasm, sperm.* They were as common to me as *yellow, blue, rectangle,* and *square.* She didn't want me to be like her, turn thirteen years old and come home crying because a boy had accidentally brushed his khaki-clad Penis against me in the school hallway and thinking I might be pregnant. So two weeks ago, while I stood on a chair playing with my dad's long black hair, twisting it into twin mounts on top of my head and giggling, I caught myself when my mom walked by and asked, "What are you doing?"

"I'm making him horny." I heard it, my try at making a joke—horns to horny—turn to filth between my lips. I knew it before I saw the shift in his eyes, before I felt the silence shoot at me from my mother's presence. And I said nothing, just let go of his locks and scooted back down off the chair.

"What are you doing?"

My dad had come into the bathroom so quiet I hadn't even heard the footsteps in the hall. He could do that, unlike my mom. Move like a cat, like a big sneaky thing. Her footsteps always announced themselves from what felt like miles away, a lumbering lack of grace before her musky smell announced itself.

"Nothing," I told him. He stood before the vanity mirror, the one that opened with a soft press to reveal his green Barasol can that turned the shelves dark red. His old razor. My mom's dull tweezers and silver hair clips. His back to me, he watched me in the mirror as he lathered his face. Like snow spreading across peaks and mountains. Something had changed in him. This mask, the snowy one, I'd seen hundreds of times. But always, I'd known what was below. Thought I'd known. It was my dad, the one who would drink an entire liter of Coke and half a can of peanuts. The one who took me to the Red Barn Auction on Thursday nights, to McDonald's for their spongy pancakes and warm syrup on Saturday mornings after the first best garage sales had been ransacked. The one who flew me around like I was a plane in the photos, who grew that moustache because I got to watch *Born in East L.A.* and thought he looked just like Cheech Marin. "Grow a moustache! Grow a moustache!" I'd begged of him, and he had. It came in slow, so we all got used to it together. Now, it was the dad in the photos that looked like a stranger. I couldn't remember what his full upper lip looked like anymore, but I knew what his moustache looked like after he ate all those peanuts. Dusted in salt and little nut skin flakes.

What are you doing? What are you doing. He said these words for a different reason than my mom. Because it made him sound like he cared, and he knew my answer would be short. My mom asked because she had to know everything, didn't realize that children came with their own deep-inside personalities that she couldn't keep choke-collar tight. I'd seen that after the horny incident, saw her face scrambling to contain the wild animal she thought she'd spotted in me. I wanted to explain that it was a joke, that my words came faster than my head could manage, but that would just make it worse. Wouldn't it? Wouldn't that just make it worse?

My dad's face was half white snow now, the top half the same brown skin as always and those green-gold eyes. They crawled over me like insects, and I could feel the itchy dead bodies at my legs again. They had disappeared when I'd first lowered myself into the water. But now that water was cool, the bubbles gone, and the false blue wasn't enough to offer any comfort. There were dark bits floating at the surface now, too. What body parts might those be? Maybe tiny little alien eyes, or a leg all akimbo. Flecks stuck to my skin where the water licked at my belly. My sides. Right below my nipples. And I was ashamed.

It was like in Sunday School, how they tell you about Adam and Eve. Eat the wrong thing, and you get embarrassed all at once. Not over time like you're supposed to. I don't know if my dad had ever changed my diaper. Given me a bath when I was too little to do it myself. I know he'd never hosed me off—that was my mom's job.

"You gon' stay in there much longer?" he asked as he picked up the razor, held the blade to his cheek. It was old, and I knew he'd cut himself. Leave the bathroom with bloody bits of paper stuck like bows at the sharpest angles. His Oklahoma accent spilt something fierce through his snow-flaked lips.

"I don't know," I said. *Penis. Vagina.* I could see the start of my vagina at the depths of the blue, blue water. His eyes kept marching over me. Down my throat to rest in the hollow of my collarbone. Across my shoulders, peeling from the early summer shine. He carved out a piece of brown from the white, the soft scrape-scrape sound echoing in the tiny room. He'd shut the bathroom door. Why had he shut the door? It was too small with two people in here, the raindrop walls moving uncomfortably close. It was pouring.

"Hmm," he said, revealing another section of skin. His chin, the one unlike mine. Mine was like my mom's, a slight dimple. *Butt-face*, that one boy had called me at Vacation Bible School. Jesus hadn't cared, just kept staring at the ceiling from the big cross up front, eyes faded and looking bored. Not like my dad's eyes. They moved to my upper arms, the ones I already knew were too big.

"You can always tell when a girl is gonna be fat by her upper arms," my mom would say, pointing out girls my age, younger, older, it didn't matter. "It's all in the arms," she'd say, with a sad shake of her head. "It's a terrible thing, to have to watch your weight your whole life. God, what I would give to be thin and rich. That's all I want in my next life."

In my water-logged fingers, the hollow alligator nuzzled close. I could fill it with one hand, I'd been practicing. Like an army man, and I hadn't even known a war was coming. Just knew, like instinct. I had to be able to load this gun one-handed, simple as that. Slow, careful, tucking the alligator against my hip I pulled his orange syringe like I was lapping up all the poison. He grew heavier in my palm, didn't want to pop up to the surface anymore. He was so full with the water, he was happy to stay weighted and deadly 'til I was ready.

My dad moved the razor against the long moustache hairs, careful to keep each side equally thick. It must have been hard to do without looking. Or maybe you get used to it. I wanted to see if he'd locked the door or just closed it, but I couldn't. I couldn't look away, or his eyes could race too fast to somewhere they shouldn't be.

To my elbows they went, the crooks of them at the water's surface. The razor slid to his throat. His eyes to my nipples. Now. The alligator attacked.

It was perfect, not a sound or a splash. I took aim like I always did, arm stretched out, trigger ready. But I shot for his face, the one in the mirror with the searching eyes, and the alligator vomited a blue stream all across his back.

"Goddamnit!" he yelled, raking the razor across his barely-there Adam's apple and it went from white to bright red in a second. "What the—Rhoda! Rhoda!" he yelled, calling for my mom. Her heavy feet slapped against the linoleum in the kitchen, just a few steps away.

"Jimmy? What is it? Is Justi—" she screamed from behind the door, and it flew open. It wasn't locked, wasn't locked, wasn't locked. "What happened?" she asked, scanning him as he clutched a wash rag to his throat, me sitting with my knees drawn up to cover my nipples.

"She shot me!" he said, like he couldn't believe it himself.

"Justine! What the hell are you doing?" she asked.

"No, I—I didn't do it. It was the alligator." It was the truth.

Animals, they work together—especially after Man crept up so close, he pushed the Wild Ones to act unnatural. It's why they pair cheetahs with abandoned dogs at some zoos, putting on a freakshow as the two beasts race after fake rabbits on worn-out trails. Skunk knew this. Coyote knew this. It didn't matter that they were both still wild things. In each other, they saw salvation.

Skunks bed down together to suckle on each other's warmth. It's only for the cold seasons, otherwise they roam unattached, digging through garbage cans or noses tucked into dog dishes on patios with their cactus tails straight up. Coyotes, well, they eat anything. A death thing. A rotting thing. Steal the slowest chickens from urban farmers.

"Don't look at me like that," said Skunk, keeping his black beady eyes on Coyote who slunk behind a fall-apart plastic slide.

"Like what?"

"Like I'd fit between your teeth." Unlike so many of the others, the ones designed to blend into their world and disappear, Skunk stood out. His stripe let them all know to stand away. Stay away.

"I'm not," said Coyote. "I was just thinking … you know, we could both have a lot more. Eat a lot more. If maybe we teamed up."

Skunk looked up from the bowl, the expensive kibbles tumbling down his oily black chest. "You want to be my partner?" he asked. "I know what you'd get out of it. What about me?" Skunk knew so many others shrank back into the darkness when they saw him. Gagged and forced vomit to stay in their throats when he stamped his foot and raised his tail higher.

"Same as you," Coyote said. "More food. Fresh food. None of this stolen dog food shit."

"You want to kill with me," said Skunk, tasting the idea in his salty mouth. "I can't kill the big ones. You know that. What do you have in mind?"

"Make me look dead," said Coyote. He'd practiced this whole speech. "Then tell everyone else. Lure them close, get them all excited. Adrenaline, it makes the meat sweeter. Like those Korean dogs they torture before they make them into stew. Then, you'll smash their heads in when they're all drooling over me." He liked this detail. The idea that thinking they could have him would made them go mad, override their senses.

"Huh," said Skunk. "It could work."

And it did.

Skunk covered coyote's body with dirt, grabbed fistfuls of the wet red mulch from the rose garden of an old woman who lived on the corner. It made Coyote look smothered in dried blood. "Let your tongue hang out," Skunk told him.

"Like this?" Coyote asked, lopping his tongue onto the cooling pavement. They'd chosen an abandoned basketball court, one where a hoop was dangerously hanging on and the smell of Man was almost entirely gone.

"Perfect," said Skunk.

Skunk didn't like it, rallying all the stupid beasts to fawn over a fake, dead coyote. And he swore, he swore he saw Coyote's rib cage rising and falling. But nobody else noticed.

"How do we know he's really dead?" asked Cat.

"Yeah," said Raccoon. "How do we know?"

"You eat garbage, what do you know?" asked Fawn, the runt who'd so stupidly stolen away from her mother when Skunk had whispered *Come with me, come here. I have something for you.* Too young, too dumb to realize she didn't eat animals.

"What, you think I don't have anything better to do than make up stories for you?" said Skunk. *Hurry, hurry, hurry,* he thought.

"Well," said Raccoon. "I mean, I guess he *looks* dead."

"I've never tasted Kay-oh-pee," said Fawn.

"Obviously," said Cat.

Skunk ran his long toenail along the gardening spade he'd tucked below Coyote's flanks. "That hurts!" Coyote had said when he'd shoved it there, hard. "Shut up," Skunk had hissed.

"Seriously, you don't believe me?" said Skunk. "Look closer. When Coyotes are dead, their teeth turn to cherry pits."

"Bullshit," said Raccoon, but he and the others leaned closer. Their shaking little back-heads to him, Skunk yanked out the spade and beat them fast, moving from Raccoon to Cat to Fawn, the most dangerous to the least.

"You get 'em? You get 'em?" Coyote asked immediately, hearing the breaking of their thin skulls, their dead weight on his limbs.

"I got them," said Skunk.

Together, they dragged the bodies to the fire pit in the park, the ones used to overcook hamburgers and split hot dog skins in the summer. Skunk had to admit, Coyote was useful here. He could carry more quicker and easier. It was like having a personal assistant and cook in one mangy, dense package. But it took a long time to get their prizes roasting. Coyote wanted to dump them right on the grill, didn't care about the acrid smell of burning hair. Skunk was the one who demanded a proper cleaning, even as their stomachs railed in the quiet night.

"I'm *hungry*," said Coyote.

"We both are. Just wait."

"No, I mean, I'm really, *really* hungry," said Coyote. "Hey! I have an idea."

"God. Let's hear it."

"What if—what if we have a race? To the school bus parking lot and back. Whoever wins, they get all the food."

"What? That's stup—" began Skunk, but then he saw it. Coyote was getting desperate, not thinking straight. And Skunk was hungry too, after all. *Screw it.* "Actually, fine," said Skunk. "Okay. But let's make it to the ugly memorial by the river. And your legs are so much longer and you're so much faster. I get a one-minute head start."

"Yeah, yeah," said Coyote, foam speckling across his black lips already at the thought of having all the bodies to himself. "Whatever."

"Okay," said Skunk. "You count down from five, and then I'll go."

He didn't even need the one-minute head start. Didn't think Coyote would be truthful about it anyway. He just needed enough time to slip into the mole tunnel he'd nearly fallen into helping to drag their kills to the fire pit. When he heard Coyote ramble over the hole, smelled the excitement pumping through the air, he waited another thirty seconds. Just in case. The ugly memorial by the river was a ten-minute round trip run, much farther than the school bus parking lot. He had plenty of time.

The bodies on the grill were on the redder side of done, but that's how he liked it. With practiced hands, Skunk carved out the choicest pieces for himself. The eyes of the Fawn, the blooming chest of Cat, the heart and hindquarters of Raccoon. Eating as he went, smacking his lips and tearing off the best roasted bits, he buried everything else he could in the mole hole, covered it up with leaves and pissed all around it so Coyote couldn't sniff it out.

But the best part? The best part was when he climbed the tree and waited for Coyote's returned. Listening to the hunger howls and screams of betrayal that rained out of Coyote's mouth.

"Idiot," whispered Skunk as Coyote circled, circled, circled in disbelief across the cracked pavement.

Chapter Two

In 1996, the internet was a new thing. I'd already learned how to kind of use the card catalogue at the library, and my mom had demanded my dad overpay for the outdated Encyclopedia Brittanicas at a garage sale, even though the "S" book was missing. Neither of them had gone to college. They'd barely graduated high school, and my dad went straight from the Indian boarding school to prison before he was twenty. Still, it was my mom's greatest hope—her requirement—that I go to college. She couldn't say why or how. Couldn't map out what college even was or how to get there, but I was her last hope for a decent reflection and I couldn't fuck it up.

The small Oregon town was suffocating me, the valley walls closing in. Just a few miles away, less than an hour, was California, but that hope had dried up. It wasn't like I'd thought. Just cross the border and there would be beaches, pretty girls with tan skin, and a hangover of what I'd dreamt the teenage years would be from 80s movies. No, I'd found that out on those Godawful family road trips to Great America where my mom yelled the whole time and would only let me each the ham and cheese sandwiches she packed because gas station food was too expensive. I was fifteen, it was summer, and I instantly despised the big, lumbering box my dad had dragged home from the electronics store.

It was a big deal, getting something new and from one of those overpriced stores. But, "Justine needs a computer!" my mom had told my dad in her harsh, cracking voice. She didn't know what they were for, not really, but they were the future. Plus, if you got a certain kind, it came with 50 free hours of internet on an AOL CD. You could buy more hours later if you wanted. But I didn't know what any of that meant.

The computer was set up in our tiny living room, nesting on the old mahogany desk between the vinyl divan and bookcase that cradled my dad's cigarettes and dozens of video tapes my mom had taken over the years. *JC tap dance, JC bday 1987, JC GS camp and saxaphone recitel.* Her shaky handwriting with the big, swooping C's were plastered on every tape and I hated it. Hated the wobbly top of her J's and constant misspellings.

But now I had the internet. Like the starved, it didn't take long to find the chat rooms.

My handle was VelvetBelle. Belle for beautiful, velvet because my favorite pair of underwear, my most grownup ones, were a green velvet thong. Like my panties, the secrecy of my handle roots were the most delicious of all. My mom had no idea what it meant. My dad didn't care.

Being on the computer, no matter what you were doing, was a positive sign. It meant your kids were soaking up skills and knowledge that they'd surely need for—well, for something, certainly. For a week, my mom hovered over my shoulder. "What's that?" "Do this." "Try that." She adored the Paint software, wanted me to spend hours creating a masterpiece she could print out and hang on the wall. Like the past ten years of forced watercolor and sketching classes weren't enough, all in that old woman's house who force fed me oatmeal raisin cookies.

"Oh my *God*, do you want to do this?" I'd ask her, and she'd smack the back of my head.

"You little shit," she'd say. "Pick up your fucking glass over there." It was worth it, the sting of her palm and the bite of her words. Even the stupid walk from the living room to the kitchen to dump the diluted Diet Rite into the sink, because I knew when I went back she'd be gone.

We had the computer just three months before Don found me in the Teens chatroom. "A/S/L?" he asked me. I could tell by how he talked, the adultness in his voice, that he was out of reach.

"20," I told him. "F, Oregon." The icon for a private message popped up, and just like that this stranger stepped in and saved me.

He was 19 from a tiny town in Texas I'd never heard of. Years later, it would be a hot spot for a hate crime dripping in homophobia. He had a single photo of himself, and it was blurry but you could tell he was a *man*. The hints towards broad shoulders and thick thighs were unlike any of the boys in my freshman class. Even unlike most of the seniors that rambled into the dirt parking lot in their dented-up trucks.

When I told Melody about him, her eyes shone for the first time since she'd started dating Chaz.

"Oh, my God!" she screamed. "Are you gonna meet him? You should make him come here, and we can go on a double date."

"I don't know," is all I could tell her. Because I didn't. I wanted to impress her, this girl I'd glued myself to since sixth grade. Part Hawaiian with big lips and hair so long and thick it had to be thinned every time she went to the salon, I knew Melody was above me. What I didn't know is why she put up with me, let me cling to the hem of her social skirts while she wafted down the hallways with all those jealous, wanting eyes on her. I'd been hoping, for a while now, that some of what she had would rub off on me. Maybe it had, now that Don hadn't seen her, couldn't see her first.

He and I moved from private chat rooms and email to phone calls fast. If I had any doubts that he wasn't who he said he was, they disappeared with that deep voice. He was originally from Colorado, not Texas, so there was no drawl to remind me of my father. It was just steady, rocky deep man voice. When I sent him photos, he told me I was beautiful. I chose ones where there were stampedes of other girls around me, pictures from last year's Miss Junior Oregon pageant I had been forced into, or class field trip photos when I happened to be assigned to sit next to the super tall girls. They'd look older, make me look older, but I already had the excuses ready to go. "They're older photos," I told Don and he'd say, "I thought you looked young."

I wanted to open my world to him, so I took photos of all the rooms in the house and gave the roll to my dad to develop, too trusting in my stupidity. "These look like crime scene photos!" he'd yelled when he got home, splaying them out to my mother. "You trying to get us robbed?" he'd asked me, and I refused to speak to him. Even though, seeing the photos, he was kind of right.

After five months, Don began to break. Always talking about his ex-girlfriend, a Broncos cheerleader, who was total perfection in her hapa skin and slinky black hair. "One time," he told me, "we just stared into each other's eyes for hours. It was so romantic. Would you want to do that?" I said yes because it's what he wanted. I'd never even kissed a boy, and I was sure Melody had already given up her virginity to Chaz, her cocaine-adled boyfriend who was already eighteen. She didn't say it, not outright, but hinted so heavily with drawing of "correct" cocks in science class that she was begging for me to ask. I wouldn't, wouldn't give her that leverage.

But she just wouldn't shut up. Not about Chaz, not about how sad it was that I would turn 16 after everyone else, not about how Don would come to Oregon if he really, really loved me. Not that he said he loved me, or even hinted at it. The hours we spent on the phone every day seemed to be adding up to nothing. He worked, sometimes, at a video store but otherwise hunkered down into his grandmother's spare bedroom. I never asked why he was in Texas now and not Colorado, or what happened with his cheerleader girlfriend. Why they weren't together. I was happy marinating in the little world we'd created, one where my joy was dictated by the ring of a phone.

Don almost always called me, so my mom never questioned who I was talking to. Simply basked in the knowing that her daughter was talking to someone, anyone. That I must have friends, be popular—or, even better, evoke jealousy in others at school. It was my dad who figured it out.

"She's going wild," I heard him tell my mom, the thin wall between our bedrooms as effective as a veil.

"She's fine," my mom said.

"Rhoda, I'm telling you … something's not right."

She sighed. "Fine," she said. "I'll talk to her."

The next day when Don called, my mom swooped on the phone like an animal starving for prey. "Is this Don?" she asked. I could hear his thick voice on the other end, but not the words. "Uh huh," my mom said. "Do you know she's fifteen?" My heart changed tempo, went from an upbeat mad race to that dull, aching throb that happens when fear of getting caught turns into the happening of it.

For some reason, I don't know why, she still gave me the phone. Don still talked to me. But something had changed, and it wasn't all in his voice. I was losing him. Losing him, even when Melody still had Chaz. Even when I'd never seen more of Don than that one grainy photo, his dark blond hair to his earlobes and cargo shorts hanging off hips. "I thought maybe something was up," he said.

"Yeah. I just … I don't know."

"Me either," he said. The phone calls didn't stop all at once, but they shortened. He was working more, and my embarrassment made words stick in my throat.

"Hey," I whispered to Melody after I hadn't heard from Don in three weeks. "Guess what?" She leaned toward me, eager for any kind of gossip to distract from what we should be doing, firing up Bunsen burners and writing down pointless numbers.

"What?" she asked.

"Don came this weekend."

"Are you serious?" she asked, dropping her pencil and turning her full body towards me. This was it, what I wanted. Her total attention on me.

"Yeah."

"Did you—did you have sex?" she asked.

"Yeah."

"Seriously? Where? Why didn't you call me?"

I had the whole thing drawn up in my head. This is how it happened: Don kind of surprised me with his visit, though he'd hinted at coming for a while now. I didn't want to tell Melody in case it fell through. But he stayed at a hotel, the local one in Central Point with the peeling green paint. No, my mom didn't know. Neither did my dad. I told them I was walking to Suzy's house, my Kindergarten friend who lived in a hoarder house half a mile up the street. Melody hadn't ever met Suzy, but she'd heard of her— Suzy dropped out of school in seventh grade. But, really, it was Don who was picking me up in the church parking lot with all the good, hidden parking spots. Oh, the first time? The very first time? No, it wasn't in his hotel room. Actually, I never even went in his room because it was such a small hotel and the owner worked the registration booth. We didn't want her getting suspicious, because what if she could tell I was underage? (And what if Melody somehow knew what the insides of those hotel rooms looked like? What if she asked?). Instead, it all played out in the local Medford pool—yes, the one that was closed this time of year but didn't have the permanent cover on it because they were prepping it for summer hours. Oh, it was easy! Really! Just climb over the fence. Everyone knew the wires were so thick and loops they were made for climbing, even though nobody we knew had actually done it. That's where it happened, right in those cool waters. Yeah, I guess it hurt a little. Blood? I'm not sure, what with the water and all.

"Wow," Melody said, and it seemed so anticlimactic. "So, when's he coming back?" she asked.

"Oh, I don't know," I said. "Actually, I don't really know if we'll see each other again."

"Why not?"

"You know," I said. "I kind of got what I wanted from the whole thing."

iii.   *The Suckling of Lizards*

Lizard wasn't always like this, crawling on clickety claws while his white belly licked the dirt from the floors. Long ago, he was a monster fish, the kind that doesn't exist anymore. The kind that inspires stories like Nelly and make fishermen weep. As a fish, Lizard ruled the oceans, knocking over boats and giving sharks pause. But the saltiness made him too hard, too crazed, and he watched in amazement as legs, feet, toes and tail exploded from his scaly body. All that was a long time ago. He remembered his old life immersed in water as well as we remember being monkeys, being amoebas.

"Why do you wear that lipstick?" Fly asked Lizard now. Lizard didn't answer. Fly was stupid, didn't he know it wasn't lipstick? Like Lizard was one of those freaks on the corner, crowned with wigs and padded bras. "You don't apply it very well," said Fly.

Lizard's tongue lashed at Fly, snapped him up and shoved him between lips. He didn't much like winged creatures anymore, their bodies too crunchy and not enough meat. He used his wicked tongue to shut them up, prove his power. Let it be known the crumbling casitas he roamed across were all his while the Tico Spanish flew all around him.

"You shouldn't do that," said Tarantula, resting fat, hairy legs on the warm earth as he peeked out from his ground burrow. Tarantula knew better than to let his whole body show. Instead, he waited with an unGodly amount of patience for his own dinner to waddle by.

"Why not?" asked Lizard.

"It's beneath you," said Tarantula. "Who cares what Fly says?"

Lizard's eyes darted all around, and he moved to a sunnier spot on the orange house. An excuse to get farther away from Tarantula, who knew Lizard had to constantly seek out the sun to keep from trembling. From this angle, abreast the hot metal window guards, he could see the family inside. The plump abuela who was nearly blind. The four kids, two screaming over who got the bigger scoop of purple rice and beans, the third hunched over her bowl of cold cereal and the baby drugged, head lolled as he processed the milk that tongued a stream down his chin. The father, Lizard knew, had already left in his rumbling truck, machetes and canvas bags in the back. Where was the mother?

There she was. She was beautiful, one of the few human women who hadn't gone round even after four children. Her waist still nipped in like she wore an invisible belt, long black hair oiled and braided. Lizard pulled back from the window, didn't want her to see him. He couldn't help it, when it happened. As soon as a human spotted him, his body swelled with their blood, the coppery red taste flavoring his lips. No matter the distance, the lack of touch, all it took was a look. They were stained for good, and it wasn't his fault. He got no joy from the magical suckling.

"Why do you wear that lipstick?"

Jesus. Another Fly landed three bars across, rubbing its legs together and cocking its red eyes at Lizard. So curious, so curious.

"Shut up," whispered Lizard. Inside, the mother flipped the sizzling palmito cheese in the cast iron pan. Her arms were thin, fingernails long and strong.

"I wanna know," said Fly. "How come?" Really, Lizard would be doing everyone a favor if he lapped up this pest, too.

"Be quiet," Lizard said loudly. The mother swatted at another Fly that circled above her, wanting to know what was in the pan. What sweetness coated her hair. She moved in fluidity, like a swimmer, a veil of sweat from tending the heat emerging at her hairline. *I love her*, Lizard realized. He loved her, and could never tell. Couldn't let her look at his macabre red mouth, the roughed up calluses on his belly.

"Why you gotta—" Fly began again, and without thinking Lizard gobbled him up. Fly's body crumbled like a brittle leaf in his throat. He could hear the soft *tsk, tsk* from Tarantula below.

"Mamá! Mamá, lagartija! Lagartija!" said one of the children, pointing to Lizard and forgetting the counting of rice, of how many beans she had compared to her brother. Before she could turn, cover her child's eyes with her long brown fingers, the child was already slumping to the depths of the chair. Lizard felt his belly swelling with warm human blood, could taste the gallo pinto in the cells.

Before she could look, before she could see, before her screams rang through the little garden, Lizard let go and let his heavy body fall to the hot pavement. Bolted like a thief to the hiding spot behind the washer.

From there, he could hear the tears start to season her screams. "Mija, mija—oh, my God!" And the grandmother, the pounding of her cane and asking, "Qué pasa? Qué pasa?" The other children joined in the screams, their scared little voices harmonizing with their mother's.

Lizard was too full of the child's blood to move, his body stretched painful at the stomach, aching his back. He needed to find sun, a good hot spot, to force the digestion.

"Look what you did," hissed Tarantula, blanketing Lizard in shame.

"Qué pasa?" the old woman demanded again from inside.

"Lagartija," said Lizard's love quietly. He couldn't see them anymore, but their voices rang clear from the other side of the wall. He imagined her cradling the child, all the blood sucked clean, the little body as hollow and light as a fly's.

"Dios mio," said the old woman. "Oremos." Let's pray.

"No, Mamá. No," she said, and Lizard's heart broke right in two, but the halves couldn't float apart. The bulk of his love's child was so thick, it kept them pressed together. Kept his heart right on beating, no matter that he wished for death.

But then ... but then ...

He had a piece of her. Her best piece, a piece that she's created herself with love and pain. And that was something. Wasn't it? That he would carry a part of her with him, in him, always? In time, by tomorrow, by next week, that piece would become a part of him. Would course through his body like it was home.

"Just look at what you did," said Tarantula again, shaking his head before dropping fully down into his nest.

Chapter Three

At a small town high school, they do what they can. We didn't have a great football team, nor the big rivalry that fueled us like the North and South Medford high schools, but we had this: AP classes. An annual trip to Washington DC where we were supposed to soak up history like good little pieces of chicken. Off-campus lunch privileges for everyone, and a senior trip to Disneyland. Me, I never made it to my senior year. The off-campus lunches I spent holed up with another outcast, Teri, in her mother's box of a house just two blocks away, skipping afternoon classes and hunched over a Ouija board. But, in my mother's insistence of taking those AP classes, I *did* get Washington DC.

To qualify, you had to be in the combination AP English-US history class taught by a mouse of a woman, Mrs. Dittan, and a middle-aged man with severe male pattern baldness woven into his kinky long curls. He looked like a clown out of makeup, but Mr. Bobienski was adored by everyone else. I think it was his complete lack of self-consciousness, his eagerly willingness to be a fool. But I hated him, hated the way he looked at my thighs, couldn't lift his eyes from my chest. Did he look at other girls that way? I don't know. I only had one friend in that class, Melody, but the assigned pod seating kept her and I apart. Plus, she wasn't speaking to me sophomore year anyway. Not since her lips had exploded with cold sores and I had said, too loud in geometry, "You know that's a kind of herpes, right?"

Yeah, it was a shitty thing to do. I regretted it right when it happened, but I'd never had to say I was sorry and meant it. The words didn't come. I'd been forced to apologize to my mother my entire life. Still found folded up apology notes with quarters taped into them from when I was five. Even then, I'd tried to buy my way out. Melody stopped talking to me quickly, but without any dramatics. Instead, she just shifted to the pretty girls and gangly boys with saggy jeans and bowl cuts, drawn to those she was always meant to be with. And that left me alone.

"Now, remember," said Mr. Bobienski from the front of the classroom, "everyone needs to be in good standing if you want to make the trip to Washington DC. That means turning in extra credit if you need to and staying on top of assignments until then. There's just two weeks left." Two weeks. It would be my first time on a plane, at least that I could remember. My mom was freaking out, demanding that I made a "to-pack" list a month in advance. "You don't want to forget anything!" she said. I hated making lists, it made me feel like her. Her, who pinned notes to the screen door daily of jobs for my dad to do. "Make sure you get a window seat," she said. "Don't let one of those shitty little brats push you around."

Really, I don't know what sex ed had to do with English or US History. Okay, I could come up with a link if I had to. But shouldn't this be in PE class? A separate, special seminar or something? Instead, Mr. Bobienski chose a day when Mrs. Dittan was off

("Seeing the dermatologist for a full body mole check like we all should!" said Mr. Bobienski), to slip in a twenty-minute slideshow of close-ups of diseased genitalia. There was no real precursor to this, and as he set up the projector all I could think of was Mrs. Dittan with her crepe skin naked in a white, sterile office. Showing all her flaws without a hint of embarrassment.

Some of the slides were pictures, others were brief videos. Sometimes a text would pop up declaring, "Herpes! Gonorrhea! Crabs!" and tiny little black dots would dart through bushy pubic hair. I felt like it should be blurred out, like some of the Japanese porn we'd found in Teri's brother's room.

"Justine," Mr. Bobienski said, pulling up a chair and sitting next to me. The room was dark, all eyes locked on the screen. None of our eyes had adjusted yet, the only flashes of light coming from shots of pale thighs.

"Huh?" I asked, not looking at him. I'd been put on the outskirts of the room, folded into a corner. I liked it there. It gave me hope I'd be forgotten.

"I'm glad you're going on the trip," Mr. Bobienski said.

"Yeah." His knee knocked against mine under the table, and I moved as slowly, softly away as I could. The cheap desk was cool under my forearms. You couldn't see what was happening under the desk if you'd wanted to.

"Are you doing any more extra credit beforehand?" he asked. On the screen, an oozing penis made its debut.

"I don't know," I said.

"I mean, not that you need to!" he said. "But, I just thought …" Ariel, a girl I'd never spoken to, glanced at us from my other side. And I was ashamed. An angry, red vagina spread open across the screen.

"I don't know," I repeated.

"Okay," he said. "Okay." His too-big, dry hand jumped out like a snake, wrapped itself around my wrist. "But if you want to," he said, "just, you know. Let me know. I'm here."

"Okay," I said as a diseased-looking pair of testicles appeared before us. *I'm here, I'm here, I'm here.*

I sat as far away from the window seat as possible, in one of those big middle rows where the attendants had to really reach to give you a food tray. The plane was huge, but mostly empty, so we could sit wherever after take-off. A red-eye flight, the only other passengers seemed to be a tired troop of military men, their beige fatigues making them all look alike. Funny, I thought fatigues were always bright greens seasoned with browns.

But at least I didn't have to sit by someone I was supposed to know. Get through those few seconds of time where normal people talked to each other, and I never knew what to say. There's a small window when you either speak to someone or you don't. I never did. These people, some of them I'd been in classes with since I was five. And I didn't know a thing about them.

Really, I couldn't believe it. That they would take a bunch of fifteen- and sixteen-year-olds to a huge city, give us hotel rooms and let us spill onto the pavement like that. Weren't they afraid one of us would get drunk, get raped, wander away and refuse to go back to our cloying little town? Apparently not.

I was lucky, there was an uneven amount of girls and I got a room to myself. I wasn't supposed to, I was supposed to share with Erin Taylor, but she got sick at the last moment. I was happy about it. Her and I had done a science project together in fifth grade, but hadn't talked since. No real reason but, like most, she could sense my strangeness and kept her distance.

Immediately, I unpacked, filled the drawers and closets with my best clothes. Stacked Mary Janes in bright vinyl, rolls of thigh highs, miniskirts and tight baby-tees. "It's a walking city," Mrs. Dittan had warned us, "and it's hot." But I didn't care. I wore the highest heels I could every day to school, kept my balance with the plastic mini backpacks or furry ones shaped like animals. To me, I dressed like Cher Horowitz, like a rich girl in California. My mom didn't care, would say, "Look at those legs!" and "My God, how tiny your waist it." Her envy coated me, covered me, even all the way over here.

Mrs. Dittan was right—this was a walking city. And my God, did we walk. To the big statue of Abraham Lincoln, which I just didn't get. Yeah, it was big. Yeah, he was an important president. But wasn't it just a big statue? After you take a photo of it, what else are you supposed to do? To the Holocaust Museum, where there were real measuring tools to tell the Nazis which noses were okay and which were too Jewish. Where real video footage showed non-stop, a horror show that never ended. All day, you could just watch people die. Listen to survivors talk about almost dying. It was sickening. Afterward, the whole class went for ice cream at Larry's Ice Cream and Cupcakes. I got chocolate.

What I loved most those first few days were the cherry blossoms. They flanked the streets with their pinkness, rained down petals like a fairytale. It didn't matter, the homeless men digging through the trash beneath them. They didn't care about the men and women in wrinkled business suits and wet hair half-jogging to something important. Their beauty existed for no one, for everyone. I wanted to be like them, even as their petals dropped at my feet.

But, what I was really waiting for, was Free Day. It was the last day of our four-day trip, when everyone's toes were swollen with blisters and the new kind of sun had burned our cheeks and turned our necks crimson. For the whole day, we could do and go wherever we liked. I heard everyone talking. They were going to the Smithsonian, the White House, the Capitol Building. I was going shopping, and didn't tell anyone.

The subways were easy to figure out, my backpack stuffed with cash and a credit card "just in case," my mom had said. I would buy something amazing here. Almost everyone in the mall was black, and I was really aware of how short my skirt was. How fair my legs were. We had two black families back home, but I'd never seen any of them up close. But really, the whistles and catcalls and *Come here, baby* whispers were no different than passing the Mexicans at home. I soaked up the attention, wrapped it around myself, and kept on.

My mom had thought sixty dollars in extra spending money would be enough, and to her it made sense. She was all Goodwill shoes and K-Mart blouses, never spent more than ten dollars on any piece of clothing. Sixty dollars wasn't much, I knew, but it was enough. Enough to buy those staggering black vinyl heels in a store whose name I didn't recognize. I'd wear them tonight to the class trip to a play.

They were my first pair of stilettos and it took all my strength not to open the box and peek at them on the bus ride back to the hotel. I blocked out the stares, the lines, with a discman and headphones. My ears rang with Adina Howard and Tupac, and I pretended like I belonged here. Like I always took this bus alone.

Getting ready, I missed Melody. I always missed Melody. Our best times were getting ready together, always had been. Ever since she'd taken me in at eleven years old and gave me a makeover the first time she came over. My mom, she hated her for that. For making me look a little more normal, straightening out my poodle bangs and layering on the makeup.

The heels, though, they were perfect. Unlike platforms or clogs, they made me look like a real grownup. The skintight black dress and plunging neckline helped. This was what Sophistication looked like.

I was always ready early, always. It was one of the habits my mom forced into me, and I couldn't let it go. I didn't have anyone to pass the time with, so I headed downstairs to the lobby where you could order a 7-Up and pretend it was a cocktail. But when the elevator door opened, Mr. Bobienski was there, alone. Dressed like he always did, with a cheap tan jacket and pilling tie.

"Justine!" he said, as I let the doors swallow me up. What else could I do? *Pretend like you forgot something in your room.* Of course. Fucking idiot. It was too late now.

In the confines of the elevator with its mirrored walls and heavy woods, he was everywhere. I was everywhere. His knee could touch mine and there was nowhere to go.

For what seemed like an hour, he let his eyes loose on me. They explored everything, the shadows of my breasts. The swell of my calves. The rise and fall of my collarbone. The forced arch of my ass in those brand new, too grown shiny shoes. And he sighed.

"Damn, I wish you were eighteen," he said as the doors opened up to the lobby, letting noise and shame flood in.

iv.   *The Cricket in the Maternity Ward*

Cricket couldn't help it, he loved watching the womens' eggs pile on. Knowing he was part of all this beauty. They didn't want anything from him, he knew that. Or maybe they just knew not to expect anything. This one, he didn't even remember her name. It had been a fast hook up, a brief one, the kind he liked when the darkness wove them together, kept them wrapped and swaddled tight. When he'd heard that he'd been the first to gift her the hundred, the first to make those handful of eggs pile on, he couldn't help it. Just leapt so fast to the birthing grounds it made his legs sing.

"What are you doing here?" she asked him, annoyed as she pushed the eggs through her ovipositor.

"I just—I just wanted to see," he said.

"I think you've seen enough."

"Don't be like that," he said. "I didn't, you know ... I just did what's normal. What we all do."

"Yeah. Whatever," she said.

"How many—"

"Ten. There are ten." That seemed to always be the case. "Are you just going to stand there? Wait for them to come?"

"I don't have anything better to do." It was true. The others, they were brushing him off more often now. He wasn't sure if it was the cold, his getting older, or something else. Maybe this one, she'd talked about him. Told them about his hurriedness, or that his spiracle wasn't strong anymore.

"That's a first," she said. He couldn't ask her name now. Not now. He looked around, hoping someone she knew would come by, call out to her. Say her good name so he didn't have to ask.

"How long does this all take?" He really didn't know, he'd never stayed the whole time before. Sure, he'd always stopped by when he could, watched the others hide the leaves in burrows, the stem of plants. These days, the soft soil was a more popular option, rich and imported to make the gardens grow. Cricket wondered if it helped, all the stuff they put in this foreign soil. Nutrients. Minerals. Maybe it would make his offspring braver and tougher than any other generation. Or maybe it would kill them, he just didn't know.

"Now that's a question better suited to you," she said, dropping what he counted as the eighth egg into the earth. "About two weeks."

"What—what are you going to do? You can't go that long without eating!" Two weeks, goddamn. "I mean, that's a really long time ..."

"Idiot, you think I'm staying here? You remember your mom ever being there? After this, I'm gone. They're on their own. I did my job."

He furrowed his brow. No, he couldn't remember his mom, but he thought that was normal. Wasn't it? He'd just been too young, and then—shit. Was this how it always happened? Just leave the little nymphs to make it on their own?

"You're getting soft in your old age," she said, this time a little more warmly.

"I'm not that old," he said, shrugging off the insult bathed in pity.

"What are you? Sixty-five days now?"

"Hardly." He was seventy. He'd just turned seventy. He *was* an old man now.

"Well," she said, a sweetness in her voice. "You should make the most of what time you have left. Leave, go, have fun. Find some new, pretty, stupid thing."

"I think ... I think I'll stay," he said. Didn't even know he meant it 'til the words fell out.

"Seriously? That's ... weird."

He shrugged. "Says who? It's what I want to do."

"I don't know. The universe, the Gods. Everybody."

"Screw everybody."

"I thought you had."

Two weeks was a lifetime for some, but he adored watching the eggs change. Start to twitch. In the mornings and evenings, he'd go on brief food runs for himself. Got a new spring in his jumps avoiding the tongue of Frog. The glistening web of Spider. He'd make it, he was sure of it. Knew he'd be one of the few that made it all the way to the end. How many little nymphs of his had crawled their way out of their shell only to be snatched up by someone so, so hungry? He didn't know. Maybe most of them, maybe all of them. He'd never met a single one of his children. He wasn't going to die with that truth.

"Hey ... hey, guys. Children," he'd say, curling up close to the eggs with his empty belly. "I'm, well, I guess I'm your father." He could almost hear their little voices greeting him. Almost feel their legs wrapping over him.

"You're being ridiculous," said Aphid, chewing through the most perfect looking leaves he could find nearby.

"I don't care," said Cricket, but for the first time he did. He cared a great lot.

"You know—you do know what will happen, right? When the nymphs get big enough?"

"Of course," said Cricket, though he had no idea what Aphid was talking about.

"Well, okay then. I'm just saying. You better watch your ass if any of them are boys."

"Yeah, yeah." Why? What would happen if they were boys? Cricket didn't know, but he wasn't about to ask Aphid, the dumb green thing who just kept on eating plants that looked just like him.

Finally, the eggs were really shaking, he wasn't imagining it. Slowly, like they'd practiced it, his little nymphs began to emerge from their chambers. They looked nothing like him, nothing like any cricket. Cute and adorable and the size of a tiny fruit fly.

God, Cricket could really go for a fruit fly right now. He'd been hungry, hungry, hungry, not letting himself hunt or forage very far from the eggs. But never mind that now.

"Hi!" he said, nuzzling each one. "It's me, I'm your—I'm your father." Shit, they all looked alike. Cute, but they were all the same. How could he tell which were boys? Did it actually matter? "Can you, I mean, can you talk? Do you understand me?"

"I understand you," said one, the others nodding in agreement. "I know your voice, I heard it from in there."

This was amazing. Incredible. What he'd been searching for his whole life.

For two more weeks, he tried to keep them safe, corralled them and told them about the best places to find food. How to make their jumps even higher. But they seemed to just tolerate him, not really listening.

"Hey," said one of the girls (he'd figured out which were which now, and six of them were boys), "don't worry about me. Okay? I'm fine." She didn't want him, didn't need him. The ungrateful little brat.

That's what made him spin out, it wasn't his fault. She was just so little, so soft. He couldn't help it. Guilt spread over him when he did it, but the worst part? The worst part was when the others came back, saw her insides still rolling in his mouth, her broken antenna at his feet. And laughed.

"You ate her! You ate her!" one of the boys squealed, delighted.

"I didn't … I didn't mean to!" he said. A monster, he was a monster. But it had been so good, and she'd been so sweet.

It made sense then, didn't it? Nobody could blame him, nobody would dare. And really, it was an offering.

A week later, when his boys were big and the scent of youth washed over them, he let it happen. Hunkered down in silence, head bowed, while their stomachs roared and they tore him apart, swallowed his body piece by piece. For an instant, he saw it happen, saw a leg ripped off and disappear into his eldest's mouths. The first egg to crack. "Thank you," he said. Or thought he did. Now he'd be a part of them forever, live on in their bodies, fuel them, feed them. Now, he would never be forgotten.

Chapter Four

There's something I didn't say. Something between Mr. Bobienski's sex ed show and the elevator incident. It happened on the plane, in the darkest of night (like these things tend to do). After the plane's wheels kissed away from the pavement, after we were let up from our seats, stumbling like cattle in the abattoir into the darkness. I wasn't supposed to be in that middle row, my mom had made sure of that. Refused to leave the airport until the plane scurried away, asked the poor woman at the gate four times if she was "really sure about the window seat." Honestly, I was indifferent about the window, about seeing the earth get smaller and the houses turn into toys. That was strange, though. I should have loved it, should have felt my heart soar at the leaving of the valley. But I just didn't care.

I should say this, everyone should know, I got there first. I sat down first. The row of ten seats was abandoned, and I checked behind the one I'd chosen to make sure nobody was in that row, either. Funny, how we settle into our night areas the same way animals do. He didn't come until after, and he moved like he knew I was there. Knew the seat was for him.

The light brown army fatigues were a shock of lightness against his dark Hershey skin. "Marines," he'd say. That's right, sorry. Marines, not the army. Like there was a difference to me.

I couldn't figure it out and didn't have a tongue strong enough to ask, but didn't military people have to keep their hair short? Didn't they have to be American? Kareem had dreadlocks, twisty black snakes, that slithered to the small of his back. His lilting Caribbean accent sounded wild and foreign.

"How yuh stay? How old are you?" he asked as he shook my hand, offered up his name.

"Fifteen." I could have easily lied, but I didn't. And it wasn't to shake him off, it was a challenge. A plea for a compliment that he bit into and held on tight.

"Man, man," he said, shaking his head and sending the snakes into a frenzy. "You look older, yuh know?" Yeah. I did know.

Maybe it was the tired that washed over him, or the fact that our class was small and had dispersed like hungry mice into the black cabin as soon as the seatbelt lights went off. Either he didn't know he was sharing a plane with a bunch of high school sophomores or he didn't care. Mr. Bobienski and Mrs. Dittan, they'd gotten seats in first class, happy to have that thick velvet curtain drawn between us. Once, just once, they had poked their heads back to us, reminding us to meet at baggage claim in DC. It was a direct flight, and they had hours or free champagne and movies waiting for them.

Really, I don't know how it happened though. But I wanted it to.

Kareem kept asking questions, probing questions, and I could feel the setup in them. I'd still never kissed a boy, I was way behind everyone else, but some things are balled up tight inside all women. I let him keep asking, kept telling, because I wanted to let it happen.

"Yuh the silent bu' deadly type," he said, and when he smiled his white teeth flashed in the inky air like a beautiful warning. Right then, I knew why the angelfish worked in the deep. Why that blinding glow drew everyone near, even though they had to know the sharp teeth that waited just beyond. I smiled back.

"I'm twenty-four," Kareem had said, but it could have been any number. Eighteen, forty-two, it didn't matter. To me, he was just grown. Alien with his knotted head and syrupy accent. Even in the moment, I didn't know if he was really beautiful. I thought so, but I couldn't see for the mane, the imported skin, the voice I could barely understand.

When he kissed me, his lips consumed mine, drier than I thought they'd be. I hoped, in a flash, that Mr. Bobienski would catch us. Not to stop me, but just to see. See *I* was the one who chose the men who could touch me.

Kareem's tongue explored my teeth, discovered my inside cheeks. There was a safety in the plane, the soft snores from the row ahead of us. In the fake stars that peppered the ceiling. Here, I knew I could puppeteer the whole show, could push and start and stop as I pleased.

Isn't this what every girl wanted? A first kiss miles above the earth, bridging over midnight with a grown man who knew what he was doing? My dad, he'd have one of his rare screaming, ashtray-throwing fits where my mom ended up getting choked as he pressed her against the wall and he sought out my current favorite thing to destroy. It would be sweetly worth it.

"See them porch monkeys?" my dad had began asking, pointing to the rare black family or couple trudging from Food 4 Less to their car just like us. He was only this wildly full of hate when my mom wasn't around. After all, she'd been a white who married an Other. Who was he to talk?

I never said anything, but when my dad would drive by them slowly, roll down his window and make monkey sounds, I'd slip off the seatbelt slowly and let the shame drag me to the floorboards. "You sit up straight!" my dad would yell. "You need to see this. You need to know." I only looked once, and that was enough. The middle-aged couple pretended not to see my dad, not to hear him, but the bristling of their backs said they were filling up with something loathsome. Thank God I never saw their eyes.

And now a man whose skin was blacker than midnight had his pink, pink tongue flicking across my bicuspids. His sparkling white teeth crashing against mine.

My mom, she'd told me this story over and over. She'd already been married twice when she brought my dad home to her parents. Her first husband, he came back from the war bad. She married him at twenty because that's what you did, and she'd been a good girl.

Sealed up tight 'til marriage. So she didn't know if he'd always been a sadist, or the war had made him one. I figured all that killing and pink mist could do that. He raped her, bruised her and bloodied her for a year before she got the nerve to divorce him. Said he slipped away easy, like he was waiting for the leaving. Her second husband, well, he wasn't much better, she said. He was in love with her older sister, but Cassie was married with two babies, so my mom was the consolation prize. That husband, he went for a beer run one day and just never came back. Just like those old milk and cigarette stories you hear.

So my dad, when my mom brought him home at thirty-four years old, was strangely and quickly accepted. Still, my grandmother told my mom, "No darker." Those were the only words she said after that initial meeting, when my dad stepped outside for a cigarette and my mom searched my grandmother's eyes for approval.

No darker.

My grandmother didn't know. Didn't know when my mom finished her waitressing shifts, she'd take her free house drinks (vodka on the rocks) and start suckling the cigarettes she hated with a side of amphetamine to stay thin. For extra measure, she'd go nearly every night to a dance club where black men passing through fell to their knees for her. It was her thick, auburn hair to her waist. Her pale, pale skin, the same shade she'd given me. The shyness in her posture. "Those black men can dance!" she'd told me my whole life. "I never did understand why, so much of the time, no other girls would dance with them. This one, a sailor, it was like sex right there on the floor."

Sex on the floor, sex on a plane, decades made no difference. Kareem had stopped asking if I was alright, took his big hand and began circling my collarbone. Feeling out the territory. I wondered if this was what he did in battle, how he fingered a gun. Where was Mr. Bobienski? The snoring got louder all around us, a cacophony of dreams.

For the first time, I wished my neckline wasn't so low. That I hadn't put the pilled plane blanket over my lap, the only defense between his searching hands and my too-short skirt. *Now, Justine. Do it now.* When I brushed his hand away, just as it inched barely below my shirt, he laughed.

"Yuh a tease, nah?" he said. It wasn't a question. I felt like I should be ashamed, but I wasn't. I just wanted him to kiss me again.

He did, but it wasn't the same. And he must have thought it was better than awkwardly sitting side by side talking about the weather anyway. When the sun turned the windows pink, when the lights came on and the smell of eggs and bacon filled the cabin, life returned amongst us. There was yawning, scratching, lines piling up for the restroom. I had to pee, I had to pee so bad, but I wouldn't let myself get up. There was something too embarrassing about letting him know I couldn't control what was between my legs. We'd learned, in biology, that us and almost every mammal on earth takes twenty seconds to piss. Didn't that sound just about right? The great equalizer was between our legs.

And yes, I'd imagined it. Pictured Kareem landing and staying in DC, too, giving me his number or asking what hotel I was at. I'd give it to him, my virginity, because it was just how I pictured it. I wanted to offer it up to someone who I'd never see again, someone I wouldn't get attached to. It was a powerful thing, that bleeding and pain, and I didn't want someone to have it who'd lord it over me. At this point, I just wanted it over. I wanted it to be done. But he didn't give me his number, and he never asked where I was staying.

"Ah, yuh a pretty thing, thank you much," he told the attendant when she handed him a juice and apple. I shook my head, nothing for me. I shouldn't be mad, should I? She *was* a pretty thing. All thin limbs, blonde hair and that kind of effortless look I'd never reach. I felt fat, plain, young. I could do this though, I could not eat in front of him. It was too difficult, managing the food into mouth, liquid sucked between teeth, filling the space where just an hour before his tongue had occupied.

Mrs. Dittan stumbled from first class right before descent, sleepy-eyed and hair a mess. "Okay, guys? Everyone? Baggage claim, remember," she said, clapping her hands just like she was at the front of a classroom. Kareem glanced at her, but didn't connect her with me. I watched her and him from the corner of my eyes, pretended to be going through my wallet instead.

There was something magical about feeling the rubber touch the tarmac. I was as far away from my parents as I could manage in this country. Thousands of miles, three time zones, and I was free. With a strange man's spit in my mouth, I was free.

The walk off the plane seemed to take an hour, with Kareem in front of me, the dreadlocks swaying and tangling together. *Look back, look back at me.* And he did. Right as we shuffled into first class, he did.

"A suh di ting tan," he said. I nodded slightly. I had no idea what he said, but those would be the last words he spoke to me.

I lost him at baggage claim, though surely he must have been headed the same direction. He walked fast, so much taller and legs so much longer than it had seemed sitting down. For a minute, I traced his oil-black head moving through the crowd, and then it was gone. He'd been swallowed up by a sea of other beige-clad passengers, other bobbing heads going every direction. I wondered if he'd remember me. It was only then I realized he'd never asked my name.

"God, that took forever," said one of the popular girls to one of the football-playing boys. "I didn't sleep at all."

"I know," he said, falling into stride beside her. I kept exactly four paces from their heels, just enough to follow their conversation but far enough away that they wouldn't suspect.

"I mean, I've taken a lot of long flights before. A lot," she said. "But this one, I don't know. With all those military people on board? I felt like I was going to war."

The boy laughed. His name was John, James or something. I couldn't remember. "My brother's in the marines," he said. "Apparently getting on a regular plane like this is a big upgrade for them. Means, a lot of the time, they're headed home. Or off duty for awhile. Something like that."

"Well. I'm just glad I got a window seat," said the girl. I think her name was Brianna. I think she'd been our grade's homecoming queen this year. What must it be like, to be named the most loved girl of all?

"I hate window seats," said John-James. "Give me the aisle seat any day."

"Don't drink so much of that free soda, and you wouldn't have to go to the bathroom all the time!" she said, laughing. "It rots your teeth out anyway, you know."

"Hey, now," he said, elbowing her gently. "I've got great teeth, my dad's a dentist. See?" He liked her, bared his teeth at her like a chimp. She laughed gently, shaking her head. Did she know, I wondered. Did she know that this lovely boy, this popular boy, would do anything for her? Probably not. She probably didn't know anything except everyone was always kind to her. Everyone was lovely. The world and all its inhabitants, they were there solely to please her.

My lips were dry, the skin of my chin hurting and raw. She didn't know, but God. What a life that must be.

v.   *Otter Teaches Bear to Ice Fish*

Otter never understood the others who loathed the winter months, complained about the crunch of frozen snow between their hooves or the chill in the air. He loved it. The fish got lazier, almost in a drunken stupor, and floated in slow circles right below the ice surface. By spring, he knew they'd be awake and fast again. Plus, the cold kept the Humans away. Only the most dedicated dared trample out in the blizzards, puffed up like freakish yetis in their down jackets and just a sliver of face showing. No matter, he thought. They didn't have what it took to get to the best spots anyway. Let them have their barely-off-the-bank fishing spots, scooping up a meager pile and not even caring if they got the juiciest catches.

It only took Otter a few hours each to create a pile of fat, flopping fish that would feed his entire family. Keep them all fat and warm through the winter.

"Hey! Hey!" Bear waddled to the bank a few yards away, his mouth foaming with desire, big bushy tail wagging. "How'd you get all those fish? You gonna eat all those fish?" God, Bear was a lumbering dolt. Otter tolerated him though, like they all did. After all, he knew his place on the food chain. Knew Bear could chase him down if he really wanted, snap his neck like it was honeycomb.

"I'm not, but my family will," said Otter. Thank God he was pretty much done for the day anyway.

"Oh," said Bear, setting on his haunches in the snow, mindlessly combing his glorious tail with his thick claws. "Looks good," he said.

"Yeah," said Otter. He knew what Bear wanted, but wasn't going to offer it up just like that.

"I wish I had some fish," said Bear.

"Maybe you should go fishing," said Otter as he tucked his own prizes into the little woven knapsack his wife had gifted him.

"I can't," said Bear. "I can't break through the ice like you. Couldn't catch the fish anyway. I'd fall in." Well, he had a point there. Even the soil shook with Bear's weight, only the thickest of ice would even hold him. Something softened in Otter, but just for a moment. The hail began to pour, and hardened him right up again. Bear sighed. "Well, you know, if you ever find that you catch too many ..."

"And who's ever said that?" asked Otter.

"That's true," Bear said, laying down and curling his long, glory of a tail around him. "It's just that, you know, I'm *really* hungry ..."

How hungry was he? Hungry enough to stamp Otter down, steal his lot and leave him for dead? Quietly, quickly, he surveyed the land. He wasn't sure of the thickness of the ice any farther out, and Bear blocked the only sure route to land. He'd have to walk right past him, knapsack fat with meat, to get back home. Otter could smell the fish clearly, even pick up whiffs of the aliveness of them. He knew Bear's nose was even stronger. Maybe, even if Bear didn't really want to, his hunger would make him snap. Otter didn't want to die.

"You know ..." began Otter. "That old saying? Give someone a fish, they'll eat for a day—"

"Teach them to fish, they'll eat for a lifetime?" asked Bear.

"Yeah, that. I mean, we could do that. I guess."

"Really?" asked Bear, perking up. "You'd do that for me?"

"Sure, why not? I've already got my food for the day anyway. And I know the route to this hole I made is super strong anyway. It'll hold you."

"You promise?" asked Bear, sensing a trick. He was smart, but not smart enough. There was a trick, of course, Otter was blessed with trickery. That, and the gift of igniting curiosity.

"Of course I promise," said Otter. "What do you think? I'd have you come out here, break the ice and leave me stranded so I can't get back? I don't know how thick or thin the ice is everywhere else! I haven't checked." Bear glanced around the ice, looking for signs of Otter going off-course. He was right, there were no tracks besides the single one from the back of the ice hold.

"Well, alright," said Bear, heaving his weight up. "Thanks!" He waddled, slowly at first, across the ice, picking up speed as confidence grew. Otter prayed it wouldn't crack. He hadn't been checking for ice that held Bear weight when he first came out here. And how was he to know that Bear wouldn't kill him now, steal his fish and run away? But it was his only choice. "What do I do?" asked Bear.

"You take your tail, like this," said Otter, pretending to dip his own tail into the water. "Wiggle it around and the fish will think it's food. When they bite, pull them up!"

"With your tail! Seriously?" asked Bear.

"Yes! Haven't you seen us fish before?" Please, please, please don't let him have seen us fish before.

"Uh, no, not really ... does it hurt?"

"The bite? No. Fish don't have teeth. It's just a nip," said Otter.

"Okay, okay," said Bear, beaming his rear towards the icy water and dipping his tail in. "It's cold!" he yelled. "And I feel stupid."

"Be quiet or you'll scare them away," said Otter, slowly wrapping the knapsack over his shoulders, priming his legs to spring.

"How long does this take?" asked Bear. "It's getting really cold."

"It depends, I don't know," said Otter. "Sometimes it's fast, sometimes it takes a while. But look, I have to get going. Okay? I'm supposed to be home soon. Just keep your tail in there. It's uncomfortable at first, but you'll get used to it."

"Alright, alright," said Bear, his eyes tearing up from the icy waters.

The next day, belly full and taut, Otter saw Bear—or what he thought was Bear—keening softly in the bushes as he made his way to the lake.

"What—what happened to you?" asked Otter.

"I did what you told me! I did it just right!" said Bear, turning slightly to present his rump to Otter. "And look! It froze my tail right off. My beautiful tail! And I didn't get a single fish for it."

Otter couldn't help it, he began to laugh. "Stupid!" he said. "Do you believe what everyone tells you?" Bear, he knew, at least in that moment, was too scared, too ashamed, and too destroyed to chase him.

Chapter Five

I decided to give away my virginity like someone decides to take their vitamins or go to the gym—quickly, without trying to think about it much. Just getting it over with. Already, I heard the hisses of *Slut* in the hallway. *Why you dress like that? Fucking whore.* It wasn't about Kareem or the knee-knocks in US history or anything else. *You look like you need to be taken down a few pegs.* That one was from a girl, a senior, with tight blonde curls and mean blue eyes I'd never even noticed before, but I think she's the one who got it right. They looked at my lace-topped thigh highs, my peek of a midriff, and mistook my armor for peacocking. Like they couldn't tell how afraid I was.

Jason, I met him at the mall. I don't know why my mom consistently dropped me off there, for hours, so I could circle the two stories endlessly like a wormy dog, lapping up the whistles and compliments from all the grown men who would lean over the top railing, raining their stares down on young girls with taut thighs. It was like open pedophilia, a hunting ground where the prey was stupid and easy. For me, it was an oasis. It was my home.

"Nice tattoo," said the boy with greased black hair and startling blue eyes, thin whisper of a moustache riding his lips.

"Oh," I said, "thanks." I'd forgotten. The end of sophomore year, I'd taken to drawing flowers on my ankle with markers. It was easy, outlining a rose with the thin black ink. Filling it in with a bright red, decorating myself like a look-at-me insect. "It's not real," I said. I don't know why I had to confess.

He shrugged. "Doesn't matter."

Jason was the same height as me, and I towered above him in heels. He smelled of cigarettes, had one tucked in his ear like a 50s hoodlum. He was eighteen, a high school dropout. Worked at Arby's slapping together meaty sandwiches. I'd never been to Arby's—the only fast food place my mom would go was Wendy's, where she'd been ordering me a plain junior hamburger, ketchup only, since I was three years old and would cut it into quarters for me. Years later, she refused to let me have anything else. Said it reminded her of *When you were a doll. Just a little* doll. *Before you became such a shit.* Only my dad took me anywhere else, and it was just McDonald's for their sticky, cardboard-y breakfast.

Jason, he did all the right things. Asked for my number, called me the next day. Picked me up in his rusted-up car and drove me to his friend's house in White City where everyone smoked joints and drank, but I was too scared and just held his own warm can of beer when he'd disappear for what seemed like hours to smoke in the front yard of the broken-down trailer.

"You want to go to the spring dance with me?" I asked him a week after we met. It had been seven days of him kissing me too deep, too hard in the car. I let him feel me up only at the chest and only once, while Ginuwine's "Pony" poured from his crackling car stereo.

"Yeah, sure," he said. But the next day, when I asked if he'd go to my mom's old Chinese restaurant with my parents and I before the dance, he looked astounded. "Oh. You were serious," he said. But by then he was too embarrassed to actually turn me down.

My dad was okay with him because, even though Jason was Portuguese, his skin was as fair as mine. And he didn't have "One of those wetback accents." He sounded white, looked almost white, and that was good enough for my dad. My mom said nothing, and her eyes only hinted at her insides once. Jason and I were making out, leaning against his car when he dropped me off. I don't know how long she had been hovering on the concrete porch, staring and poking her head from behind the bushy tree full of black widow spiders. But when I finally saw her, she was a blank. Just reeled her head back in with its short, spiked nearly-mullet and disappeared inside the screen door.

But she bought me a dress for the dance, my first with a date and corsage and everything, and it wasn't even from a thrift store. Instead, it was turquoise blue and sparkly, draped to my knees and skin tight. It even had spaghetti straps, though she insisted my arms were too thick to pull it off. "But you have a tiny waist. Look at that little waist!" she'd said, as if she were admiring her own. "Such an hourglass," she said.

When Jason came to pick me up, he almost did it right. He had the button-up shirt, the fistful of flowers, but a spray of hickies covered his neck. "My ex," he said when he saw my eyes latch on to the purple and blue explosion. "Don't worry," he said. "I didn't sleep with her." Because he thought that made it okay, so did I.

The drive in my mom's minivan to the restaurant was steeped in silence. Why had I picked a place so far away? At least twenty minutes, and my mom carried all the talking. She was good like that, could listen to herself power on, on, on, without even a hint of interest from anyone else. My dad, he just seemed enchanted by the street signs.

I ordered what I always did, the comfort food of my youth. Just a bowl of the chicken and rice soup and a plateful of those buttery rolls. "When she was little," my mom told Jason. "God. She was so breathtaking. She loved this stuff," she said, gesturing to the food before me. "I'd bring her here, and she's just eat packet after packet of plain butter." Was that true? I didn't know. But my arms felt big and heavy suddenly underneath my thin coat.

At home, getting into Jason's car, there were no empty threats about getting me home at a certain time. No *Be careful* or anything. My mom just waved us away and my dad walked straight inside.

One thing I'd forgotten when planning this whole faking of normalcy—I didn't have any friends. Not at the dance. Melody was still ignoring me, and my little clutch of outcast friends, Teri and a redhead we'd claimed strangely named Maria, they'd never go to a dance. I was there alone, showing off to nobody who cared. I made Jason stand, stiffly, for a formal photo. There. At least I'd have that.

He lasted for forty minutes before the constant shifting of feet and glances to the door told me he was done. We had one dance, but only the last minute of it. I didn't want to stay there, not any more than him. But I didn't want to let him lead me into the deepest of night, either. Not yet.

I was on my period. Didn't want to disgust him, couldn't think of an excuse to keep from giving it away that night. What timing, right? So I just let him finger me as he pressed me up against the scratchy exterior of the gym wall. It was late in my cycle, and as he kissed me I reached the string from behind me, pulled it out and threw it as discreetly as I could on the ground. When he slipped a finger inside, my first—I hadn't even done it to myself—I prayed that the hymen would tear apart. It didn't hurt, the drying up blood lubing me up, and I saw little flocks of people I didn't recognize clutch their coats tight and race to the parking lot just a few feet away. Couldn't tell if they saw us or not. Didn't really care.

I tried to brush my hand across the hardness in his pants, but he pushed my hand lightly away. For that, I was glad. When he was done, I wove my hands through his, forced it against my dress to try and get rid of any blood he might have layered across his knuckles. That was the first night.

The second night, the hickies on his neck were mostly faded. It was less than a week later, and I couldn't take it anymore. The taste of his mouth was too full of ashes, the forced conversations no easier than the day we'd met. We'd only known each other a month, and by now he felt entitled to me and I could count the days until I turned sixteen. Just over ninety. I would not turn sixteen a virgin.

It's like we talked about it, like it had been decided already. I never met his mom, his twin brother or any of his friends that mattered. But I knew he lived with his thirty-four year-old mom who pulled double shifts at a dispatch company in a little manufactured home in Gold Hill. He took me there on one of the nights she wouldn't come home 'til dawn. Forgot his keys inside and jimmied open the door with ease. It was dark, nearly ten o'clock, and I could barely make out the shape of the place. The steps leading to the door were shaky, and one of the boards was missing. I couldn't tell if the yard had grass or was barren. He didn't even pretend to show me around or let me sit in the living room where an ancient plaid couch seemed so sad in its sagging. Apologetic about the rips and tears held together with duct tape.

Jason just led me straight to his mother's bedroom, which somehow squeezed in a queen-sized bed with all white everything—from blanket to pillowcases—and pushed me down hard. His mother's room smelled of chemical roses and a peppering of cigarettes.

His hands gripped the thin threads of my underwear, yanked them off. He kept my skirt on, hiked it up, and didn't even try to remove my jacket.

"Do you ... do you have something?" I asked him. I'm not sure where that courage came from, but flashes of diseased genitalia strobed across my inner eyelids. He sighed, annoyed, "Yeah, okay," and pushed off me into the little bathroom around the corner. Fluorescent light streamed in through the short hallway, lighting up the room. An old dresser vomiting up scarves. A photo of a middle-aged man who looked sad and angry all at once. Everything was foreign.

Jason came back, switching off the light, and the sudden re-entry to darkness made me blind. I could see him unbuckle his jeans, but the halation made it hard to see anything else besides the flash of buckle slapping against my thigh. This was it. I never even saw it, but this was it.

He rammed into me, hard, his penis feeling too pointy. Hard yet wobbly all at once. He didn't know. I'd never told him.

And the pain, the pain was incredible. I knew it would hurt, had heard all the stories. I took pain well, was proud of my high threshold, but this. I wasn't prepared for this. It felt like a seppuka had been taken to my innards. The blood was a lubricant. *He must think I'm so wet*, I thought.

It was over fast, less than a minute for sure. Jason said nothing to me, just rolled away, fished off the condom with a wet smack and wrapped it in a tissue from his mom's bedside before heading back to the bathroom. My eyes had adjusted, were taking in the room again. Those white bedsheets, they glowed like a warning. And in the middle, my God. The blood looked black, an oil spill. It was a murder scene, the puddle at least the size of two basketballs. *Shit. Shit, shit, shit, fuck.*

I couldn't let him know, didn't want to show him. Between the rocky pain between my thighs, wiping up the blood that began to trickle down my legs as I stood, I made my way to the bathroom where he was silently combing his hair back into place. "Hey," I said. "I need to go home. Now. I forgot, my mom wants me back early tonight."

"Okay," he said. The bathroom was crowded. Messy. Black hairs littered the sink, cheap beauty products were scattered everywhere. He slid the comb back into the mess of a medicine cabinet and led me back outside. It was cold for May, but still I slipped my jacket off and sat on it. Let it soak up the blood that was now starting to flood out of me so it wouldn't get on his car seat.

That was the last time I saw Jason, and for days afterward I bled. It was like my period, but with pain that never stopped. Not that up and down cramping I'd gotten used to. I was too scared to use tampons, so stole my mom's thick, fluffy pads instead.

Jason called, sure. I'll give him that. But I screened his calls, told my parents I didn't want to talk to anyone, and after three days he gave up. It was that easy.

Two months later, my period was all over the place. Didn't want to come, seemed all bled out from the horror show I'd created. On one of those nights when my dad wasn't home by six, when my mom and I knew he'd gone on one of his benders and might not be back for a week, she slept in the next day and sat like a corpse in their California king, letting the neon lights from a sitcom dance across her face. I poked my head into their room and over the raging on the television said, "I think I'm pregnant."

"What?" she asked, aiming the remote up to the television with a stiff arm.

"I think I'm pregnant," I repeated.

"Whatever, Justine," she said, turning the volume back up.

Two days later, the blood came again and it thundered hard.

vi.   The Yellowjacket Who Hunted Children

There are all these documentaries about bees, and just a whisper about yellowjackets, wasps and hornets. Everyone talks about them rarely, and when they do it's with disgust—just as it should be. Most humans, they think all these stinging monsters look similar because they're from the same family. How wrong they are. Bees are the Gods of the yellow and black world, working themselves to death to bring the sweetness. Risking their lives daily for sips of water. Worker bees and honey bees, gardeners put out watering dishes for them made with clean, cold, clear taps and fish pebbles to keep them from drowning. They plant trees and flowers that draw bees near, praying for pollination. It makes them feel better when they buy their organic, local, raw honey from the stores for eight dollars. A little less like it was stolen.

What they don't say in documentaries, in children's books, is that yellowjackets and their kind are far from the bee family. Instead, they were designed to look like them to steal that honey. There are bees, guard bees, whose only job is to stand at attention at the honeycombs and fight to the death to preserve that sticky goodness. That sugary vomit the worker beers spit up and turn into something wonderful. Yellow jackets are thieves, murderers. Not martyrs like the good bees, who only have one sting before the act rips out their innards in a macabre display of the ultimate sacrifice. Not yellow jackets. They can do it over and over again. The poor bees.

But this isn't a story about bees. It's the story of the yellow jacket.

Once, not that long ago, there was only one. A massive yellow jacket the size of a mature elephant—bigger, even. It lived in the mountains. Maybe it was the Rockies, maybe it was the Smokies, nobody knew for sure because it was spotted everywhere. How it flew from range to range without anyone noticing, without planes crashing into it or the winds bowing at its strength, nobody is certain. He moved his huge body like smoke, like Santa. It must have been in the darkest of the night, and he must have moved as beautifully as a moth.

Yellow Jacket had a taste for children, a hunger so deep none of the other animals could fathom. But most feared him too much to ask directly. It was like approaching an acting pedophile head-on, knowing his ammo was stacked and you'd have your throat sliced.

Once, a Guard Bee did ask him as he circled a honeycomb at dusk. "What's your problem?" Guard Bee asked, clenching his body in preparation for the squash. "Need our honey for the children, do you? They taste better in a marinade?"

"Fucking fool," Yellow Jacket said, crushing the Guard Bee easily with his leg. He barely felt the bee's first and last sting. For Guard Bee was right. They did taste better with honey.

He knew, he'd heard, the Human hunters were getting restless. He knew about their guns, knew they could destroy him with their metal bullets and sharp knives. But their young, their littlest ones, they didn't have the strength. Were too stupid, too trusting, to give him any pause. He couldn't help it, his cravings for them. The best, the most tender, were the ones in between. Half child, half grown. Especially the girls, especially when their blood was running. It was the last stages of innocence, a flower in full bloom, that he just couldn't resist.

But the hunters, the strongest of the human flocks, were tired of the sacrifices. Couldn't handle the disappearing children anymore, the complete breakdowns of their spouses. There were rumors all through the mountains that the Humans were gearing up for an attack. The Deer, the ones who escaped the gunshots, came back to their dens with stories of human words murmured. *Gonna get that yellow jacket. Gon' smoke him out and make him pay.* The whispers were so heavy, so thick, that they even reached the ears of Yellow Jacket. But what could he do? Stuff himself with nothing but honey, try and develop a taste for Buffalo and Rabbit? No, he couldn't. His body ached for the pieces of young girl flesh.

It was dawn when the hunters found him, circled round the mouth of the cave abandoned so long even the Spiders had given up on it. It was here that Yellow Jacket had called home for half a century. Just like his father before him, just one of them. One at a time. That's all the Greats would allow. One at a time. It was a lonely, desperate life. One that glowed only in small pieces when he'd drag a girl back home. And now, now. Their bones and hair, fingernails and teeth, decorated his cave like tchotchkes.

Yellow Jacket could smell the smoke before it crept into his eyes. He was dreaming, and it felt like the campfires he watched from a distance. He could almost smell the s'mores, hear the laughs of the young Humans. Fire, it comforted him. It was a beacon in the night, a sign of easy pickings. By the time he realized what was happening, he'd already lost himself in his head.

"My God," whispered Blue Jay to Sparrow, watching the Humans toss in more and more smoking sticks to the Yellow Jacket cave. "Do you think—do you think it's working?" he asked.

"I don't know," she said. "I hope so."

Slowly, the animals gathered. An unnatural gathering. Cougar beside Buck, Snake beside Mouse, and there was an agreement. This was something holy, or something damned. Until they knew which, they'd embrace peace around one another.

This even it? asked one of the Humans. Another chortled and spit a long stream of brown into the leaves. *Fuck 'fi no*, said the Human with the jacket that looked like leaves. *S'wat steev sed.* The animals couldn't understand those words, but they felt the worry, the distress. The trouble in the sounds.

And then it happened. Like a hurricane come on too fast.

From the smoking mouth of the cave, thousands—no, millions—of tiny yellow jackets burst angry from the black hole. Stormed over the heads of the Humans, made them scream but not for long. Jetted off in every which direction, swarming past the animals with the occasional tiny prick and sting but nothing, nothing like what big Yellow Jacket used to do. These pains, they hurt, but could only possibly kill the smallest of things.

"Did it have babies? Are these its children? Oh my God—" screamed a voice from the branches.

"It's me!" screeched one of the tiny yellow jackets. "It's me!" echoed another. "God damn! God damn! Look what they did!" And they saw, all the animals saw. Evil had been broken into a myriad of pieces, millions and millions of tiny pains instead of one big one. Was this better?

Was it?

Chapter Six

I stayed with him four years because I didn't know any different. Wait, that's not true. All I knew was Different. Josh was the opposite of my father in every fathomable way, from his grass-green eyes against my father's melting honey ones to his recklessly outgoing demeanor to my father's quiet reserve—his only woke up after the magical number of drinks. Josh turned nineteen the day before I turned sixteen, and we thought that was some kind of kismet. Destiny, perhaps, that I swung like a pregnant pendulum from my father's absence and neglect to Josh's mounting verbal abuse, emotional slaps, eventual physical confrontations. But it didn't start like that. It never does. I was young, I was stupid. I was a child oblivious that seething hatred was falling from the sky.

You'd think, after my one online-based debacle I'd be done. But I was way too stubborn for that. I went back for more, and it's like Josh was waiting. Probably he was. Lurking with oil slickness in the darkest of the AOL chatrooms. Before he was Josh, he was Rusty999, the name of the family dog.

This, remember, was the days before smartphones. Before selfies, before Facetime, before catfishing, before anything. Yes, of course you could send images online, but it was still taboo. Still took a lot of work. We talked for six months before any concrete plans to meet, although Josh was just 250 miles away in Portland. And we promised, romantically, not to exchange pictures 'til then. That was the foreplay of teenagers the year "One Sweet Day" and "Because You Loved Me" pushed for the chart tops.

But we described each other, of course we did. He said people most often said he looked like Blane in *Pretty in Pink*, and I thought I could manage an Andrew McCarthy. I told him I was told I looked Mariah Carey, though I didn't see it. After two months, he asked for a lock of my hair—today, that would be the mark of a serial killer. Then, I thought it poetic.

Josh drove down in his shuddering '81 BMW on a weekend his mom and stepdad were out of town. He was a high school dropout working as a busser at Red Robin, yet still had to ask permission to leave town. We told my parents that his were okay with it all, and my mom made up the spare bed for him in the makeshift detached garage cum rec room. My father, he didn't like the idea, but he went along with it. Who does that? Stretches clean sheets and pilled blankets across a pull-out couch so a stranger could fuck their daughter?

It was four years together, and they were increasingly horrific. When Josh arrived, we were both relieved neither of us looked like monsters. But what can you tell by looking? He pulled a boom box out of the trunk and we danced on the patio by the decrepit pool to "Everything I Do (I Do It for You)" and I thought I had *made it*. To me, Josh was alright looking. About five-foot nine, a mop of sandy brown hair, patrician nose and squinty green eyes. A body that suggested it could go V-shaped, but hadn't. And his penis? It was rather lovely with a flat mole at the base.

Of course we'd talked about sex, and I'd trimmed up my one incident the best I could. For the most part, I didn't have to lie. No, I hadn't loved him. No, it wasn't good. Yes, I wish I'd waited for Josh (that was the only lie). I didn't wish that. Until I did.

He was a virgin, that's what he said. I didn't know any different to tell if he was lying or not. But it didn't hurt much that time. After three days, his parents came back and found him missing with Rusty hungry for food. In a thirty-minute phone call, they'd negotiated with my parents to let Josh stay. He moved into the garage permanently, got a job at the Pilot gas station that had just opened up. I was turning sixteen and living with my boyfriend.

He was gorgeous to others, I saw that quickly and he became my beacon of what could have been. Dropped me off and picked me up from school every day, until the end of sophomore year. Brought me flowers that he stole from graveyards. Began sleeping in his car between classes and lunch until the principal told him he had to go. At almost nineteen, he was an adult man lurking in a child's parking lot.

The control started slowly. As it does. Josh bought me colored contacts, brown ones, because that would make me look more like Audrey Hepburn. Started tearing out magazine pictures of Natalie Portman, made me find outfits that matched hers. Told me to straighten me hair, no, "Kind of crunch it up with mousse like this one girl did at my old high school. She was beautiful." Me, I never was. Bit by bit, he replaced my entire wardrobe, my makeup, every part of me. All while my father tried to catch us fucking, but he never quite did.

"I don't trust the guys at your school," Josh told me the day before I turned sixteen. It was August, school wouldn't start for another month. It came from nowhere, hours before the freedom of a license was within my grip.

I failed.

"Are you fucking retarded?" my mom screeched as she drove the three of us home from the DMV in the aging minivan. "Even fucking *morons* can get driver's licenses." Josh looked at my sympathetically, squeezed my hand. Rolled his eyes. Did all the right things. The guys at school were nowhere near my brain's apex. Not that they had ever paid me much mind anyway—it was the girls who bellowed, "Whore!" down the hallway. Whispered, "slut" as I passed by. The most attention I'd gotten from a guy at school was when one, a chubby redhead who was preternaturally quiet, found me online and sent long descriptions of what he wanted to do to me out of nowhere. *I want to spread those thighs and dive right in*, he wrote. I never replied.

When I did get my license, Josh slipped in. "The car she has isn't safe," he told my mom. It was an '85 red Mustang convertible I'd saved for since I was twelve, scooping nachos at the raceway in the summers. Selling all my Barbies and toys at garage sales. "She needs something sturdier," and my mom blindly followed his words. It was swapped for a Ford Probe with pop-up lights and an ugly burgundy interior two weeks later.

The loss pangs cut me when a middle-aged woman drove the Mustang away, and I hated the Probe. I despised Josh for forcing it on me. I had no idea it was meant to be an escape vehicle.

In late August, when Josh did the big reveal, proved my dad was having an online affair, the last of the wobbly walls crumbled. My dad ran away for good, escaped up north to Scio. My mom went insane. Pierce her nipples, buy a dog collar and invite men from the newspaper over to whip her and take photos, tattoo on her ass insane.

"That psychotic boyfriend of yours needs to go," she screamed at me while Josh was at work. "Now."

"You tell him," I said.

"No, you little cunt," she said. "You choose. Right now. Him or me." What a fucking idiot to think I, to think that anyone, would choose her. Really, I thought she was bluffing. She thought I was, too. So when I came home from school the next day to find the locks changed and random clothes of mine in a black trash bag on the porch, a jolt of freedom shot through me. This was it. I was free.

She poked her head out the screen door as I slammed the bag into the trunk, her graying inch-long hair spraying every direction like a mad scientist. "You want to come back now?" she asked, her voice that mean little kid sing-song like she always had. I hated that. Hated how she said something was "yummy, yummy, yummy" instead of good or delicious. Like the four-year-old in her had been clinging on airtight for years, too stubborn to let go.

"You fucking bitch!" It was the first time I'd ever yelled at her, the first time I'd shown what I really felt. She slammed the door behind her, clicked it shut. I knew, right then. Knew I only had a few minutes.

Josh was at work, but could sense the urgency when I whipped into the parking lot. "We need to go," I said. "Now." For the first time, he didn't hesitate, didn't ask questions. Just got in.

For six months, we lived in that Probe. Stole and re-sold items at pawn shops. Showered at other Pilot gas stations in California and central Oregon. Slowly worked our way back up to Portland where his family begrudgingly took me in. "You need insurance," his mom said, an all-together woman with deer eyes. "And at least a GED. Something." Before we'd arrived, she had been in contact with my parents. Tracked my dad down to his runaway cabin in North Carolina with his new girlfriend. Both my parents had, in writing, relinquished all parental rights to me, and Josh's parents became my legal guardians. I got my diploma through independent study at the community college and lied on job applications to say I was eighteen so I could get hired. Before I was seventeen, Josh and I were living together in a little one-bedroom that I paid for in full. He spent his days playing video games and sleeping 'til the afternoon.

Twice, I got pregnant. I didn't realize the birth control hormones were making me sick, didn't figure out that throwing them up meant they didn't work. The first time, I cried an ocean before settling into the idea that maybe it was alright. "How do I even know it's mine?" he asked. At least, he took me for the abortion. I was barely eighteen. It happened again less than a year later.

When he eventually got a job at Abercrombie, he immediately began an affair with his manager. She left messages with a sickly sweet voice on our answering machine. I'd started beauty school, and when I skipped one day to surprise him back at home, I came in just in time to hear him say, "I love you." Three months later, he began sleeping with the sixteen-year-old who worked at Walgreens across the street.

It got real bad the day I found out he was taking the Walgreens girl to prom and he tackled me on the kitchen floor to keep me from leaving. As his knee pressed into my throat and my eyes began to water, for a second I thought about just letting it happen. Just letting it go. But I wasn't that. I wasn't my mother.

Some superhuman strength sliced through me, giving me the ability to throw him off long enough to grab a kitchen knife off the counter. "Hey, hey, hey," he said, backing away. Letting me get to the doorway. Down the stairs. Into my car, though his blocked me in. He liked doing that. Also liked to pet the hood of my car to make sure it wasn't warm unless he'd pre-approved some place for me to go. Either work or school.

"Come out," he said, pulling at the handles of my locked car. I kept the knife in my left hand, gripped the steering wheel with my right.

"Move your car," I said, the calmness in my voice shocking me.

"No, just come out—"

"Move it or I move it for you." He didn't believe me. How stupid he was.

I rammed into his car with a hatred that had been stewing for years.

"Oh my God!" he screamed like a little kid. "You fucking bitch! You're just like your mother!" And just like that he moved. I drove, with instinct, directly to a friend's house. The only friend I had in Portland. Josh hated her because she didn't fall under his words, worship like a child.

"Did you pull a knife on my son?" his mom asked when she called me at work.

"Only to get him off me while he was choking me on the floor," I said. It sounded so matter of fact. Like it happened every day.

"Did you hit his car?" she asked.

"Only when he refused to let me out," I said.

She sighed. "That's not the story he says." I felt the briefest desire to apologize, but I just sat there, silent, until she hung up.

Twice, I saw him again. Once to get my stuff and he tried to negotiate for sex. "You know how sometimes … some people … old couples, they still, you know? Just for fun?"

"The kid not fucking you?" I asked as I shoved my few possessions into soft paper bags.

"Well, her dad's a *minister,* you know," he said. "So she's staying pure 'til marriage. And I can't marry her 'til she's eighteen."

"I wouldn't fuck you for all the money in the world," I said.

"Well. At least I was your first," he said.

"I lied."

It was true. He'd called me a slut so many times when he first came down to Medford that I began to feel like one. Told him I'd made up the whole thing about losing my virginity before. It was exhausting, just listening to him, I'd have said anything to shut him up. Anything.

"Are you—are you serious?" he asked. The last cheap nylon shirt was crammed into my bag.

"Yes."

"I always knew you were a fucking whore."

vii.   Snakes, Sun and Sin

Humans have always been smitten with sacrifices, and Snakes make the best offerings of all. Most Snakes, they're content. They wriggle in their terrariums and perch below heat lamps, or slide through the desert sands baking in the heat. Misunderstood, that's their real protection. Not the shoot-out fangs or the few that carry poison in their scaled bodies. People think they're slimy to the touch, bite for pleasure, stalk big, beefy bodies that would never fit into even their most stretched-out long, long stomachs.

And the sun, the sun. Its ego grew just as fat, round and blindingly bright at itself. It began to rain down on the earth like a crazed monster, intent on burning everything on up. They called it global warming, heat waves, and made a game of seeing what could be cooked on the sidewalks. All the technology, the science, the knowledge Humans had accumulated over the centuries didn't add up to a solution. And so a sacrifice was decided.

We need a volunteer for glory. You'll save the earth, save us all. That was all that needed to be said, and the people began lining up. Humans are quick to give up their most precious possession for a shot at glory, even if they'll be dead and won't see it for themselves. We wonder why some hold still for their own honor killings, how it can be so easy to recruit suicide bombers. We shouldn't. We've always been quick to offer up our hearts in the hope that maybe this, this ultimate offering, will be enough to buy us forever.

They chose the man because he seemed the least crazy of all. Almost normal, with just the right amount of friends on social media. A basic American upbringing complete with a dog name Scribbles, a brother and most of his grandparents still alive. *What does your family think of you doing this?* he was asked. *I don't know. I haven't told them yet.* It was a boring, nice answer.

The recruiters scoured his history, pulled up his grades from elementary school and quizzed his closest friends and every girl he'd ever fucked (heterosexuality without even a brief petting of a friend's penis in middle school made him delightfully even more mundane). Still, they found nothing. Nothing. He was nothing, nothing, nothing. And in that lack of finding, they found their answer.

He was perfect.

The television crews and podcasts crowded around his last day. His family cried, his friends took their last selfies, and one of his most recent bed partners (the one before the most recent) took off her engagement ring to stammer over coffee with him one last time. But for the main event, it was just him and a smattering of faceless lab coats.

Are you sure you don't want to know how this works? asked a female lab coat armed with a syringe. *No last questions? As you know, we're not certain how communication between us will work after—*

No, no. Nothing at all. I'm fine, the man said. He knew his mission, that the risks were high and the rewards unknown.

Two hours later, he was the biggest Snake you've ever seen.

Go towards the light, a voice whispered into his body. He didn't have ears now, and picked up the message through his whole skin, muscles, even his bones. There were hangovers from his Human life already, fading and drunk. The voice sounded like Penelope Cruz. *Abre los ojos, abre los ojos.*

And so he did. He was a giant snake, a monster, a God and he shot through the universe towards the sun like a meteor. This was what he was made to do, by the Gods, by the Humans, by every force in the galaxy. To simmer the sun, lower its heat, save the world from extinction. He was close, so close, the heat blasted between his scales and scalded his new eyes that couldn't see color but drank in a sharpness he'd never known before. He was an angel, a savior, Icarus soaring towards the heat.

He got close, so maddeningly close, before he could go no farther. *You think you can swallow me like one of your mice?* asked the sun, its voice brimming with laughter. *I keep you warm, cook your belly with my fire. Pull the rabbits from their dens so you can taste their thin skulls and rusty blood in your throat. You are nothing to me, a charity. May you crawl through the dregs of the earth in your worship of me.* He was cast from the stars a failure, blinded by all he'd seen.

By the time he reached earth, the words of the Humans were slipping faster from his brain. Only a few he could make out. *Try again? ... failed ... embarrassment ... in a rescue ... let him go. Let him go.*

Maybe it was a, what, a rescue? Conservation camp they sent him to? He didn't know, he didn't know what Home was supposed to be for a Snake. Other living things began to split into two groups, those that were Eatable and those that were Not. More so, two other groups, those that were Dangerous and those that were Not, came nipping at the first group's heels. He had three reasons to live, and they drove him daily, daily, daily. First to eat, next to avoid the Dangerous. Humans, Bears, Mongoose, the names sometimes spurted into his mind at random, but usually they were all called Dangerous to him, and they all smelled the same.

And third? To seek out the sun, the heat. To bask in its glory.

In clips and fits, 'til the end of his days, he had moments of Human clarity. Some mornings he awoke confused why his arms didn't work, why he couldn't flail his legs over the bed. *Oh, yes. Oh, yes,* he recalled, and the Human words began to fade faster.

But why *can't we see the Snake, Baba?* It was a little one, a—a child, that was it. On the other side of the barricade. The voice sounded foreign, lilting at the wrong letters. *I've told you,* said a bigger one, exasperation thick and wet. *Ever since the ... incident ... it'll make you go blind. Just trust that it's there, okay? Look! There's its picture.*

Not 'it'. He, thought Snake. *I'm a he, a he, a he.*

Chapter Seven

I left Josh for good in spring, moved onto the couch of a woman I barely knew who'd shown some type of kindness to me at work. I couldn't help it. I had nowhere else to go. Besides most of my clothes, what I used every day, I left it all behind. All the shit Josh had put on the credit cards he'd applies for in my name, even when I was sixteen, seventeen, those sweet ages when the credit card companies should have noticed my birth year didn't match my social security number and they kept sending the cards anyway. There were four, five little ones with five-hundred-dollar limits, but that added up fast to someone just barely toeing up to twenty years old.

Lost and flailing, I enrolled in the local state school in downtown Portland because what the hell else was I going to do? They let me in with my sympathy application and because, with my independent status, the financial aid Gods favored me thick. There were four months to stab slowly with a dull knife before the autumn quarter began and my sliver of a single dorm room would spread her creaky wooden legs to me. Four months of taking up as little space and making as small of noise as possible so, hopefully, my martyr of a roommate wouldn't notice me.

Four months to fuck anybody but Josh, wash his slime out from my insides. But I couldn't. I had no practice in seduction, not even in bumbling and overt sexuality. I did nothing.

It wasn't until I'd tucked into that closet of a dorm room, bought cheap nylon bedding and strung Christmas lights around the odd little sink in the corner, faked my way into a sorority and began the long string of failing classes when alcohol (my new best friend and confidante) gave me permission to let a stranger take me.

It was early October and I'd padded myself with stranger-friends whose last names were just starting to get imprinted in my brain. Sorority sisters, the same ones who trudged to Sunday meetings with me hungover and moaning about classes the next day. As much as we wanted to, as much as I wanted to, we weren't allowed to wear our letters when we drank. Nationals stripped us of that armor, and we were feared into following them, especially at open fraternity parties. What if someone from the rival sorority saw? Everyone seemed to be experts at ramming each other under oncoming busses, developed super human strength like those mothers you hear about who lift cars off babies with one steady arm.

The Kappas were having an Around the World party and, even though they terrified me with their stories of sledding off their roof and they had the best-looking guys of all the houses, I still went. Didn't even know what an Around the World party was, but like I'd been doing for the past four weeks, I dove into the initiation of it without blinking. When we arrived, we were given cheap paper passport printouts describing the theme and drink in every room. You had to follow the map exactly and had to drink the entirely of whatever cheap, sugar-laden drink they'd thought up before being allowed to move on. There were eight rooms in total. But first, arm hooked through Bianca's, the dumbest girl in the entire sorority (the dumbest girl I'd ever met), we scouted the old, sprawling Victorian for a place to hide our purses. The half-full washing machine made the perfect treasure chest.

Room one, some kind of tropical theme with dollar store leis and a guy going towards beer belly in a grass skirt and coconut bra. "Pirate's boo-tay!" he roared, pushing a red Solo cup towards us that reeked of bottom shelf rum and Hawaiian punch. There was the jungle room, which served Jungle Juice of course and had "Welcome to the Jungle" on repeat. We shotgunned beers in Detroit, took lukewarm shots of sake in One Night in Bangkok (did they have sake in Thailand? I didn't know), drank watery margaritas in Mexico. By the time we stumbled out of Paris is for Fuckers, the walls were trembling. But I wasn't drunk, at least not drunk-drunk. Not yet. I'd only had my first drink ever two months ago, but my tolerance had shot up surprisingly fast. The fact that we'd stuffed ourselves with pizza beforehand to ward off the blackouts helped.

Bianca disappeared, as she tended to do. She had a penchant for pulling down her tight jeans and fucking fraternity boys in their dirty bathrooms. Already, she'd drummed up a nickname for herself. Springs. Not that anyone ever really heard the creaking of the mattress coils when she took them on, but eighteen-year-old boys have vivid imaginations.

"What are you supposed to be?" He was crazy tall, the tallest boy who'd ever spoken to me. I could tell already, even though he was somehow sitting beside me on the ratty couch. Had he always been there? How had he lowered his greatness onto the complaining cushions without my knowing? His thigh was almost touching mine, was twice my femur's length.

"Oh," I said, looking down. What *was* I supposed to be? Every party was a costume party, and for Around the World it was a crapshoot. "I don't remember," I said. For some reason he thought this was funny and his smile lit up the room like a firecracker.

"Me either," he said. He wore sunglasses with a bright orange frame, a Hawaiian shirt that let the outline of the top of chest muscles shine through. "You go to school here?" he asked.

"Yeah." Of course I did. Why else would I be here?

"Huh," he said. "Not me. My friend. Troy? He does and brought me along. We were supposed to be at a strip club tonight." Was I supposed to know who Troy was?

"Sorry to disappoint," I said.

"No disappointment," he said. "I'm Kyle." Kyle. I'd always loved that name. Had a crush on a middle school Kyle with black hair and eyes, prone to fat and who (last I'd heard) was a helicopter pilot for the local Medford news station.

When he shook my hand, like we were meeting over important documents in some brilliant Windex-glowing office, they were nothing like Josh's. His palm swallowed mine whole in one fast bite.

He was a banker at the downtown Wells Fargo. A real one who didn't work in a branch or anything like that, but did Important Financial Stuff that he summed up in nugget-sized pieces but I still couldn't follow. I was mesmerized by his voice, deeper than any I'd known. He was twenty-six. Should I be concerned that a grown man was slumped into stained fraternity couches when he could already have a master's degree? I didn't think about it and I didn't know anyway. He soared above me. And when he pulled those thick lips back into a grin, the shock of his perfect smile shot me into blindness. I'd have followed him anywhere.

Bianca re-emerged as the mythical Troy sunk down on the other side of Kyle. No, I didn't know him. Didn't recognize him. Turns out, he wasn't a fraternity member anyway, but did go to school there. His body reminded me of Josh, but he had thick blond hair and dark blue eyes. Surely Bianca would take him.

The negotiations happened like I thought they would. Who would drive who, how far away Kyle's apartment was (just ten minutes), pretenses of what we'd do. It was nearly one in the morning when we crammed into Troy's little brown truck and rumbled off the base of the West Hills to Kyle's one-bedroom on Barbur Boulevard. Bianca and I ducked into the fading rooms on our way to the fraternity bathroom, me needing to re-up my courage before letting it all go. By now, the card tables weren't manned and every room was perfumed with vomit.

Kyle's apartment wasn't much bigger than some of the college housing apartments I'd seen, and it looked like a man lived there. Everything was beige, from the carpets to the chipped paint, and the whole focal point of the squashed living room was the television. Half-empty beer bottles littered the plyboard coffee table, and I took the cold one he offered me so I'd have something safe to wrap my hands around. He sat next to me on the short couch while Bianca curled into Troy in the big, cracked recliner. They started necking immediately. Funny, I never used that word, that dinosaur from the 50s, but that's exactly what it was. Her neck, the one Troy began covering and claiming in hickies, looked long as a swan's.

Kyle had asked if we'd seen *One Night at McCool's*, a "bomb-ass movie," and we hadn't. It didn't matter anyway. There's no way I'd be able to even remotely follow a storyline. By the time Liv Tyler was seducing Matt Dillon in his dead mom's house in her tight red dress, Kyle big hand was on my thigh. By the time John Goodman had fallen for her, too, his entire side was pressed into mine. By the time Paul Reiser was describing the cherry-dotted dress she wore to a barbeque, his mouth was on mine.

This is what being with a real man is like, I told myself. It was easy, letting him take control. Take charge. Take whatever he wanted.

"You okay?" he asked as his dry hand slid up my thigh.

"Yeah," I said. Willing nonchalance from my voice.

"We're going," he said suddenly to Troy who was drowning in Bianca's straw hair. Kyle took my hand, pulled me from the couch, and directed me down the narrow hall to a bedroom so black my eyes couldn't adjust. He never turned on any lights, and the bedding was deceptively softer, cleaner than I thought it would be. Another person's bed is always strange, it doesn't matter if they'll be sliding between your thighs or not. It's here where you suffocate in their real smells, where you figure it out their pillow or lumpy and how thick they like the comforters. How worn their sheets are, what kind of laundry detergent they use. If they add dryer sheets.

He didn't remove anything but my underwear, and for that I was grateful. Even in the dark, even in the blackness, I wasn't ready to be really naked. Instead, he just kept kissing me, tongue diving into my mouth in little spurts. Light, like an appetizer. Slowly, the glow from the blue-lit digital clock began to outline shapes in the room. 2:42 and the chair pregnant with button-ups and basketball shorts appeared. 2:48 and a crowded desk with unplugged electronics came into shape.

From the headboard, a heavy old thing made of thick wood, Kyle grabbed a condom, it's loud packet crinkling against my ear and (I imagined), slipped it onto his cock in a second. Really, I couldn't see anything. Never did see it. Just heard the noises, felt his arm moving against mine.

By 2:51, he was inside me and I could feel the heat from him struggling through the cool, slick condom. He nuzzled his face into my neck, and I could taste the sugary concoctions from the fraternity house mixing with his saliva. Watching the clock made it seem like it lasted longer. As the numbers ticked closer to three, I pulled at his back, made the sounds I knew I was supposed to, and just wanted it to be done so I could tick my first one night stand off my life. Replace Josh with someone else so I could shoot like lightning into my new life.

He never asked if I finished (thank God), or said much of anything when he pulled out and I heard the slap of the condom being taken off. "I gotta take out my contacts," he said, and disappeared into a bathroom that I hadn't noticed before. In the bathroom mirror, I could see a quarter of his shirtless body reflected back at me. It looked strange and grown.

A few hours later, in the harshness of morning light, he slipped out of bed and began banging pots in the little kitchen. Eggs and meat began to sizzle and crackle, muffled voices began to emerge. I wish I'd taken my contacts out, too, but I'd been too embarrassed to ask. Now, they stuck like dry leeches in my eyes.

"Breakfast?" Kyle asked as I walked carefully into the living room. Bianca and Troy were strewn across the couch. I'd done my best to fix my hair and makeup in the bathroom mirror, but I knew I looked a mess.

"Uh, no. I'm not hungry," I said. I was starving, but I wouldn't eat in front of him like nothing had happened.

Troy drove Bianca and I back to campus, Kyle offering up a kiss at the door. Like he was a housewife and I was off to sell vacuums door to door for the day in my too-short skirt with the hem starting to rip.

For two weeks I thought about him. Knew where he lived and made excuses to myself to take Barbur when I headed out of downtown instead of the faster, more convenient highway. It wasn't him I was hooked to, I knew that. It was all he represented.

Bianca had Troy's number and finally, after ten days, I wanted a do-over. It didn't take much to convince her to call Troy and ask him to hang out. He nearly lived with Kyle, his own home being miles away in Eugene. If he was in Portland, I knew where he'd be.

"He said okay!" Bianca said as she hung up. "Friday night."

I drove us, not even having to slow down to check to make sure it was the right apartment complex. This time I'd do it right. Ask for a spare contact case like I had the right to it.

When Kyle answered the door, he was dressed like a pimp—feather boa, big hat and all. He was shocked to see me. "Oh—hi!" he said. I couldn't read what was behind these sunglasses.

"Hey," I said. "Just ... picking up Troy," I said, even as Bianca was already pushing past to hold Troy tight.

"Oh, yeah," Kyle said. "He, uh, he said he was going out. I just didn't—I'm going to a costume party. With friends," he said. I don't want you here.

"I can—I can see that," I said. He was different, oceans away. He scared the shit out of me, and I saw nothing of the brief moments of tenderness he'd showcased earlier that month.

"Well," he said as Bianca pulled Troy to the car. "You kids have fun!"

Show me your eyes, I wanted to scream, to demand. *Show me your eyes.*

viii.   Crane Seeks Love

Every day he watched her from the waters, his eyes curling around her as she walked with shoulders-back, chest-forward, hips squared yoga body across the carefully manmade bridge. Draped long piano fingers along the splinter-less railing. Wondered at how she kept her expensive shoe treads so white, her black leggings so free of snags. To Crane, she was perfection—but he was far from alone.

"She'll never love you," said Hummingbird as he sprinted from bloom to bloom, long tongue suckling and whip-fast wings ablaze.

"I know that," said Crane, although he prayed that he was lying. Held tight to fantasies that the woman could look beyond his ugliness. Those long gangling legs punctuated by knocking knees. Drooping looking tailfeathers and hunched forward head that made him look like he was always sorry.

"If anything," said Hummingbird, flashing around Crane's head, "she would fall in love with me. I mean, if I wished her to." Hummingbird was probably right. Everybody loved him. They thought there was something magical, fairytale like about him. They hung beautiful glass tubes flanked with beads from their French doors and windows, hoping to lure him close. Cooked up homemade sugar water concoctions stovetop, let it cool, and dripped it slowly into their window dressings for just a chance to glimpse him close.

"Then why don't you?" said Crane. Crane would, if he could. In an instant. He thought he saw Hummingbird cock his head, though it was impossible to tell since the damned thing couldn't stay still long enough to let any subtleties leak out.

"I could," said Hummingbird. "I could. What about you? Why do your females lay two egg but just raise one? Too lazy?" That was just like him, to take two incomparable things and smash them together.

"Why are you asking me what women do?" asked Crane. The truth was, he'd wondered it himself, but had never asked. Didn't want to pique his own mother's interest in wishing she'd raised his brother instead of him. He just assumed it was a brother in that other egg, although he couldn't even remember the shape of it. Whether there were oddities or speckles that made it stand out. If it had shaken with life or not. What he could recall of childhood was doled up in spits and flecks. His mother's gentle feedings. Learning to fish. Figuring out how to balance on those spindly legs.

"Well. I guess it's too late to figure that out," said Hummingbird. "You'll likely never know. I mean, it's not like you'll have chicks of your own."

"You know what?" started Crane. It was time, about time. His love would come to the bridge at any moment. "Let's just ask her then. Ask her which she'd prefer. But not just like that. We'll make a bet of it. Prove our devotion to her."

"I wouldn't say I'm devoted—" began Hummingbird.

"Nevermind that," said Crane. He was tired of waiting. He'd been watching her for two years. Not once had he seen her with a partner. Never heard her speak into the phone about dates or boyfriends or anything.

"Well, what kind of bet do you have in mind?" said Hummingbird. "If it's fishing, count me out!"

"No, no," said Crane. "A race. Whoever wins the race wins."

"You really are stupid," said Hummingbird. "But okay."

"Okay," agreed Crane. "But you ask her."

The eye roll, even if it wasn't really there, was palpable.

As she approached, Hummingbird zipped around her. He made her smile, made her laugh so easy. "Gorgeous morning, gorgeous," he said. Why couldn't Crane make it as easy as that?

"Good morning," she replied. Her voice, it sounded like the best dreams.

"Are you the romantic sort?" Hummingbird asked.

"Aren't we all?" True. Aren't we all.

"My friend and I, we were wondering," began Hummingbird. "We both find you the most beautiful woman we've ever seen. But we're friends, so ... we don't want to make things difficult between *us*."

"Oh?"

"So we decided, whoever wins a race gets to ask you on a date. Would you accept? With the winner?"

"Who's your friend?" she asked. Already her body language was screaming yes for him.

"Right there," Hummingbird said, nodding to Crane.

"Oh. *Oh*," she said. His heart slammed to the ground. Even though he was used to it, those pity stares. It stabbed deeper coming from her. "Uhm. Okay," she said.

He knew why she said okay. It was the same reason Hummingbird accepted the bet. They didn't know, nobody knew. It was his best, last secret. They didn't know he could fly.

The race was set for the next morning at sunrise. When she came, she wore a flowing yellow dress he'd never seen before, gold sandals peeking out from the hem. A vision. It was a clichéd simile, but it matched. She looked like the sun itself.

"Ready, go!" she yelled, and at first Crane let Hummingbird sprint ahead. To him, so tiny, it must have felt like he was soaring, like nobody had ever moved so fast. Crane took a reaching step into the water. Then two. Just as her smile began to break into something made of the Gods, he flapped his expansive wings and took flight. "My God," she whispered as he took to the air. Within seconds, he overtook Hummingbird, reached the far end of the park and turned in an arc so full of grace he looked nothing like himself.

"I didn't know you could fly!" Hummingbird said when he returned. "You cheated."

"I didn't cheat. You never asked," said Crane.

"Whatever. Go ahead. Ask her, then," Hummingbird said in a huff, speeding off, angry at the loss of the race much more than the loss of the girl.

"Oh, sorry. You know. Actually? I don't—I don't like this whole idea. Of being a prize," she said, raising up from the bench she sat on and wiping the dust from her legs. "Sorry."

Sorry. Sorry, sorry, sorry. Crane kept watching her the rest of his days, but from the shadows. From the dampness below the leaves. He never did see her with a partner, with a ring, with the flush from morning sex. Was he really worse than that? Was he worse than loneliness?

Chapter Eight

I let Parker get ushered towards me because I wanted to wear a pretty dress and didn't want to be left out. I'd never been to prom. Josh had consumed the whole of my teenage years. "Are you going to the black and white thing?" Allison asked me. Another new so-called sister, I was still working all their names over my tongue. Making them taste like familiar comfort food instead of something too spicy and foreign.

"I don't know," I told her. There were five of us gathered at a worn vinyl booth in the biggest student lounge area. It had somehow become our booth in just a few short weeks, and no matter what time you showed up, one of us would be there. It was the kind of porch light left on, homey feeling I'd never known.

"You should!" said Nicki, a girl who was perpetually stoned and lived with her parents in their monstrous West Linn home. "Why wouldn't you?"

I shrugged. "It's not like I have a date …"

It was true. It had been three weeks since my second and last Kyle confrontation, and although that wound had scabbed over, I still liked to lick at it. "So?" asked Nicki. "I have a lot of guy friends. I can set you up."

"What about me?" Allison asked, recently single after her born again Christian boyfriend said he was a little sad they wouldn't be going to heaven together. Her going to hell and all.

"Yeah, both of you," said Nicki. "I know a lot of guys."

She did. We were given names, Parker and Stephen, and no description beyond that. Nicki had gone to high school locally with Stephen, and Parker was his friend she'd met four times. "They're nice!" is all she would say.

The day of the black and white ball, we crammed into Nicki's parent's multiple bathrooms to pile on more makeup and spill beige powder down our inky dresses. The local black sorority and fraternity hosted this floating ball yearly on the Portland Spirit and invited the other Greek houses out of regretful social obligations. No outsider ever went though, and we didn't realize that's how everyone liked it. For the first time in years, we—a mixed up crew of non-black girls and their non-black dates—would be attending and making a spectacle of ourselves. Nicki's parents ordered pizza for us, and when it arrived an hour late we only had ten minutes to gorge ourselves with cold slices before the guys showed up.

That night, I hated Nicki. I hated Allison because Stephen was cute. Parker looked like everything I found unattractive in a man. Semi-tall, very thin, with a beak nose and hay-colored hair riding milky blue eyes. It was the kind of hair that would make him bald by thirty.

"You're thinking I look like someone famous, huh?" he asked me after shaking my hand limply. His palm was been cold and wet.

"Uh—" I didn't want to insult him immediately, but what was I supposed to say?

"I'll help you out," he said. "It's Andy Dick." He was right. He looked incredibly like a taller Andy Dick.

Even though the buzz of alcohol was already clawing through me, I took three more shots in the bathroom to get through the evening. Sitting on laps and pretending we couldn't feel penises between cheap suit pants and thin rayon dresses, the drive to the Portland waterfront was full of laughs and screams and clear alcohol perfuming our wrinkling clothes. It was only the second floor-length dress I had ever worn, sleeveless and black to show off my fattening white upper arms, and in the car it got stuck under someone's mangy heel. Ripped before we even arrived.

The actual ball was just a ninety-minute cruise where sideways glances were tossed at the intruders, us, while we were largely ignored. The two presidents thanked us briefly for coming in their opening speeches, and all our worries of being overdressed died fast. The real members in attendance had bouffants that must have taken hours, full-body sequined dresses and suits that were custom made. We were just playing dress up. At the big round table that seated eight of us, it was easy to be minimally polite to Parker. After all, he had Stephen and Nicki to keep him company. He laughed fast, showing a gummy smile I hated. It was too much like mine. But the champagne was bottomless and something about the rocking big boat lulled us all into a false sense of alcohol-proof security. By the time we de-boarded, I was almost at blackout status.

"Let's go to a party," Nicki said, clinging to her own date, an ex-boyfriend who still looked at her with smitten eyes. "I have a friend who's—hey, watch the fucking dress!— what was I ... oh, yeah. A friend is having a party, like, five minutes away." It was thirty-five minutes away, but it gave me time to sober up. The party was the classic sticky floors that suck at your shoe type, everyone there was way drunker than us by the time we arrived, and it was broken up within ten minutes. Before any of us even got drinks mixed in the kitchen.

"Alright, let's get going," boomed a voice from the front door that could only belong to a bored sounding cop.

"Is everyone twenty-one?" asked a female cop voice. Hers was ripe with excitement for whipping out MIPs.

"Oh, fuck, oh, fuck," whisper-shouted Nicki. "I'm holding! Come on," she dragged me to the basement that was already crammed full of people. Suddenly Parker was on one side of me, Nicki on the other, in a sweating basement so pregnant with drunkards that the only room for us was balancing on the old wooden steps leading down. For what seemed like an hour, nobody spoke besides the occasional, "Be quiet!" and "Are they gone yet?" Even if we couldn't hear the person retching and vomiting in the corner, the smell would have told us about it.

By the time the group brain got bored enough to crawl out, the cops were still standing in the front yard but must have gotten cramps from writing all those tickets. At this point, they just herded us out to the street.

"Okay, well, bye!" yelled Nicki as she clung to her ex-boyfriend's arm and let him lead her away.

"Well, that was ... interesting," said Parker. We were alone together. How did we get alone together? Loneliness, though, it was waiting for me back at the dorm. I wished he were Kyle, Stephen. Anybody.

"Yeah."

"So. Do you want to—go somewhere else?" he asked, checking his watch. "It's one, though, so I'm not sure how late anything will be—"

"We should go to Canada," I said. I have no idea why.

"Uh, yeah! I mean, next weekend I—"

"No, tonight. Right now."

"Now?" It was a challenge, and a cheap one. I didn't care. "Sure!"

And just like that, we took a cab that happened to be rolling by—sheer luck or a sign—to my car parked on campus. I didn't even go in to change. "Can we stop at my mom's first?" he asked. "It's on the way, in southeast. I want to get something." He was bothering me, making me wait for him.

"Okay," I said. We snuck into his mom's seemingly abandoned vintage home like bandits. I couldn't see much as he rummaged through what looked like a sprawling storage basement, but was somehow on a strange landing.

"Hold this," he said, shoving a fat wallet at me, before picking up a relic of a VCR.

"Why are you taking a VCR?" I whispered as a strange cat wrapped around my legs.

"We might need it?" Was he asking me?

By the time we were running low on gas somewhere between Portland and Seattle, I knew it was a bad idea. Maybe not bad, but stupid. Another stupid idea. In the middle of the night, we waited for ten minutes in the car for the attendant to come out before remembering you had to pump your own gas in Washington. Parker did it while I stayed inside, listening to the same pop music on the radio and pulling at my now itchy dress. Janet Jackson's "All for You." "Peaches and Cream" by 112. What the hell was taking him so long?

"I got it," he said finally, sliding back into the passenger seat. It was colder than what an early October should be, wasn't it?

The sky was starting to go to pink well past Seattle, and in the blooming light the stains from the vodka and whiskey were beginning to shine on both of this. *Let's turn around, let's go back.* I couldn't work the words through my teeth.

"Hey, look!" he said, pointing to a sign. "Just a few more miles 'til the border." Well. We couldn't turn back now.

I flew my little Hyundai across the line and just like that we were in Canada. Was it that easy? It looked the same. Everything, from Portland through Washington to British Columbia, it all just looked like a version of home, slightly diluted.

The tired had caught up with both of us, so I just turned into the first Best Western I saw. It couldn't have been more than fifteen miles from America. Feeling badly for dragging this stranger to another country in the middle of the night, I paid. It was already early Saturday morning, and check-in wasn't until eleven, but they let us in anyway. Maybe they thought we were prom refugees. Maybe they thought we had just eloped.

Would I have to fuck him? Did I owe him that now? Jesus. In the sober morning light, he looked even worse. I would have swapped him for the real Andy Dick right then if those were my two options. Exhaustion kept me from making that decision, and we fell asleep side by side in the big king-sized bed without touching. Neither of us moved until mid-afternoon.

Shuffling in some weird, extended walk of shame, we just made it a couple of blocks away. Bought overpriced bottles of little hard alcohol at the liquor store and a discount movie at a Blockbuster knockoff. I guess his fast VHS machine grabbing had been a good idea after all. The hotel charged ten dollars a day to rent theirs. We ate greasy Chinese food and told each other it was good. Tried to go on a pleasure drive, but the bright sun shot pins and needles through our recovering, liquored up eyes. By five, we gave up and just went back to the hotel.

I gave him what he came for while the Sylvester Stallone movie we'd bought rumbled on. It was getting easier, giving sex away like this. The miniature bottles helped lube things up and make it happen faster. He kissed me and I let him, because it was better to get blinded by his blurred, too-close face than to see him. Really, it wasn't that bad. Was it? It didn't take that long and it was a relief to at least get out of that dress for a little while. I forgot the details, the mechanics, as soon as he was finished. The real pleasure of it was getting to wear his too-long undershirt the rest of the night while my poor black dress hung like a beaten dog on the chair. I only had to fuck him once. He didn't ask or try much after that.

On Sunday morning, I angled the car back to the America border where there was a line miles long. "What the hell?" I said. "There were—there were no lines coming in. Were there?"

"I don't think so ..." he said. "But, it was in the middle of the night when that happened."

"No, it wasn't," I snapped.

"Oh, my—oh, my God. Oh, my God," he began to repeat. "Where's the—where's the wallet I gave you? My wallet?"

"In the glove compartment! What's your problem?" I asked. Didn't he know I just wanted to get home?

"There's weed in it," he whispered. Fuck. In the rearview mirror, Canadian police (were they called Mounties? Or was that only if they were on a horse?) walked car to car with German Shepherds at their side.

"Hide it!" I said.

"What do you want me to do with it?"

"I don't know! I didn't even know you had it."

"I thought we might—never mind. Fuck." With the least amount of subtlety I'd ever seen, he pulled less than a dime back from the fat brown wallet and stuck it deep between the carpet and floorboard, spraying air freshener over it and nearly smoking us out.

"Passports?" the cop said when he came to us, glancing at the American license plates.

"Uh, passports?" I asked as Parker pulled his from the wallet and handed it to the police, brushing my chest in the process.

"Yes. Passports."

"I don't—I don't have a passport," I said. Fuck, fuck, fuck. I hadn't needed one for Mexico. "We didn't, I mean we didn't need one when we came to Canada last night ..."

"Americans don't need passports to get in," the cop said, sounding exasperated and I realized he'd given this speech hundreds of times. "You need one to get back."

I was just way too tired. I couldn't do this, I didn't want to do this, and I didn't want this strange guy in my car. I don't know if the cop sensed I couldn't take anymore, if he was just trying to push through the line of sometimes honking cars, or if we had some kind of telepathic conversation I was too exhausted to remember. *Please, officer, just let us go. I can't. I just can't, I can't, I can't.*

It's okay, it's okay, he must have soothed me. *You can go. You can go. You can do better.*

"You know what?" he said, snapping Parker's passport shut. "Just go. And don't come back without a passport." The bushy dog yawned and watched a crow perched on a short pole.

"Thank you! Thank you!" I said as he waved us away.

"Can you believe that? Can you believe that?" Parker asked.

"A goddamned miracle."

I dropped him off at his mom's house, which looked only a touch cheerier in the day. He took his wallet, but forgot the VCR player in the trunk.

For two weeks, he called me. Daily. More than daily. "Did you give Parker my number?" I asked Nicki on Tuesday at the booth.

"Yeah! He said you still have his mom's VCR."

"Yeah. Not on purpose! I mean, he forgot it."

"So call him back, give it back to him."

"I can't," I said.

"What do you mean you can't?"

"He's nice and all," I said. I didn't want to disappoint her, or make her feel bad for setting me up with someone so unattractive. "It's just—I don't want to see him anymore. You know? Again."

"You're stealing his TV!" said Bianca, looking up from her breakfast of macaroni and cheese she'd surely vomit up in a few minutes.

"I'm not *stealing* it. Well, not because I want the VCR. I just … you know. It's too awkward to see him again."

"So you're stealing it," said Nicki, but with a laugh.

He left voicemails, and at first they were sweet, like he assumed we'd see each other again. After ten days, they were desperate. He begged for it back, said his mom was pissed as hell. I learned to recognize that breath he'd take before starting a spiel and deleted them before I could hear his voice. Instead, I began to college the cheapest movies at the store down the street, even movies I didn't want to see.

The weed I didn't find beneath my floorboards for years. Not until a dealership was inspecting it for a trade-in value.

ix. The Panther Party

Sometimes when two hunters collide, their worlds end. Sometimes it ends for just one of them. And sometimes, sometimes, a kind of magical craziness takes form. The Human had been hunting within the reaching pines and painted hills his entire life, graduating from clutching BB guns alongside his father to his very first rifle so obviously wrapped under the Christmas tree. Now, edging close to thirty, he'd seen the cities get so fat their thick thighs had spread to even the remotest parts of the state. He saw his first black man move into his town, and then the next. He'd subconsciously picked up hits of Spanish from his peers at work, knew what a selfie was, and begrudgingly liked his fiancé's posts on Instagram (otherwise she'd make a scene). But soon, what he hated began to seep into his pores and became normal. Just like his receding hairline and his hunching back.

You're going again? His fiancé asked as he laced up his favorite boots. Of course he was going again. Next weekend was squared off for barbeques with "friends" he just tolerated. Hunting was his alone time, his special time, a time when all his childhood wildness ran free.

I won't be long, he muttered to her.

That's what you always say.

Panther felt the same way, but for him the invading cities meant more than being uncomfortable. He knew they were a sign of his demolition. They'd want to stick his stuffed body in a museum, or cage him up "humanely" by dumping him in one of those dusty conservation places where he'd pace a desire path straight into the ground. That's why he'd done it. Why he'd magic-ed up that townhouse that was impossible for Humans to touch. There, he'd be safe. Could continue to live like the wild thing he was. And in comfort.

Human and Panther hunt the same prey. Big game. Juicy does, hunks of bucks, and the most tender of fawns when they could.

It was the start of the Human hunting season (how stupid they had rules like that), and Panther knew that if he wanted a luxury feast before they swarmed the shared woods, he'd have to leave early. He didn't care that his kills from the previous days were resting heavy in his belly, or that he was aging even better cuts for the endless parties he threw. More was never enough.

He saw Human before the squat man saw him. As it always was. He knew he could take him with ease, knew that hunters tasted the sweetest of all Humans. They ate more pure, and he could suck the juices of the Human's own kills from the blood. But still,

Human was far from his favorite of meats. Too much fat, too many chemicals, and the bones were hard to crack.

The man moved with a kind of grace that was shocking in his kind of frame. He was somewhat beautiful, thought Panther.

"There's no game here," said Panther, slithering up to the Human in his slinky black body and jewels of eyes.

Oh, shit, said Human. *It's okay. It's okay, stay calm,* Human said as he backed away. Was he talking to himself or Panther?

"You're the one who should stay calm," said Panther.

I—I am. I am! said Human.

"I can smell your adrenaline. It's sour," said Panther. "Would you want to eat something soaked in sour?"

Well ... no ...

"Neither would I," said Panther. Human, he was kind of sad, a scared and pitiful animal. Panther rarely took on such philanthropy, but he must be getting soft with age. "Look," he said. "I have no interest in you, nor do I care much to race you for kills. I have more than enough, better than any deer, elk, bison or moose you've ever managed. Won't you come with me, to my townhouse? I'm having a party." His glittering eyes mesmerized Human, made his tongue thick and the words "No" impossible to pronounce.

I, uh, okay! said Human, and followed Panther back into the fold of ivy like it wasn't blasphemous.

Panther hadn't lied. He really did throw the best parties. Gatsby level parties. The kinds where skewers of meat were rushed around by gauchos, the wine flowed like cut arteries, and the sex was the seasoning that went with everything. Somehow, Human fit in, his milky skin striking a skunk-like contrast against all the black-black bodies that slithered around.

I should get back, thought Human to himself. But then one more drink. One more long-stemmed glass of wine. One more foreign dalliance with a beautiful black beast that made him feel alive, though he couldn't quite piece together how it all worked.

I should go, he told Panther, finding him chuffing at the barbeque pit.

"But you've only just arrived."

I know, I know. But I—I gotta get back, Human said as he stumbled towards the wrought iron gates.

"But you've only just arrived!"

Human didn't quite know how he made his way back, but the weather had changed drastically. Snow littered the ground, and there was something off about everything. The worn paths he knew so well, and some landmarks had grown while other had shrunk. How long had he been gone?

Seven years. That's what a newspaper date told him. He'd lost seven years. Somewhere in the mess of it, he'd dropped his gun, and a new, alien looking bank had popped up on the trail back home blinking the date, temperature, and a message about a coat drive.

His fiancé was gone. His home taken over by an elderly Mexican couple with a penchant for horseshoe knickknacks and a kindness too deep to turn him away. For six days he struggled in their guest bed, sweating beads the size of horse pills while the old woman force fed him rice in chicken broth. He didn't want rice. He wanted big bites of red meat, bottomless gobs of wine. On the seventh day, he changed. Or started to.

"El diablo," said the old woman, dropping the tray of coffee she brought to him daily. As dramatic as a telenovela, he thought.

It took all he had to struggle to his elbows (why were they facing the wrong way?), to glance in the mirror as she ran screaming for her husband. "Javier!" she screamed. In the mirror, he saw black fur was creeping across his face. "Javier!" His canine teeth were dropping lower. "Javier, dios mio!" Whiskers long as needles stretched from his face.

Don't let me die like this, he begged in his head. Let me be all the way. Let it happen all the way. He willed the words to come out, but they stuck like glue in his throat. Javier couldn't hear, couldn't listen. Couldn't understand the warbled language that was half-person, half-panther. The old man raised a gun, shot him between the eyes, the ones that were fading from a river blue to its own special sparkling gem color.

"But I've only just arrived!" he cried as the bullet began to split his head skin. Even he heard the words come out a roar.

Chapter Nine

I stayed for seven years, counting down each little milestone—the day we met, Valentine's Days, summers during the undergraduate years that he spent in Fossil instead of Portland—like there would be some kind of participation trophy at the end. As if I would be gifted a gold watch and a pension package that, one being very useful and the other a pretty knickknack to wear at black tie event, was just another to-do to check off my list.

Jeremy wasn't a bad guy. He was just the exact opposite of Josh, and that's all I wanted after the Josh years.

He was brilliant (truly), with a domineering IQ and flanked in stories of how he would take apart his family's most complicated electronics at age six to see how they worked and then put all the pieces back together again. That's what I thought he could do with me.

Jeremy and I met, technically, on Halloween our freshman year of college. I was still heady with the thought of Kyle and shamed with the dalliance of Parker. Pair that with my getting tired of treading, and I consider myself lucky to get ushered together with what I thought was at least a nice, normal guy. The night we met, Jeremy was wearing a sparkling, stretchy prom dress he'd borrowed from a girl in his dorm, bright pink lipstick, and dirty Van slip-on sneakers. He hadn't bothered to wear a wig, letting his black hair look like a pixie cut set off with the most startling blue eyes I'd ever seen. It was Halloween, and he was blackout drunk while Cherish, an ogre of a big black woman in my sorority lavished him with her tongue probing at his wisdom teeth.

Our courtship was pulled directly from a modest instructional manual on How to Get an MRS in College: The Shortcut. He began hovering by our booth after the most drunken of college holidays, following me as if someone had waved my scent captured in a dropped scarf beneath his bloodhound nose, the one with all the pores blocked with black gunk. I said yes to a date, yes to him being my boyfriend, yes to spending that first Thanksgiving with his family, and yes to us both pretending I didn't get incredibly fat by sophomore year because what else was I supposed to say?

The very first time we had sex, it was after a mild-mannered date of bubble tea and jelly desserts. In his dorm room, while he played what could only be called a Makeout Playlist way too heavy on the Nine Inch Nails, that it happened. His sheets were thin and the material of t-shirts, fast to lap up any spilled over liquids. We only used condoms the first week until I figured he was safe enough with just a high school girlfriend's vagina under his belt. Surely, he was clean.

I hated every time we had sex.

Not that it was bad. His cock was average in every which way but, strangely, I kept comparing it to Josh's. Not that I missed Josh, but I missed how everyone had found him so good looking. Missed how, at least for first impressions, I could show him off with his always perfect hair, flawlessly pulled together outfits, and penchant for grabbing the spotlight. Jeremy had none of that. I was embarrassed to be linked to him, overtly self-conscious that he was half an inch shorter than me. Whenever I wore heels, I felt like his babysitter, holding his hand as we walked down the sidewalk and throughout campus as if I were scared of him toddling into traffic and getting creamed.

Jeremy would eat pussy on a semi-regular basis and act like he liked it well enough. Like it was the spinach dip of appetizers at a chain restaurant. Not really offensive, and when you're really hungry it can be very filling until something better arrives. That something better wasn't unveiled 'til our senior year, though, and by then I'd become expert at developing excuses to not fuck him. My stomach was upset from too many sugar alcohols (by senior year I'd gained over one hundred pounds, then dropped it and a little more through Atkins and relentless self-body-shaming), my head hurt, could we raincheck for a morning (one that never came)?

But I have to hand it to Jeremy. I piled on the weight of a child or anoretic model, and he never said a word about it. Even fluffed up a tiny bit in his own cheeks and belly.

Why didn't I leave him when the thought of him touching me with his grubby, nail-bitten fingers made me want to be sick? It's simple. You don't just get up and leave the person who has cancer. You just don't.

Sophomore year, and Jeremy was diagnosed with Hodgkins Lymphoma, the same cancer his sister had taken on when she was fourteen. The doctors said it wasn't known to be genetic, but what else could you call it? His mother was convinced it was from them growing up in Wisconsin farmland, playing in the corn fields dripping in pesticides. Maybe she was right, but it didn't really matter.

He moved in with me because you can't fight cancer while living in a fraternity house. He moved in with me because his treatments would be in the children's wing of a nearby hospital (Fossil barely had a town doctor, let alone a hospital or clinic). He moved in with me because that's what you do when your boyfriend's eyelashes start to fall out and his paunch gets bigger while his limbs get even thinner, making him look like a sickly little tyrannosaurus rex. And once he'd moved in with you, it's not like you can go back. The wheels of forever start rolling, and it's not making you motion sick yet, so you stay on board.

By junior year, he was declared cancer-free and I was coasting on the fact that he hadn't wanted or asked for sex for most of his treatment. I guess eight hours of chemo per day Monday through Friday can do that to a person.

As he lost his hair, I lost the weight. Slowly, my pant sizes dropped from a twenty back to the normal eight I had worn in high school. I kept my hair long and virgin, like I were compensating for him. By senior year, I was teeming with resentment. Not that he'd asked, but I dropped out of the sorority and took only online classes for the entirety of his treatment so I could sit on the squeaky vinyl couch in the children's ward all day, proving what a good girlfriend I was. By senior year, I was drowning and flailing my arms, crying in my poetry professor's office because I couldn't figure out what to do next. By senior year, I was writing both of our essays for a master's program and filling out applications to intern in London for two. I shaved off all my own hair just to see what the shape of my head was. Thankfully, it was quite a lovely head.

And I bullied him into proposing to me. He did so with a ring from the 1960s that cost under a thousand dollars and instantly added too much weight to my hand.

I despised going down on him, his uncircumcised dick pink and always, always, faintly tasting of urine. I hated how he looked when I was on top of him, eyes half-closed and mouth slightly ajar so you could see the spaces between his crooked teeth. I couldn't stand his smell, or hos his keratosis pilaris made his arm skin feel like a fresh-plucked goose. Maybe that's why he did it.

I went to visit my sister, the one I found out about only when I was eighteen and who spent her forty-five years in and out of jail, being drunk and high on drugs, in Kansas City for a Thanksgiving weekend. While there, she got drunk, ran her car (with us in it), into a median then called the cops the next morning to say it was stolen. Jeremy, it turns out, had an equally exciting turkey vacation.

It was the end of our senior year, and I was expert at dodging any form of touch from him, when it happened. And it happened like it always does, with email and carelessness. Home alone in our shared little duplex, I grabbed his computer to get a class assignment printout because my own wasn't booting up. I was in a rush, needing to make sure a file was in my sent folder so I could print it out at the campus library. When I opened the email and found the whole virtual box entirely blank, I began to panic. When I opened the sent folder, that's when my world's walls began to shudder and crumble.

"What do you have in mind?" was the first of just six emails in the folder that I opened. It was sent to an anonymous Craigslist Casual Encounters email. The original link was still good and embedded in the message. When I opened it, it was a posting from what was clearly a dominatrix or prostitute who was looking to peg someone new.

"How about these?" asked the next email, linking to a pair of thigh-high patent leather boots in Jeremy's size.

It was his email account, one I'd never heard of before. These messages were all sent during the time I was ducking the curious cops with my sister. It was Jeremy's most secret of worlds I'd opened up.

That night, we had the ugly fight with the monster tears. I locked myself in the bathroom and scuttled as far away from the door as I could. As far away from him as necessary. After five hours, I didn't have any more wetness in me. I was tired, just tired, and wished I'd never found what I did. So I promised him I'd never bring it up again after he made sad attempts to blame me for what happened ("You're the one always saying sexuality is on a spectrum!") and swearing he wasn't gay. That he never went through with any of it. That it's perfectly normal to send yourself questions as you shopped for next year's Halloween costume. That he was, perhaps, maybe a cross dresser—but didn't I remember that most male cross dressers are straight? Many have wives, and a lot have wives that encourage this habit and even take pictures of their husbands in ridiculous flowing skirts.

That night was my leverage to get him to propose, get him to let me rent a flat in Brixton before we even arrived for our internships, get him to power through grad school with me because I didn't know what I wanted to do yet. Didn't want to grow up.

After two years of grad school and terrible sex in our little flat that barely fit a bed, sink and square shower stall, I still wore that cheap ring on my finger and was desperately searching for another extension. I found it in a year-long teaching contract in Seoul. We were placed at the same school, one floor apart. Those teach abroad programs prefer couples because they're less likely to pack up and disappear like ghosts in the night when they realize they can't hack the culture shock. In Seoul, I got head lice and pink eye and a wrist permanently damaged from the police-grade handcuffs I had him use on me in bed in a try to make me feel something while he was inside me. Pretending he was a stranger that had scaled the glass walls to our twenty-third floor apartment to rape me was better than facing who I was really screwing.

We were married on the beach in Hawaii, and a storm rolled in as I sat in the backseat of a rental sad that it was now too windy to wear my veil. There was so much alcohol and happening that I got out of sex on our wedding night, too.

Six months later, back in Portland as we both worked dead end jobs (him in software, me at a failing non-profit), I just woke up and said it. "I'm done."

"Okay," he said, as if the past seven years hadn't even occurred.

x. Lynx: The Runner Up of Sinners

The Lynx only hints at fatness, like a puppy with too-big feet gearing up for a growth spurt. You can't tell, between his oversized fur tufts, distracted by his elfish ears, that below the beauty lurks blubbery fat layers a seal pup might envy. The Lynx was a glutton, a binge eater—you could find him huddled between the rich thighs of a mature tree cramming any foodie bits he could find down his slippery throat. But like any glutton, it wasn't just his tongue, his belly and his throat he was stroking. He had a taste for women too, for sex, needed them to try and satiate his lower half while he gorged the upper. Still, he killed and ate everything he saw, which made finding a wife impossible.

That was before the female Human came with the chestnut hair braided to her waist, and fingers so long and thin she could stretch them across more piano chords than anyone else.

You find me beautiful, don't you? she asked Lynx, sliding onto the park bench beside him. Lynx was tucked into a spread-eagled red hawk, slopping up its intestines, mopping the entrails in blood. She knew, like they all did, to only speak to him when his lap and mouth was already full.

"Of course I do, everybody does," he told her, pushing a feather-laden chest piece into his mouth. She was lovely. But he knew better than to try and impress her. It was pointless.

So why not ask me out then?

He laughed, flecks of blood flying from his sharp teeth. "Aren't you kind of old for such schoolyard dares?" he asked. "Stop bothering me. I'm eating."

I can see that, she said, catching herself dipping into sarcasm and pulling herself out before she got stuck. *But seriously. Why not? What's the worst that could happen?*

Lynx sighed, annoyed that she was making him lift his head out of his current prize. God, she really was beautiful, with those melted chocolate eyes and cheeks that looked sprayed with a sparkling rose wine. "Will that make you go away?" he asked.

Find out.

"Fine. Can I take you out sometime?" He could feel the heat from the bird fading away. He hated that.

When?

"I don't know. Tomorrow. How about tomorrow?"

I don't know. That's awfully short notice—

"I'm not going to play these games with you. You have everyone else for that."

Uh, okay ... tomorrow, then. Okay.

Six weeks later, he married her. It might have just been two witnesses they paid twenty bucks for, near-vagrants loitering outside the courthouse, but it was the marriage that lit up the town. Through their entire courtship, she did nothing but feed him. Held her breath when he kissed her at first, initially praying he wouldn't snap off her face, then transitioning to praying the most recent thing he'd packed into his jaw wouldn't make her wretch. But, goddamnit, she was going to do it. She wouldn't get the other half of the fifty thousand until her whole job was over.

Let's go camping. For our honeymoon, she'd told him. *Just you and I in the wild.* Eager to avoid long drives, airborne rides, and locations where he didn't know the best places to eat, he'd agreed. She'd proven to be astonishingly agreeable. Maybe being with a woman wasn't so bad at all.

The campground she chose was a desolate one, miles of nothing but sand dunes pushing against the Pacific waters. "Where am I going to hunt?" he asked her when they arrived, tent poles strapped to his back and her carrying the sleeping bags. "Where the hell do you expect me to hunt?"

Would you calm down! I packed plenty in the cooler.

"It's not enough! It's not enough! You know that."

It wasn't. He went through the entire cooler designed for fifteen people in the first two days. On the third, he set off early to hunt, enraged at his new wife who could subsist on nothing but four granola bars per day. *Where are you going?* she asked, pulling her sleeping bag up to her chin.

"To find some food in this desolate place you picked out," he said, stalking out of the tent to get slapped in the face by the salty air.

Finally, it was time. He hadn't questioned the little axe she'd packed. *You need these for camping!* she'd said. He didn't argue. He'd never done this before.

The smaller trees were easy to fall, and she knew he wouldn't be back 'til dusk. Methodically, she stacked a modest pile in the tent, poked at the embers of the fire until they roared, and made up a stake-out spot behind a nearby dune, digging a hole in the sand for comfort. She slathered herself in pine needles, not caring about the sap that stuck her fingers together. She had to smell like nothing, like the earth, like anything but food. And she waited.

Lynx came back right on time, harboring the gait he only carried when he was still hungry. "I couldn't find nearly a goddamned thing!" he yelled towards the tent. Already it was working. He thought the stacks of logs were her. Quickly, he pulled out a makeshift spear, the pointed end likely hand-carved with the dull pocketknife she'd also packed. Without another word, he stabbed the stack of wood through the tent. A faint pain soared through her chest. That was meant to be her heart. "What the hell? Hey—"

he began, stabbing a few more times and not getting that soft give of flesh he craved. "What happened? Where are you? Where are you!" he paced in circles around the fire. "You fucking bitch, I'm *hungry*!"

It didn't last long. Well before dawn, he let the fire die and wore a deep ravine into the earth. As the last flames flickered, his pacing slowed and he became an ouroboros before her eyes. First, he chewed lightly on his little stub of a tail, and she thought it was an anxious habit. But then, then ...

He took a curious bite out of his sturdy back flanks, like he was tasting a new recipe and wasn't sure he'd like it. The blood stained the sands a sickly black, spread farther as he bit of one rear foot and then the other. He made it nearly to his belly before the self-consumption stopped him entirely. She waited another thirty minutes after his head hit the earth, his own blood and bones sticking out of his teeth, before she ventured to him. Snapped a photo. Took her wallet and car keys, shivering, and began the five-mile journey to the car. Her wedding ring, in its endless circle, dangled loose to her middle joint from the dehydration of a job well done.

Chapter Ten

Chris had been fat—real fat—his entire life. I met him six weeks before I left Jeremy at a swing dance class held in an old masonic lodge. This was well past the swing revival of the nineties, and classes were usually crawling with confused couples trying out options for their first dance, retirees huffing towards their glory days, and a sprinkling of desperate semi-single men lapping up the excuse to wrap their hands around strange women's waists knowing they'd let them. Chris was well over six feet tall, all slim limbs and big brown moon eyes that seemed too deep for his delicate skull. And his teeth, big and perfectly aligned, were made for biting.

He was the opposite of Jeremy, and the weight of my engagement and wedding ring sautered together made it difficult to keep my hand on his shoulder.

"You're married!" Chris had said when guilt forced me to bring up Jeremy. We'd already had six dances and it was pure immersion between us. I didn't have to hear about the future of 3-D printing, how he needed to get home early to plan the storyline for Dungeons and Dragons this weekend, wonder if Chris liked dressing up in ratty pull-on dresses every Sunday.

"Yeah," I said, embarrassed.

"Good!" he said. "I always think, well, worry ... you know, that women come to these classes for dates ..."

"Oh, no. No!" I said. As if being attracted to him were so ridiculous.

He told me he'd been fat like it was some kind of accomplishment. It was the bond that sidled us closer together. We exchanged fat pictures, and I could barely see the skeletal looking man I knew beneath all the blubber. We compared how we did it, and he (a calorie counter) was fascinated about low carbing it. A week later, at a salsa club where Jeremy dropped us both off before jolting back to his friend's house to continue battling dragons, Chris asked, "Can I smell your breath?"

"What?" I screamed over the thumping music.

"Can I smell your breath?"

"Why?" It was the strangest ploy to taste lips I'd ever heard.

"Ketosis."

"What?"

"People who don't eat carbs, they go into ketosis. It's supposed to make the breath smell sweet."

I opened my mouth, he ducked close and breathed in. Around us, couples cumbia-d and women teetered on suede-bottomed shoes while watered-down drinks were sloshed onto laminate booth-tops. "I don't smell anything," he said.

When I sat up in bed a month later and told Jeremy, "I'm done," it's like he already knew. He just didn't ask. I was leaving him, but not for Chris. Not really. No lines had truly been crossed, but I was free now. Free to push at them, nudge them in whatever direction I liked with him or anybody else.

Being freshly arrived in Portland, an EMT trainee who worked odd hours, and a cloying need to Experience and Meet New People made Chris an easy target. He said yes to everything—he had no other options. Once, I picked him up to take him to my favorite gay club, miraculously parking my little red Nissan facing downward on the steep hill where he lived near OHSU. It was a stick shift, I was slightly buzzed already, but sobered up enough by the time he got to the car to be too scared to get back out. "Want me to do it?" he asked, and I nodded. He slammed directly into the car in front of us. "I didn't know it was a stick shift!" he said. A group of smokers watched the whole thing, forcing me to leave a note and raise my insurance, and Chris didn't say a word.

He friended me on Facebook, and occasionally, as if he were doling it out, would message me innocuous appetizers. "Check out this article on existentialism." "Have you been to that one Cuban restaurant?" "What's the name of that one hike you were telling me about?" Because I was his personal, free, and willing tour guide, maybe he felt obligated to say yes when I asked him to an overnight stay at a tucked away McMenamin's bar, restaurant and hotel for a friend's birthday.

I booked a room and left the details vague about when everyone was leaving, who was staying where, and stepped back to see how my work would play itself out. We got drunk, or at least I did. Roaring drunk. I didn't even like the girl whose birthday it was, but it was an irresistible excuse. Somehow, after last call, Chris ended up in my single bed (the only size they had left), spooning me while we slept fully clothed. It was the closest we'd ever been. In the morning, children screaming through the thin walls, I stayed as still as I could trying to stretch out the moment.

"Oh, man," he said, rolling onto his back. "Is it morning already?"

"Yeah, I think so," I said, watching the too-bright rays penetrate the dusty curtains.

"Let's go get some breakfast," he said. Breakfast was easiest for me, low-carb options everywhere. "I gotta meet Laura at noon."

"Who?" I asked.

"Laura? The girl I told you about last night? The one from that dating site." I didn't remember any of that. Why was he on a dating site? I was right in front of him.

"Oh, right. I forgot her name."

"Oh, sorry. I think I only called her Vanilla last night."

"Vanilla?"

"Yeah, you know—I mean, maybe it'll get better. She's just real vanilla in bed." So he was fucking and I was divorcing. But she wasn't fucking well. That had to at least put something in my favor. Suddenly I was in some kind of macabre race with Vanilla Laura, who'd somehow gotten him between her legs but only to disappoint. She was equally so far ahead of me and just as quickly falling behind. Lauras have light-colored-eyes, brown hair and can be beautiful without any makeup. They're thing and were unnoticed in high school. Lauras peaked in their twenties. She was my biggest threat.

It was my one last shot, dangling a carrot in front of him I knew he couldn't resist. In a ridiculous attempt to look like a Real Oregonian, regardless of the fact that I'd been born there, I clung onto my most outdoorsy friend, Alice, and her new boyfriend who were going camping at the Oregon sand dunes. But that wasn't the worst part. The worst part was I borrowed Jeremy's jeep and held no punches. I asked him, told him who was going, and forced into a corner by my sheer nerve he said yes. It was just one night in the sands, but it was all I needed. Especially when I told Alice that we'd "just meet them in Florence" while I made up some unbelievable excuse as to why we couldn't ride together. I'd bought five hours each way in the topless Jeep alone with Chris, a night in a shared tent while the sand formed to our bodies, and a smoky fire rumbling below the flawless night.

I didn't know you had to remove air from the tires of four-by-fours to navigate the sands. Neither did he. Instead, we got stuck and had an ATV tour guide pamper us, releasing the right amount of air as he sweated inside his helmet. I didn't know barreling through the foam of the ocean would kick salt water so deep into the Jeep's insides that it almost instantly began to rust. I didn't realize how hard it would be to drink around fire and not give in to my skull splitting down the middle.

"So how do you like Oregon?" Alice asked him as her boyfriend, Brendan, expertly handled the tinfoil cooking.

"I love it!" he said. "It's beautiful. And that's coming from someone who grew up in Montana." Alice beamed, another native Oregonian sucking up the compliments as if she'd birthed the state herself.

"That's great," she said. "There's a lot of outdoor recreation here. I'm sure Justine's told you." As if I had any idea about outdoor recreation. I was cold, the smoke kept crawling its greedy hands over me, and I kept drinking because there was nothing else to do.

"Oh, yeah!" he said. "Actually, I want to take my girlfriend out here, too. This is amazing. You can't camp on beaches, well lake beaches, in Montana. Not legally anyway."

"Your girlfriend?" Alice asked, darting her eyes over to me. I just widened my eyes at her, like "Oops!"

"Laura, yeah," he said.

"Where ... where is she now? Why didn't she come?" Alice asked. Brendan never looked up from the potatoes he was tending.

"Oh, she's in Portland," Chris said. "It's her mom's birthday this weekend. We're actually doing a late dinner tomorrow when I get back."

"That's ... nice ..." Alice said, and when Chris bent down to his own drink, she gave me the *What the fuck look?* and all I could do was shrug.

It was a drunken, blurry, shit of a night. With the sleeping bags (borrowed) so thick and the sand seemingly frozen beneath us, I'm not sure we even touched, though in that tiny tent it would have been impossible not to.

In the morning, light searing my brain through my eyes, I turned down Brendan's coffee. "It's full of grinds," Alice complained as she downed her second cup. I was hungover, I was hurting, and I wanted to barrel through those five hours back to Portland. Jeremy's Jeep, a hard top, was open and exposed. In the way Oregon has, yesterday's heat had evaporated only to be replaced by a gray, chilled sky that threatened constantly to drizzle. It never did, not for those five long hours, and not even after we didn't figure out until fifty miles on the highway that we'd never puffed the tires back up.

My head screamed at me, but I did my best to act carefree. Like I didn't care that it had been a shit trip, or that I was delivering Chris back to the city in time to meet his girlfriend's mom. What the hell was wrong with me?

Back in Portland, he must have sensed something. Like he'd agreed to pony up something on his end and had failed. He helped me drag my things back into the house before I dropped him off at home. "You tired?" he asked. I was so delirious with exhaustion I could barely speak.

"No, I'm good!" I said.

"We made good time," he said, glancing at his watch. "Want to watch something before dropping me at home?"

It was a consolation prize, and a crap one at that, but I took it. I'd take whatever I could get. The house was freezing, but I hadn't figured out how to turn the heat up yet. I'd moved right into a stranger's spare bedroom after running away from Jeremy and had felt too awkward to ask in the first week how to manage the settings. Now it seemed way too late to ask such a common question.

Dragging my comforter downstairs, I repeated a thank you, thank you, thank you mantra to whatever Gods had kept my new housemate out for the day. Without a word,

Chris pulled half of the comforter over him, raised up his arm, and welcomed me into that warm corner of his armpit. It didn't matter that neither of us had showered for two days. He smelled like campfire, like the ocean, and like that warm foreign scent that had slowly started to be familiar to me. Deep inside, I knew this was it. It wasn't going to go farther than this. There would be no kisses, no meeting the parents, no assumptions that of course we would spend the holidays together. Whatever I'd been for him, I don't know, but he'd used it all up and was standing on his own now. This must be how it feels to have a child, breathe life into them, show them how to walk and which rules to follow, and then when they leave you for college or the army or a wife you just have to lean back and smile like that had always been the plan. Maybe it had been.

It was the last time I drove to Chris' place. For days after, I kept my messenger open and on while on Facebook. I'd set the alarm for one in the morning just to sit online, because that had been the most common time he'd messaged before. Half the time, I'd see him online, too and just stare at that big green "available" icon. *Message me, message me, message me.* A few times I'd open a chat window, but it's like he didn't know. Who was he talking to in the darkest of the night? It couldn't be Laura—she'd be there with him. Wouldn't she?

"Why not me?" I asked Alice over heavy pints at a pub one month later. I didn't like beer, it made me feel too heavy.

"Oh, he's just—you know ..." she began. I didn't know. Neither did she.

"What?"

"Men are stupid." It's the only thing she could say. "What are you sad about anyway? You just got single for the first time in seven years. Enjoy it! Shop around."

"But I wanted him," I said, like a stubborn child about to throw a tantrum.

"Why?"

"I don't know," I said. "I just did."

xi. The Blue Jay's Legs

Maybe we are moving backwards. Or maybe it's forwards, a swapping of cultures and tight embracement of the digital era. As Indian parents loosen the reins on their children, considering love marriages as equal with arranged, exchanging traditional hard copy biodata sheets for a shared online dating account where both they and their 27-year-old child suss out matches, American children are shuttling back under their parents' wings. Asking them for matches. Consistently signing out of their hookup apps as they flail about, wondering at nearly age forty why they haven't found a match. Humans, they're marrying less, later, and more poorly. A cross-hatch mingling of species was that egg-cracking-open epiphany that saved some.

The Wisconsin farmer hadn't ever imagined this—his daughter, asking him to play matchmaker. He hadn't been watching the corn-fed boys she'd grown up with to see which one might be the hardest working. The most faithful. The kindest, the smartest, the strongest. He'd thought, like them all, that he'd send her away to some out of state school and somehow, in the midst of the binge drinking and putting on weight, she'd find some kind of partner who would do. He considered himself progressive. Open-minded. Had toyed with the, "What if she's a lesbian?" idea just so he'd be sure to keep a straight face if it came to that. Really, he didn't care. He just wanted her to be happy.

I'm giving up, she'd told him, bluntly and without reserve. It was just the two of them, her picking at egg whites at the same table she spat up cream of wheat thirty years ago. He carved the fat away from his steak.

You're just in a slump, he told her.

No, really. I'm giving up. And putting you in charge.

What's that mean?

I want you to find someone for me.

I don't think—

Dad. Please. That was all it took.

He'd heard about all the ways people were meeting. Had even toyed with some of them himself after her mother had died, but found it wasn't for him. He didn't need a new partner, companionship. All he really needed was the weekly maid to scrub the wheat field out of his clothes. Run some errands, bleach the sink, tackle the hard water stains on the shower doors.

But he knew this much. He knew she was a prize, and if he could make others see it too, it would be easy.

The challenge he posted was open to all, and it was sweetly straightforward. He with the longest, strongest legs could take out his daughter. Yes, it was a niche site where he posted, and of course the competition had to be held in person. The demand for strength, for endurance, would ensure a healthy and determined winner. She'd already said she didn't care about intermingling, for her it was the heart that mattered. She supplied her own photos, and he handled the description, the competition, and the deadline.

For Bear, it seemed easy enough. Everyone knew of his powerful legs, those that made Olympic athletes fall into the fetal position and pray. Plus, he knew he'd make an excellent provider for a Human wife. They loved the salmon he was gifted at catching, the sheets of honeycomb, how his claws could go from fierce to gentle with the tiniest of adjustments. He'd been alone long enough. And she was beautiful.

For Blue Jay, it was something else. It was always something else. Why this challenge? Why was this—the longest, strongest legs—proof of what made the best partner? He was tired of it, tired of it all. They all loved to watch him, bigger than most of the birds that watched for the crumbs dropped along the pavement. Not a carrion eater, thank God, so he couldn't be compared to those. But not a cute, little spritely thing either. None of that was his fault, so why should he be left out?

"Why are you so obsessed with this?" his sister asked, pulling her chicks closer to her. She didn't get it, and she didn't need to. She'd already established her life.

"I'm not *obsessed*," he said.

"You are. Who cares if some backwoods farmer wants to set his daughter up with whoever had the strongest legs? Humans are weird. You know that. Leave them be." One of her chicks, gap-mouthed and tongue lolling, rolled its head up to her as if she were holding out on food. "Not now," she said, shushing it. Her. Him. Whatever.

"I just want to prove a point. You know? It's stupid, the parameters he's set."

"So it's stupid!" she said. "Let them be stupid."

"No, I'm going to prove him wrong."

"Whatever," she said.

It was three weeks 'til the competition, and Blue Jay felt like he'd been prepping for this his whole life. Carefully, he gathered the freshest sticks, kindling and twigs for makeshift legs. He watched for his own feathers to molt, but gathered others', too. Blue when he could, but as the deadline inched closer any color would do. And he practiced, all day every day. Walking in those makeshift, long-long legs. He looked like he imagined a flamingo would if they weren't so ridiculous (and ugly, really, when you looked up close). "You look like a freak," his sister said as she watched him practice his sprints. He did, probably, but he didn't care.

On the morning of the race, he was surprised by the relatively few competitors. Did nobody want to prove themselves anymore? *Okay,* said the farmer, his daughter watching from her childhood bedroom window above, *I'm going to make this real simple. Whoever gets from here to the green tractor out there first, they get to take out my daughter.*

"Wait a minute," said Bear, "I thought this was, you know, a matchmaking thing. Not just some date."

Ideally yeah, it is, agreed the farmer. *But this ain't the Ice Age, ya know? I'm not gonna make my only daughter marry some stranger just 'cuz they won a race. She still gets'ta choose. Ya'll both do.*

"Okay, okay," said Bear. When the farmer shot the rifle at some imaginary clay pigeon, sixteen of them raced off, and Blue Jay felt like he was flying. He left them all behind— Bear, out of shape Buck, even Rabbit.

Blue Jay wins! shouted the farmer, and the others looked at him in wonder. Where'd he get those long legs? Those lengthy sure things?

"What the hell? What the hell?" asked Bear, the runner up, over and over, confused and out of sorts.

She really was lovely, too. Freckles shining and hair dark with sprouts of red. And she seemed happy enough, too, with the winner. Flushed and smiling when she emerged through the old screen door. And that's when it all fell apart.

The fake legs felt awkward, shaky after the win. As Blue Jay lifted his prize, began to take flight into some kind of ever after, the sticks gave way beneath him. He felt the straps unwind at his feet. "He cheated! He cheated!" bellowed Elk from below, and the shame got so heavy Blue Jay had no choice but to bring her down.

I don't much 'preciate a cheater, said the farmer, ushering his daughter towards Bear, who opened his arms to her with his claws limp.

"I just ... I just wanted to show ..." Blue Jay began, but the laughter drowned him out. One of the twigs cracked and broke as he shook it off, and the girl flipped her hair. Turned up her chin. Like exchanging a Bear for a Blue Jay was the most natural of things.

Chapter Eleven

I'd found myself without an eraser. A re-start button. When the whole Chris thing fell apart, I was itching to delete the years with Jeremy, and I'd thought that Chris would at least supply that. So caught up in the drowning of feelings, I'd spent one an entire night moaning to a friend, "Why not me?" while she pet my head until I quieted down and fell asleep next to her. Now, the competition was stiffening. In some sick kind of phantom limb phenomenon, Jeremy and I continued to message all day at work, although strange new walls had formed between us. He told me about getting set up with friends, and I felt not a pang of jealousy. In a sudden, seemingly drunken rage (though he never drank, and it was before noon on a Thursday), he demanded that I give him one hundred dollars. It seemed a severance package. He'd logged into my bank account and seen that I'd been spending hundreds of dollars every weekend at bars and clubs, so surely I could give him some balm to soothe his wounds. I didn't care, I'd never cared about money. He should have asked for much more.

"You want to go to Vegas?" I asked Gina, a girl from the sorority years. We'd maintained loose bonds, but had never stuck particularly close. There was something about her that kept her at a distance. But now, in our late twenties, it was becoming harder and harder to get anyone to say yes.

"Let me check with Brian," she said, her husband who must have breached those stone walls of her somehow. By that evening, she agreed and began mapping out how we'd get there. When. Who we'd stay with on the drive back up, swooping down to San Diego then up to San Francisco. I contributed the car, miles be damned, and a hook up in Vegas that could get us comped hotel rooms and show tickets. Gina relied on genuine friends peppered throughout the west coast, happy to give up spare bedrooms and couches. Mine was a fifth grade boyfriend, Keaton, who asked me years later, "Surely you knew I was gay, right?" I hadn't. I was ten years old.

I was sure, absolutely certain, that I could up my Number during that ten-day jaunt through the deserts, between the big legs of the Redwoods, at the golden beaches that inspired so many songs. It took us two days to shoot through the backroads to Vegas, stopping for photos at the trees with dangling sneakers, at the entrance to a brother that held nothing but semi-trucks for miles. We didn't see a single person, but imagined all that must be happening at the long, narrow building beyond. "Do you think the girls line up, still? Like in those old movies?" I asked Gina.

"I don't know," she said. "It makes me sad."

We saw the glittering lights just as dusk caught up to us, and from so far away the strip looked tiny. A little dollop of faked glamour in the wild and dead desert. Keaton had gotten us a room at Hooters and tickets to the latest Cirque du Soleil. I'd seen him in person three times since middle school, and there was nothing of the little boy in him that used to reply to my long, carefully crafted quizzes in Mrs. Ford's fifth grade class.

Who would you want to go to prom with? Who would you want to kiss? Who's the nicest girl in class? Who's the prettiest? Like he should, he put my name almost every time. But never when I asked who was nicest, and I never figured out why that bothered me so much. I wasn't nice, didn't really care to be. But Keaton choosing that item to give to someone else seemed like blasphemy.

Only I could not get fucked in Vegas. We were there for just two nights, and the first was a blackout of a mess. Or brownout. It came in flashes, and Gina stayed sober enough to take photos of the entire disaster. Keaton and I deciding to try to get married (it's not as easy as it sounds). Me peeing in bushes. Him trying to eat my head. The two of us making out everywhere. In a gay club, at the famous sign, in every bar, casino and pool party we crashed. All Vegas gave me was a monstrous hangover and bloating so bad half the clothes I packed didn't fit.

Tijuana was no kinder, and (there alone since Gina was too afraid to cross the border with the drug war warnings), I stayed to the main roads and spent that day brushing beggar children off my legs. In San Diego, we stayed in a house of men with Gina on one couch and me on another. The sole guy I found attractive talked non-stop about his girlfriend in Pennsylvania, and we didn't get drunk enough there for me to fuck one of the others just to get it over with. In Los Angeles, the shithole hostel across the street from Grauman's wasn't conducive to even the dirtiest of shameful acts. In San Francisco, we found ourselves surrounded by all women. My last chance was that single night in Medford, where it all began, when we split up so Gina stayed at her family's home and me with my mother. Kind of.

I've always loved the filthiest of bars. Perhaps because that's what I saw in movies growing up. Hardened men with long birds, used-to-be sexy women aging in too much makeup and unraveling clothes. I loved the looks of the dark rooms with the long bars, neon glows and whiskey in tumblers. I couldn't get enough of being the youngest, most beautiful woman in the room. It was the only place where it happened, and that made it sacred. Whiskey Lake was a too-big bar on the outskirts of Central Point where monster trucks, lifted and jacked, swarmed the dirt parking lot. Old timers had been parking in the vinyl seats so long the cracks and worn spots perfectly complemented their asses. There were fights out back every night, and even the top shelf whiskey was half the price of bars in town. Pool tables were heavily seasoned around the room, and a makeshift dance floor which only got used well after midnight was tucked into a corner. That night. It had to be that night. I couldn't go back to Portland without getting rid of the past seven years.

When I picked him, it was like he already knew. On the other side of the bar, playing pool with three other guys, they were all out of their element. Young, early twenties, and if they were from the valley it didn't show. The college. They must be from the college thirty minutes away in Ashland, slumming it here because it's so easy to get tired of the handcrafted college bars designed to make students feel like they hadn't made a huge mistake coming here.

Really, he was non-descript. Baseball cap, jeans with a wash you couldn't get in this part of Oregon. Brown hair, brown eyes, and my height when I wore heels. I walked by him twice, three times, catching his eye just long enough to let him know. After the last time, he'd finally drank enough of the discount beer to approach me, alone, at the bar.

"My name's—" he began.

"What took you so long?"

"I don't ... I don't know."

"I don't want to know your name." And I didn't.

"Can I buy you a drink?" he asked. The youth in him was palpable.

"I can buy my own drinks."

"Oh."

"Your friends are leaving," I told him. They were doing their best not to stare, but I remembered those days. "How old are you?"

"Twenty-two."

"Really."

"Twenty-one."

"I doubt it, but I'll take it," I said.

"How old are—"

"Do you really care?"

"Nah, not really," he said. I couldn't tell. Did he want me to be as young as him, so he'd feel more comfortable? Much older than I was as a conquest? I was twenty-seven. Probably not so much older to make it a genuine Mrs. Robinson story. Or maybe, to him, that felt very, very old. "My friends—I think they're going back to our place."

"Our place?"

"Well, two of us. My roommate's here, and then our other friends."

"Where's your place?"

"SOU." The college, I knew it.

"You're quite the ways from home," I said. Was that what a wolf would tell a sheep?

He shrugged. "We wanted something different."

"We all do."

"So, you wanna—"

"Yeah, sure," I said, signaling for the too-thin, blonde bartender to close me out. "Tell your friends you'll meet them there."

The cops were hungrier than usual that night as we swatted at fate along the trail to Ashland that was teeming with DUI ticket givers. It was a notoriously corrupt town where drivers were hunted like the little morsels of meat they were. The shining white Victorians were never subtle, would pull out right behind you and follow for miles, tailgating and falling back to get your adrenaline going before the sirens switched on. But if you grew up there, if you grew up there you knew. Lose them in the first half-mile they start following you, whip into a side street or parking lot, duck down and wait them out. Do that before they can log or even see your license plate, and they'll give up. It's the easy stuff they wanted.

We made it halfway there, Gina's extra bag nestled in the backseat, before I angled the car into an all-night grocery store parking lot and waited for the police behind us to keep going. "Are you drunk?" the boy asked me, thinking that's why I was avoiding the cops.

"No, but that doesn't matter to them," I said. It was nearly two by the time we made it to his off-campus townhouse on an Ashland street I'd never heard of before. His roommate was the most obnoxious of the bunch, a blond and blue kid who was probably just as loud and raucous sober as he was drunk. He'd picked up some underage girls who pulled at their skirts as they crowded around the old coffee table playing Kings. Nervous, they sipped at their Solo cups and tried to size me up from the corners of their eyes. Is this how I had looked, all those years ago? Is that what I'd been like that night with Kyle? I felt sorry for them, wanted to tell them they shouldn't feel awkward around that loud, attention-seeking ass of a boy. They could wipe off their makeup, put on boxers and a ratty t-shirt and he'd want them just as much. Didn't they know he'd want them just as much?

"You want to play?" he asked me. They all asked me.

"No," I said. That's not what I'd come here for.

I'd lied, I was drunk. Just not brownout drunk, but definitely too drunk to be able to feel anything. For that, I was grateful. And I was tired, I just wanted to get it over with. Put on my performance so the boy would have a story to tell and I could get moving on with everything else. I wasn't in the mood to teach, to lead, but I had to. That's what I'd signed on for. In his bedroom (thank God he had his own room, thank God it wasn't a dorm), I asked, "Where's your condoms?" and he had none. I could hear shrieks and laughter as he went back to the living room to ask his blond friend to borrow some. That was sweet, wasn't it? Proof of his innocence, and maybe some of that would leak into me.

"I've never done this before," he said.

"I know." I did, and in that moment I thought I was doing him a favor.

He was fast and rough and full of energy that I guess all boys that age must have, it's just that I didn't remember. And he did the right things, told me I was beautiful and went down on me, though I felt none of that, I at least appreciated the gesture. Put with each thrust, with each pump, I felt the bad years drain out of me and right onto his cheap nylon sheets. It wouldn't give me back what I'd lost and what I'd whittled away, I knew that. But it would give me permission to start again. This boy, who was so clearly out of his element, was giving me what Chris had promised.

A few hours later, the tugs of soberness woke me up. I had a vision, I always had, of sneaking out but my bladder had other ideas. By the time I'd found the bathroom and wiped the mascara from my cheeks, he was already up, too. We ran into each other in the hallway, me in his t-shirt from the night before since I couldn't find my own.

"Hey," I said.

"Good morning," he replied, and smiled. It was genuine. As much as I wish it hadn't been.

"I'm taking this," I said, pulling at the shirt I was wearing.

"Okay," he said. "Do you want some—"

"Nah, it's okay," I said. "See you around." I didn't look back, though his eyes burned holes into my shoulder blades. I didn't look back. Just like in the movies, when they don't look back at the building they just set on fire.

xii. How the Rabbit Lost Its Size

"Too big for his britches," that was the saying. Deer thought it perfectly fit Rabbit, like a pair of custom-hemmed pants with plenty of give in the waist. He was tired of the whole thing. Of rabbit getting so literally big, his pompous tail nearly the size of Deer's head and those strong, thumping thighs thundering across the trails. His ego stretched right along with him, a worrisome thing. Wasn't it enough that Rabbit had the speed, the grace, the sharp eyes and the always-twitching nose that led him directly to the lushest of greens? Deer was skittish, always watching, and although he was fast too, those trembling stick legs were called lithe and lovely—word made for a woman.

"You know," said Deer, rolling the practiced speech over his tongue as he cozied up to Rabbit bullying the fescue by the creek, "I head there are untouched flower fields, vegetable beds, on the other side there."

"Wouldn't you know for certain?" asked Rabbit. "I can't fathom you spreading such greasy rumors if you weren't sure of yourself." That was true, but it still jabbed at Deer's stomach. How did Rabbit know him so well? Rabbit was such a stranger to him.

He shrugged. "Just what I heard. I don't always have time to be fact checking for you, you know."

"Nobody asked you to," Rabbit said, his deep and smooth voice muffled as he buried his face deep in the greenery.

"I actually haven't been to the place, the area I heard about," said Deer. "You want to check it out?"

"Why in God's name would I want to go exploring with you?" Rabbit asked, raising his heavy head and methodically pulling slips of glass between his lips.

"Because all my friends are busy today, and I'd really rather not let them know about a veritable quandary a few miles away. You're always alone—which is weird, by the way—I figured you might be interested. Two of us are better than letting an entire army know." He was rambling, Deer could hear it in himself. *Stop it.*

Rabbit sighed. "Fine, fine," he said. He didn't even try anymore to explain himself, and why he was always alone. He was the last one left, and didn't that make him a monster? If you're the last of your kind, where's that line between prized rarity and total freak?

"But, you know, we have to get across this creek," said Deer.

"You think I can't handle that?" asked Rabbit. It was his biggest flaw, that he could be so easily challenged. But he couldn't help it. He existed for all rabbits that are (if any remained), were, and might ever be. He had to be strongest, longest, quickest to dare.

"I'm just *saying*," said Deer. "Don't be so defensive."

"Fine," said Rabbit. "But don't act like I'm not as skilled as you. I don't need to prove anything to you."

"Nobody asked you to," said Deer meanly.

"Can we just do this?" asked Rabbit.

"Yeah, let's go," said Deer. "I need more of a running start than this, hold on."

"Of course you do," said Rabbit, smug that he knew he could jump the creek easily, with just a few steps if that. Deer on his rickety legs. He didn't know how he managed the leaps he'd seen before. As Deer backed up, Rabbit soared effortlessly across the clear waters, felt the little splashes as the fish whipped their tails.

That's when Deer acted. He'd been practicing this, though in little puddles and pools rather than moving water. What's the worst that could happen? That it wouldn't work? That he'd have to play dumb to rabbit and say he'd been wrong about the flowers and food?

He willed it, felt the magic rising up in his bones. Deer wasn't sure how long he'd been able to do this, or if he was the only one, but with his thoughts he could multiply water. Make it grow like he was a God, the one who controlled wetness and thirst. Rabbit's eyes, on the other side of the creek, grew just as fast as the water grew. "What's happening? What's happening!" Rabbit yelled from the other side, fear strangling his voice even as the gushing waters drowned him out.

"I don't know!" said Deer, but he knew exactly. Knew this particular creek ran from the oceans to some raging beast of a river hundreds of miles away. He made the waters angry and fast, the currents deadly. Rabbit would never get back across, but he didn't want a water trail so fat he couldn't see the other side. He wanted to watch Rabbit suffer.

But nothing ever happens like we imagine. For the first few days, he watched Rabbit pace along the waterline on the other side. He wasn't killing him—there was plenty of food. He just wanted him gone, exorcised. Rabbits fast mouth moved like thunder, but the waters were too loud for Deer to understand. Instead, he kept vigil, acting like he worried over Rabbit. 'Til one day he was gone.

Deer was young, that mean spirit pushed out by the time he was fully grown. By then, he'd almost forgotten Rabbit. Had completely forgotten what he'd done. Eventually, a day came when he thought the river had always been like this, enraged and screaming.

He was old when he finally saw it, rubbed his milky eyes against the dewy grass to be certain. On the other side of the river, Rabbit had shrunk. Proliferated. There were dozens of him, little furry things no bigger than a cat. Rabbits milled about, snapped up grass and watched him, sideways, with their beady eyes. Curious, scared, and so lonely even as they seemed to multiply before his eyes.

Chapter Twelve

It was an across the room moment, the kind every drab romantic movie had prepared you for. And, just like they all said, it happened when you weren't trying to force it from your marrow. A rain-drenched April. I was with Melody, post-Delhi to Dublin show at the Diamond Ballroom with the floating dance floor and the single drink line that snaked for miles. It was nearly two in the morning, and we'd dragged some short South Indian with us because he seemed so lost and it felt so cruel to shake a clinging puppy from your leg. I wanted one last drink, a strong one, an over-priced one, from Velcro Lounge. I wanted another chance, and to push him off onto her even though she'd sworn he'd cupped her ass in a way she didn't like when we were all swaying on the dance floor.

Velcro was a misfit, sometimes teeming with drunkards well until three in the morning, and otherwise deserted like everyone knew what a whore it was and for a single night they were above it. It was one of those nights.

Melody and I had been tangled up at Velcro so many times the bartenders knew us. Knew us well enough to forgive the nights we were so drunk we ran out on the tab because we didn't want to wait for the machines to spit out the numbers. "*I* don't care," said the always-there server, Matthew, a slight gay boy who refused to age. Carmen, the sole female bartender with heavy arms stuffed with ink, acted like she remembered us, but never called us by name. I imagine that's how she was with everyone, and I wished I could pull off that kind of cool.

The Velcro crowd had either given up early or give up on the sticky-floored slip of a bar for good that night. It was just the stumbling three of us, Carmen, and a black-haired boy with curls springing from his head and a black leather jacket wrapped around his shoulders slouching at the bar. Most of us, we don't recognize a magnet by its looks. We know it by its pull, how it miraculously sticks in the most impossible of places.

A bathroom is the global excuse to thin yourself from the herd. I knew Melody. She was drunk enough that I could buy myself ten minutes, even right in front of her. I didn't even know his face, if it would match the cacao of his hands, or how tall he'd become when he stood from that stool. I was just taken to him like it was supposed to be.

One barstool away, I leaned across the reaching bar and nodded to Carmen. She knew that meant coffee sweetened with whiskey. I wondered if she thought of people by their drinks, to her so much more important than names. The man looked at me, and I reveled in the unraveling happening from the corner of my eyes.

"Ya gimme the familiars," he said, his voice a strange lilt I hadn't expected.

"What?" I asked. I couldn't help it, the aloofness slid off me before I could grab at it.

"I'm Jimmy. You look familiar," he said. If it weren't for how he held himself, how he let his eyes crawl over me and through me, fingering the wet insides of my smile, I would have sworn he was gay. His voice betrayed something feminine about him, something that didn't exist anywhere besides his throat.

"You don't look like a Jimmy," I said. From a far-off corner, Melody shrieked with laughter.

"And you don't look all white," he said.

"I'm not. Half Cherokee."

"And I'm not Jimmy. Jimit, but most people can't remember that. Can I buy you a drink?" he asked.

"Last call, Jimmy," Carmen said as we poured the whiskey into the bitter blackness.

"Put it on his tab," I told Carmen as she slid the thick ceramic mug towards me.

"Hey, wait a minute," he said. "Can I at least get your number." Melody was falling into herself in the corner booth. Any minute now she'd start looking around for me. Either he'd get the number right on the first try, or not.

Five minutes later, Melody was leaning on my arm and we were promising to drop the short boy off at his car twenty blocks away. "I can take her home," Jimmy said, gripping Melody's other elbow as she slipped across the floor.

"She's coming with *me,*" Melody said, the mother in her springing up from a deep well, like she was just as responsible for me as she was her two kids sleeping at her mother's. Jimit lifted his shoulders, like he knew that last try wouldn't work out. He was just tall enough to worm his way into my hippocampus.

It took three weeks for Jimmy to text "Remember me?" More than enough time to narrow down who he really was. I mean, how many Jimits could there be? Just one that cropped up over and over again on search engines, the first hit complete with a hospital portrait haloed above a detailed description of all the accolades he'd collected as one of the leading cardiovascular surgeons in the country. Jimit Ahmed was forty-two, had graduated incredibly young from a decorated medical school in the mid-west, and had a brother who was equally impressive at cutting open hearts in Florida.

I didn't have his number, had never taken it. But I knew. I knew instinctively, no matter how many other men I may have given my number to. "No," I replied.

"I remember you." The three words flashed across the screen.

"What do you remember?"

"Black dress, strappy shoes. You remember my name?"

"Which one?" I asked.

There was a little splinter in me that panged over the text instead of the call. Especially now that I knew he was fifteen years older than me. I could find no mention of a wife, now or in the past, anywhere online. Was he gay? Did he have one stuffed away somewhere in India, although there was no whisper of Hindi or any other far-off language in him, but you never know. You never know.

He chose Hot Box as our first place to meet, and although I'd trekked by it hundreds of times I'd never gone in. It always felt dead, and way too big to justify that kind of surely staggering commercial rental price in the gut of downtown. We were a ten-minute walk from where we'd met. Now, knowing who he was, his credentials, all the awards sprinkled over him, the stakes were higher. I was drowning.

"So, what do you do?" I asked, hell bent on proving how squarely I was in the dark.

"What do you do?" he replied. I was scrambling for control. Couldn't find it.

"I'm a director for a non-profit serving African Americans," I said. I had the mission statement, the vision, imprinted in my brain. Knew exactly how to make it sound more important than it was, sprinkle a little idealism over it all. He didn't need to know that there were only three of us there full-time, and the other two were the Executive Director and the administrative assistant.

"I'm a physician," he said. That was it. Physician, was it supposed to sound more or less impressive than "doctor." I'd always been able to keep a blasé face, whether you told me the world was crumbling to dust or I'd just won millions. *I don't care* was the toughest of armors.

Neither of us ordered food, just drinks, drinks, drinks, though I'd stopped up my stupid levels with heavy protein with Melody beforehand. Just enough to keep me from getting blackout without making me fat. Carbs, they'd block the drunkenness good, but added padding I'd been trying so desperately to lose since Jeremy. I'd never be fat again. If I was fat, what doctor would want me?

When Jimit excused himself to the bathroom, I flirted shamelessly with the Bangladeshi at the table beside me, punched my number into his phone while I imagined Jimit took his time pissing.

We made excuses, crawling from one bar to another lounge, swinging into Velcro and then wildly back out when there wasn't enough room to breathe. "Do you want to see my place?" he asked. It's just two blocks from here. Two blocks and a sky-reach up, it was the most beautiful Pearl District penthouse I'd ever seen. Not that I'd ever seen one before. With creamy crown moulding, an excess of wainscoting, and mahogany floors polished for so many decades they were impossible to dull. Still, they could only be seen in fits and bursts. His two-bedroom condo was covered in clothes, empty boxes, and at least one hundred empty Fanta bottles. What could I say but, "I didn't know they even made Fanta anymore." It was a teenager's home—a teenager who had suddenly found himself swimming in money and didn't know what to do with it. So he bought a couch and coffee table because he thought he should, but that's where the adultness ended.

He was greedier than others, consistently trying to reach up my shirt, but didn't he know? I didn't fuck anyone I actually respected—not right away. I had to get out of there, and even if I were interested in just the night, it wouldn't be like this. It wouldn't be on a littered, ratty couch that looked like a fallout survivor from some post-apocalyptic disaster. How could he have bought so much overpriced beauty and just shit all over it like this?

"I need to go," I said. He must have known the resolve in my voice, understood that any effort he put forth would be wasted.

"Okay," he said, sitting back to let me walk myself out.

"You're driving me to my car," I said.

"What?"

"You heard me."

"I can't drive," he said. "I've been drinking. I could lose my license."

"You should have thought about that before. What, were you going to make me walk home in the middle of the night?"

"I hadn't really thought about it," he said. I knew that was the truth.

It was like some kind of overwrought medical drama episode. Jimit, ranked by one medical journal as the top one percent of cardiovascular surgeons in the country, drove a 1993 Acura loaded with dust and a stethoscope on the passenger seat. The drive was short, terse and silent. By now, any numbness the alcohol afforded me was wearing off, and I was pissed. Didn't even let him kiss me when he angled up behind my red car that shouted like a beacon in the darkness.

This went on for two years. Two long years where the best of times were spent on pseudo-dates. He'd tell me about the girls he would take out, sometimes texted me in the middle of those dates with, "This girl is 22 and an idiot."

"She's 22," I would reply. Of course she was an idiot.

But he was there, there when I fell in love for the first time—for real—so hard, it skinned my knees and blasted my face with the impact of it all. Jimit and I, we settled into a kind of fake relationship where we'd lean on each other hard when we needed to, falling into each other's arms on holidays and at the end of one of our bad dates to lick our wounds. The first time we fucked, I'd somehow managed to drag three meetings out of him first, and he shut down immediately. It was like fucking a robot. The things he said, the "You like that, don't you?" could have been said to anyone. They were canned sentences filtered out of porn. And he kept sticking his finger in my ass without warning. I didn't like it, but it didn't necessarily hurt (although there was never any type of lube), so I just put up with it and hoped that the next day it wouldn't hurt too bad.

But the weird part? I was never jealous. Never. Sometimes, when I'd see him in bars with women, I'd get annoyed after a while because I wanted to tell him something and he wasn't done with them yet. But never real jealous. I began to wonder if being with him had broken something in me.

And there were gallant times, like when he swooped in as a 250-pound former professional football player got me in his target zone and wouldn't let go. May as well have been shaking me from the scruff as I squealed terrified, though it all happened over a skinny bar table. There was something about Jimit, even in his completely average height, that demanded other men fall to their knees. Women too, of course. There were times I'd cry to him for hours over my heartbreak of others and he'd accept it, soak it in.

Once, on his balcony during a hissing summer heat, he asked what my saddest song was and he told me his. Mine was Peter Gabriel's "Book of Love." I couldn't imagine a love like that. We danced on the balcony and I told him to kiss me like a teenager—like he meant it—and for once he did. In the morning, he combed my hair with his fingers while we watched old James Bond movies. That was before the worst of it.

It was August, a week before my birthday, and I was trying too hard to make friends with a Chinese girl who was pushing herself to seem all-American. Jimit found us at dusk, sitting at patio tables outside Velcro. "Do you want to join us?" I asked him, assuming he'd say no but I didn't know what else to say. Instead, he sat down and scared my new friend away. Like always, like the past two years, it ended up just him and me at two in the morning. He began to cry, bolted up and went to the bathroom. I didn't know what to do but sit in silence with him.

"Will I always be alone?" he asked. He was drunk, but he was always drunk. A highly functional alcoholic. "What's wrong with me?"

We didn't fuck that night, but I stayed over. And in the morning. In the morning. I rolled towards him, out of habit, out of familiarity, and he pushed me away like I'd wronged him. Like his shame was my fault.

"Fuck you," I said, slamming his pager that always dug into my back against the nightstand. He pretended to sleep and I pretended like I didn't take the fifty-dollar bill out of his wallet for a cab ride to my car. Those were our last words, my last words. Fuck you. It was fitting. It was all we'd done to whittle away two more years of our youth.

xiii. The Cuckolded Coyote

It's shameful, you know? Your wife having an affair. And when the affair is with Wolverine, it's even worse. In your head, you see her crouching deep to get to his level. For months, Coyote pretended not to notice the new scents. Made excuses to stay out later, get up before her and spin his imagination into some kind of binding comfort. That made her sloppy. It's like she was showing off, gloating about the bite marks that didn't match his teeth. The co-mingled scent that didn't involve him.

Their community was a small one, a dip of a valley with mountain ranges too high to allow for anyone but the wanderlust animals and a sprinkling of off the grid Humans to pass through. "She's a whore," he told Fox as the two scouted the river bank for prey.

"You shouldn't use that word about your wife," Fox said, keeping his head down. He wanted to be progressive, to think he was better than degrading women for who they slept with. But he was well aware that Coyote was bigger. Stronger. Shouldn't fully be crossed.

"She shouldn't be fucking around then," said Coyote.

He had a point there. "So what are you going to do?" asked Fox.

"I don't know. The Indians, the ones clinging to the rez for dear life, they wouldn't be very happy about any kind of massive uprising."

"Since when does an affair call for a massive uprising? Just kick his ass and be done with it," said Fox.

"It's not that simple."

"Since when?"

"Since I let it go on too long. I thought, you know, maybe it was just a fling. I mean, who cares? But it's started to stick. You know? There's an unraveling happening."

"You're thinking about this too much."

"Maybe so. But I can't un-think it."

Coyote was close to the edge, surely his wife knew it. Wolverine had to suspect it. The whole goddamned valley, even the birds, they had to be in on it. Had to sense the new clip in his movements, the clench of his jaw. And his wife, now she was just flaunting it. The night she came home when it was almost dawn, smelling of sperm and a part of the woods where the blackberry bushes seemed to come alive, the wild in him was let loose.

"Where are you going?" she asked, circling beside him to prep the floor for a dead sleep.

"You should know," he said.

"Don't—" she began, but he silenced her with a look. What power he had, buried so down, down low.

The two of them had settled in a den on the outskirts of the valley, nestled beside a mountain base and close to one of the most worn paths. Pinks and lavenders began to rake at the sky as he walked intent to Wolverine's home on the other side of the valley. Along the path were the early risers and the late nighters trekking home. Skunk, Raccoon, Squirrel and Rabbit. He killed them all.

At first, it wasn't purposeful. Not really. They were in his way and surely, surely they'd each seen his wife slumping home after one of her late nights with Wolverine over the past few months. Their blood was sweet and laced with that kind of sharp fear that you only get when they don't see the kill coming. By the time he was halfway there, he was snapping throats outside his food chain. Antelope, Calf, and Goose. He didn't care, just left a trail of blood and bodies in his wake and no one—no one—dared to stop him. By the time he came to Wolverine's home, it was just another artery. Just another chunk of meat. But he could smell his wife's scent, and her musk blended with that last kill to make it thicker and more filling than the rest. On his walk back, he snapped up the last few lingerers. Snake and Sparrow, even Worm who was wriggling into the earth.

"What did you do?" A lanky, brown-skinned Indian cocked his head and adjusted the Pendleton blanket wrapped around his shoulders. "What did you do?"

"I killed them all," said Coyote. "Do you want to die?"

"Only the sick want to die."

"Then perhaps I did him a favor."

"Who?"

"Wolverine."

"Ah, yes, Wolverine. Had enough, did you?"

"See? Everyone knew. Everyone."

"Everyone loves to gossip," said the Indian. "And your wife?"

"She's alive. At home," said Coyote. "She's the only one alive and I—I don't know why."

"What you did, it's unnatural," said the Indian.

"I know."

"And in more ways than one. These murders, all this blood, of course it's unnatural. The act of revenge, the feeling of jealousy, I thought it was a Human condition. But letting your wife live ... why? Love? Or did you think she loved Wolverine, and living would hurt her more?"

"I don't ... I don't know."

"Here's what I know," said the Indian, bending down and exposing that pulsing throat to Coyote. Wasn't he afraid to die? "What should happen now, is your death. To level everything off. Maybe I was put on this path to kill you. Your coat would keep my daughter warm, and your meat would feed my pigs. But that's not what I'm going to do."

"Then what?" asked Coyote. There's a catch. There's always a catch.

"I won't mention this to anyone," said the Indian. "None of my business anyway, not really. And the woods, they'll repopulate themselves. The valley has a way of making that happen, it's like a cup. You can't help but fill it. But here's the deal. Teach me your magic, so that I may pass it on to my elders."

"I don't have any magic," said Coyote.

"Of course you do. You have the magic of either great love, or great anger, probably both. And in an animal at that, one that we always thought did nothing but take. Since you're heading back to your home, it seems you have the magic of great forgiveness, too—or were you going back to kill your wife last? Dangle a souvenir from Wolverine in front of her face?"

"No, I ... I don't know what I was going to do at home. But it wasn't that."

"All these traits, these are forms of magic. Show me, and that will be it. The world will right itself again."

"Even if I did have magic, I don't know how to teach it," said Coyote. Suddenly he was worried. What did the Indian keep under that blanket? A big, sharpened knife thirsty for blood? A white Human's handgun that shot hot bullets through even the toughest flesh? Whatever kill-driven mission that had been fueling him, it was gone now. Coyote was hyper aware of exactly where he was on the food chain, and it was well below the curious Human with the almond eyes that hovered above him.

"It's simple," said the Indian. "Let me take one of your eyes."

"My eye?" said Coyote. "You want my eye?"

"Just one," said the Indian. "It won't hurt much, and you'll still have the other. Plus, nobody will mess with you, try to sneak up on you, once word spreads of what you've done."

"I thought you said you wouldn't tell anyone."

"I won't," said the Indian. "But the birds ..."

Yes, the Birds. Coyote had forgotten about them, unless they were hopping along the ground. They saw everything, and made stories travel on the winds. By the time he got home, they'd have made him into a mad God.

"The birds," said Coyote. "Alright. Okay. You can have my eye."

The Indian lied, it did hurt. It hurt a great deal, but worse than the pain was the blackness that washed over his right side. Instant and cloying. The light faded to a pinpoint before disappearing entirely, and his eye socket sucked at the eyeball as it was plucked from its home like a ripe strawberry. This is a mistake, this is a mistake, the words kept tumbling in his head.

"Ah, it's lovely!" said the Indian. "Like a jewel. Here, let me patch you up so you don't bleed too much. Thank you. You've taught me, us, a great deal."

"I can't see ..." said Coyote.

"Of course you can! You just have to learn to rely on the other side more. Don't worry, it'll get strong and compensate soon enough."

And he was right. By the time Coyote found his way home, he'd already become used to swinging his head more, turning his head a sharp right to take in all his surroundings.

"What the ... what did you do? What happened?" asked his wife, running to him and lapping at the blood that had stained his head to his neck. "What's all this blood? What happened to your eye?"

"My eye? The eye, I gave away. I see all, I don't need two. And the blood, it's not all mine. In fact, very, very little is mine."

In that moment she knew, and keened for only a second into the too-bright morning before nuzzling his neck, licking the pain from his wounds, and separating her lover's blood from his along her tongue.

Chapter 13

You get addicted to it, the whole bar scene, and in familiarity you're tricked into thinking you belong. With Melody, we made outlines of Acceptable Romps. "Six feet and six figures" was the ideal, but for me it was deeper. I wanted someone, even if just for a night, who I could never know completely. Someone who's childhood didn't mimic my own. With Jeremy, with every American, when they told me about their childhood I could picture it. Even if I wasn't there, even if they'd grown up playing in the corn fields in Wisconsin. I knew what they meant when they said "Thanksgiving with family" or talked about their high school graduation and talking driver's ed in those beat up cars with the brake pedals on the passenger side. No matter how different they may seem to be, I knew that one day we'd merge into one big lump where I couldn't see my end and their beginning. It was a slow killing, like eating yourself to death.

I wasn't attracted to Aakash when I saw him at the bar. But he was tall, and he was brown, and he seemed so lost. By now, the Velcro regulars had come to know one another. We acknowledged each other in sideways glances and, rarely, full-on looks when the alcohol made us careless.

It's so easy to make a man think he's chosen you. Sit close to him. Don't look away immediately when your eyes cling to each other. Make sure you're always, always alone.

"What's good here?" he asked me.

"Sorry?" I asked. I'd heard him perfectly.

"I said, what's good here?" he asked. Those three little words held so much weight. Nothing. The answer was nothing. But that's not what I said. Instead, I suggested the strongest of drinks, the ones you never see coming. These type of men, they might have practiced their way into drinking a single clear liquor, maybe even neat, but that liquor is usually whiskey or vodka. Sometimes tequila, though usually not Indians. It's never gin. Suggesting they order a drink that's basically chilled, local gin with strange flavors has one of two outcomes. They either will themselves not to wince, in which case it pushes me out of my element and makes them actually intriguing. Otherwise, they squint their eyes and shake their heads, and I know I'm in control for however long I keep them. Aakash was the latter, as I knew he would be.

"My God, that's strong," he said. I shrugged like I didn't know what he was talking about, but I did. I could still remember the years in London where I tried so hard to even drink whiskey without diet Coke. I couldn't, no matter how many pre-cocktails I'd had. It took me another couple of years to get rid of that crutch.

Aakash was an engineer, of course, but a different kind than what I was used to. He worked at an aeronautics company about an hour away, and had well-versed stories that made even the engineering aspect of it seem plausible and interesting. There's some magic in working on, near and around planes. Somehow, these massive steel birds took flight and roared over us all. He was one of the people who pushed the wind below those wings. Even so, I couldn't force myself to be attracted to him. There wasn't anything wrong with him, but the right wasn't powerful enough, either.

But I gave him my number when he told me he had a condo just a few blocks away, squarely in the Pearl District though the cut of his shirt and the wash of his jeans said he should be completely lost in such a space.

Two days later, he texted and five days later we went out. It was on a Sunday, my choice because I didn't see enough in him to give him a Friday or Saturday night. We started at a sushi place I had once been, though I didn't eat rice, and ended up back at Velcro where Sundays were reserved for lingering at well-lit tables. When I told him how much I adored their dates wrapped in bacon and stuffed with goat cheese, he ordered plate after plate.

That first time, back at his place, I just wanted to get it over with. Not the sex, I couldn't bring myself to that yet, but just that first physical contact. I could make out with anyone—had made out with anyone. It's easy. You just close your eyes and imagine. You read their body, give them what they want a few seconds too late if you want to hurry them alone. Then, with those like Aakash, you play good girl even though you know it'll make them fall for you. But he was a nice person, and he made good money, and he looked at me like he thought he saw something of merit deep inside. He was wrong, of course, but I felt too bad to tear apart his dreams so soon. I was bored already.

Aakash did all the right things, even making me a strong gin drink because he thought that was my preference. I didn't mind them, but I drank martinis because by the time I swam to the bottom of the glass I was guaranteed to be drunk. I didn't like the taste enough to down it like it was soda—that was how I drank whiskey now. Instead, the slow pulls perfectly inebriated me and I had a sure thing in a martini glass. But it still wasn't enough to make even myself pretend that I could do whatever this was for life.

And his condo, it was lovely. All exposed beams and plenty of concrete smatterings, even a proper couch that didn't turn into a bed. It wasn't pulled together by a designer, but it was far from a bachelor pad. This is a man who wants to get married, I told myself, and that thought made my bones freeze. Someone, sometimes, would feel so blessed to stumble across him. Why couldn't that be me? What did I think was so great in me to trade for a life like this?

For days after, he'd text and I would respond, but I couldn't muster excitement in the words. I replied when I felt like it, which he must have read as playing no games. Usually, that meant within thirty minutes of getting his text, lest I forget. I didn't want to be rude, and responding felt like another task I was ticking off at work. Like mailing the annual reports or confirming receipt of a grant proposal.

Then, "You free on Friday?" came and my gut flipped at the thought of giving up a night prowling. How could he do this? Assume that he should come first and I wasn't strapping on my hunting boots as soon as I escaped early on that all-important day? I rolled everything he could have possibly done wrong around in my head, looking for a reason to blame him for this untangling. Maybe it was that he'd seem so wrong in Velcro, or that he'd been so quick to text. Unlike Jimit, I intuited that he texted because he thought that's what I preferred—not because he didn't want to leave the wrong impression by actually talking on the phone. In fact, he had called, but it was after our first date. I just never picked up, and that taught him that hearing his voice wasn't what I wanted.

You free on Friday? It was just Tuesday. I couldn't pull together the right words, and so didn't reply until Wednesday night. "Have plans with a friend," I responded, and he replied immediately. Gave other options, even tried to offer up his own excuses of what he may be doing, too. I felt bad, cornering him into trying to save face like that, but I couldn't help it. I just wanted to erase the past couple of weeks with him, stop myself from taking the seat next to him, and get rid of the fact that I had ever given him my number. For a moment, I toyed with the idea of actually changing my number, give myself a brand new start, but that seemed like a terrible amount of work for one little mistake that would be easy to brush aside.

After two more days, I stopped replying completely. When his name flashed across my screen, I deleted it fast without looking. Finally, I blocked his number so I wouldn't even have to know when he tried to reach me. Thank you, thank God that I never slept with him. That was my mantra every night, even though I knew I'd have to avoid Velcro for a while. Was he the type with strung up nerves I hadn't seem that would lead him back there? Maybe he was truly worried about me, or perhaps his ego was bruised black enough that he would actually confront me in a crowded room. I didn't want any of that, and I didn't know him well enough to tell if that was in his nature. When it came down to it, I didn't know him at all, even though his saliva had surely made its way down my throat and into my belly. There, it would mix with the rest of them and what wasn't expelled in waste would surely become a part of me. Funny, how we consume and become everyone who's crossed our lips. Does the one who's come inside us stick better, or does percentage and type of fluid have nothing to do with it? Is a person who's only been as deep as their tongue in the back of our mouth just as sticky as the person who came inside us for years?

Still, I didn't have to add him to my growing list. He wouldn't become a number, and that was a good thing, right? I didn't have a particular number in mind that was too high or too much, but with each addition it felt like I was a little less of a person. With every person that become a part of me, I had to give away a part of myself to make room for them. At the very least, I wanted to reserve those numbers for someone who ravaged my heart or at least made me feel something for a little while. Maybe that's why it was so easy, to keep going back to Jimit for so many months even though he went somewhere else when he was inside me. At least a repeat meant I wasn't adding to my rag tag of a list.

I only saw Aakash again, once, and it was years later. A co-worker, Francesca, was between him and I at a long bar. But the music was so loud, she couldn't hear him properly. But I did. "Is her name Justine?" he asked Francesca.

"Huh?" she said.

"Is that Justine?" he asked, and I kept my face forward, pretending I couldn't hear.

"What? No," she said.

"Oh," he said, like she was lying for me. I never did find out what she really thought he said, but just thanked her, deep inside. But the strange part? I had looked at him, he was in my sightline again all those years later and if I hadn't already had him, I would have saw right next to him again.

Opossum had the most beautiful tale of all, thick and lavish. It rivaled Squirrel's and put Skunk's to shame, and even Fox wouldn't dare raise his tail in pride when Opossum traipsed along. Every last drop of ego was drained into Opossum's tail, keeping him home most days brushing and admiring. Conditioning and coifing. Yet it was all worth it for those special occasions, the ones where he would slip into a long overcoat to reveal the bouffant beauty that made him the most desirable of all. As a child, Opossum was first confused then embarrassed by the attention. "Oh my, how lovely your tail is!" old women would say as he trailed behind his mother. "Is it real? Is his father's like that?"

"Oh, no!" his mother would say. "We don't know where it came from. Ours, as you can see, look like Squirrel's at best." It was true, he was an anomaly. It caused him teasing through his adolescence and uncertainty as he matured, but when that day came—the day where he realized being beautiful and different was a gift, he went all in.

"Hey!" called Rabbit, hopping along next to him as Opossum hurried down the street for his monthly trimming appointment. "Are you going to the pow wow tonight? I'm selling tickets."

"Oh, I don't know," said Opossum. Was the annual pow wow worth the effort? Would there be enough eyes on him? "How many people are going again?"

"*Everyone's* going," said Rabbit.

Everyone. That sounded promising. "Huh," said Opossum. "I don't know. What seats are you selling? It's really not worth my time unless I get a center seat. You know, to display my tail."

Rabbit rolled his eyes, but he was under incredible pressure to pack the house. For each seat he sold, he got a commission, and the most expensive seats—the ones in the center—gave him a great cut. If he could sell a headliner seat to Opossum, that was twenty easy dollars.

"Yeah, yeah, I have a center seat available. Just one. It got returned today due to a family emergency." That was all a lie, but Rabbit knew how to sell, how to tap into the desires of his targets.

"Right in the center?" asked Opossum.

"Right in the center."

"Well, okay," said Opossum. "But I don't have much time to get ready. You didn't give me any time to prepare. I'll need to properly groom my tail, and I'm going for a trim right now but they don't have time to do a full prep for it. I'm not sure how—"

"I'll help you," said Rabbit. He couldn't bear to hear Opossum dole out any more self-compliments.

"You will?" Opossum was shocked. He wasn't friends with Rabbit and had been after soothing compliments, not an offer to help.

"Sure," said Rabbit. "Just tell me what time you want me to come over, and I'll help you."

"Uh, okay," said Opossum. "Be there at four, this is my address—"

"Four?" said Rabbit. "The pow wow doesn't start 'til nine!"

"I know. It takes quite some time to get ready for big events," said Opossum. "You wouldn't understand. It must not take you long at all to get ready."

Rabbit's heart was raging against his rib cage, but he steadied it. "Okay, okay. I'll be there."

Even though he had to stop hawking tickets early, even though he might have lost tax-free money, Rabbit stopped his sells early and raced home to tuck his own dull pair of scissors into his folds, hidden from Opossum's watchful eyes.

He'd never been to Opossum's before, but it was how he imagined. Well-lit, full of mirrors, and the walls were covered in self-portraits and photos, with Opossum striking the same pose in each one. Back to the camera, tail on full display, and eyes coyly looking over his shoulder.

"You came!" said Opossum, flinging open the door.

"I said I would," said Rabbit. "Now, what do you want me to do?"

"Here, I'll show you," said Opossum, ushering Rabbit into the sitting room. For ten minutes he blathered on, but Rabbit didn't hear any of it. Should he do this? He should do it. He'd be doing everyone a favor.

"I think," said Rabbit, eager to interject one of the few times Opossum paused for breath, "we should do the grooming as you say, but then how about I tie up your tail in a lovely type of braid? That was, you can untie it and do a big reveal once you get to your seat!"

"That's a great idea!" said Opossum. "I love it. I just hope, you know, the ties don't make a pattern in the hair—"

"Oh, no, I'm sure they won't," said Rabbit. "Your tail is much too thick for that. And I'll keep the ties as loose as possible, I promise."

How he pretended to prep and groom that monstrous tail for three hours, Rabbit didn't know. There were times he actually listened to Opossum as he repeated the instructions over and over. The coconut oiling, the massaging, the fine-toothed combing and so on. It was maddening, but it gave him time to make slow, quiet snips. Lock by lock, he carved hideous chunky patterns into Opossum's tail with the sharp little secret he kept pressed against his flanks. With just forty minutes to go, he tied up the tail as promised, shoving the shorn hair into little pockets so they would fall out at the big reveal.

"All done!" said Rabbit. He had to admit, it didn't look too bad with the lops of hair so well woven into the bands.

"Thanks!" said Opossum. "I can't wait to untie it. Hold on, let me just look in the—"

"No time, no time!" said Rabbit, just in case Opossum wasn't impressed by his handiwork. "Let's hurry, so you can be sure to show off all this grooming before the grand marshal begins her speech."

"Oh, okay," said Opossum, disappointed at the lack of time for admiring.

As Rabbit led Opossum through the crowds and past the check-in line, made a pathway through those who were huddled around the outer tables, he began to doubt himself. Was this cruel? Did Opossum really deserve this? But it was too late now. He delivered Opossum to his seat in the center of the room, then dashed away with an, "I need to check on something," before bolting like a madman out of the auditorium.

"Everyone!" shouted Opossum, "Everyone, I've arrived. And have I a treat for you." The loudness of his voice was enough to quiet all at the head table, though they knew what was coming. "My friend, Rabbit, and I spent several hours preparing for this evening. I'm pleased to share with you," he said, reaching behind him and pulling at the ties, "perhaps my most incredible look yet."

In an explosion of hair, Opossum's tail fluffed out before most of the cut-off tresses fell to the floor. Awkward lumps stuck to bits of his nearly naked tail at random, like confused clusters on a cactus. "What the hell?" he said as everyone began to laugh. "What? No, no, no—"

They were all around him, circling him, laughing and pointing. His tail and entire backside felt cold, exposed, and his glorious hairs floated all around him. The pride drained out as the ugliness swept over him. At a loss of words, of anything, Opossum had no choice. He laid down, curled up, and played dead until the speeches began.

Chapter Fourteen

"I thought you were a slut when I first met you," Titan said. What a stupid name, and one that didn't fit him at all. He was my height at best, his thighs half my size. Night-black skin and a hairline receding so badly at twenty-nine that it begged mercilessly to be shaved clean. We'd met at a hotel bar, a historic downtown gathering spot next to a bustling theater. It was known for having the biggest whiskey selection in Portland and a ghost that wandered the hallways.

"Why?" I asked. When we'd met, it had been early and us both seemingly alone. When he'd introduced himself, he gave his full name, Titan Libra. When my eyes must have betrayed what a ridiculous name that seemed, almost a drag queen, he'd said coolly, "Google me." And he'd meant it. I did, but found nothing of merit. A skydiving video, the kind you paid an extra fifty dollars for. Endless Facebook photos of him next to a lemon-yellow new Corvette (dig a little deeper and he'd had countless white women with mediocre bodies and ugly faces pose with it). A mention of a PhD from Arizona State and an engineering job at Intel like every Indian had.

"Why else would you be in a hotel bar?" he said. That made no sense to me.

"Why else? I mean ... it's just a bar ..." I always found myself explaining myself to him. Why I parallel parked the way I did (apparently, it was strange). Why I "only" had a master's degree, after he'd ranted for fifteen minutes about how he'd only date someone with a doctorate. Anything less was laughable.

"No," he said. "Girls who go to hotel bars, who aren't staying at the hotel, are just looking for easy fucks because there are bedrooms for rent above their heads."

"You think a woman needs to go to such great lengths? I've never met someone in a bar and had sex with them. I've only had two one night stands in my life." At that point, that was true.

"It doesn't matter," he said.

We'd had one official, real date, and now I knew why he was shaking his restless leg and looking at his watch an hour into it. He'd thought he'd done his duty, put on the little performance and now that he'd paid for a drink and a four-dollar shared happy hour plate I was obliged to sleep with him.

I never fucked him. Not once in the whole year we talked. Actually, that's mostly what we did. After seeing each other several times, he loaded me with scotch (telling me only the unsophisticated drink whiskey or ever had brown liquor on the rocks) and somehow I ended up blowing him. He said, time and again, that I gave the best head of his life. I'm not sure how much he'd ever had, but I didn't think I was that good. Is that all it took? No gag reflex, so I could never be bulimic no matter how hard I tried, and remembering to wrap your teeth with your lips?

"I'd never fuck you," he said after that one time. "I have higher standards than that. But anytime you want to give me head, text me. If I'm around, you can come over." How someone could say something like that without a trace of irony, I'll never know. How I could accept it and go crawling back after every sour date was an even larger mystery.

It was the alcohol, it had to be. It made me do stupid things over and over again. Once, we met up for drinks so he could tell me about the latest doctoral candidate he was seeing. She looked like a horse that had never picked up a pair of free weights in her life. "But she's going to be a *chiropractor,*" he said. "That's basically like a real medical doctor."

That same night, I bemoaned to him how much I hated the loose skin at my stomach. It's what they don't tell you about gaining and then losing an incredible amount of weight in such a short amount of time. Granted, mine could have been worse. A lot worse. At least I had youth on my side when I took my body on that ride. But now, now even if I could afford liposuction and a tummy tuck, I couldn't get it. Not really. After numerous free consultations, surgeons had told me they would do it—but if I ever wanted to have kids, a re-tightened stomach could cause problems. They recommended waiting until I knew for sure. Until I had children, ideally.

"That sucks," Titan said. "You can't fix your stomach until you have kids. But you can't find anyone to have kids with you until you fix your stomach." That last part he had intuited, and honestly I'd never really thought about it. Of course I was embarrassed of my stomach, but weren't all women self-conscious? I'd sucked it up and sucked it in with every man I was with, and not a single one had said a thing. But maybe they were just being polite. Later that night, as I drove him home (I always drove, so he could drink 'til his liver could handle no more and I would be the one driving for miles out of downtown wondering if I was over the limit), he put his hand on my thigh. And looked at me.

"What are you doing?" I asked.

"Nothing," he said, taking his hand away. Maybe, for just a moment, he'd forgotten horse face and I was enough.

It wasn't all bad times though. It couldn't be, otherwise what woman would get caught up enough in it all to stay? There were hours we'd spend at his waterfront condo, drinking scotch and not much else. "Do you want to see some magic?" he asked one night.

"Sure." He didn't seem the magic type.

"Here," he said. Shuffling a playing deck and fanning it before me. "Take a card and memorize it."

When I gave it back to him, he re-shuffled, fluttering the cards without paying them much mind. Whatever trick there was to it, he must have done it so often he didn't even need to think about it anymore. Slowly, one by one, he flipped each card over. About a quarter of a way into the deck, he said, "This one." It was. The nine of clubs.

"Yeah," I said. I'd never understood magic or anything like that. Never tried to. I just trusted that the other person knew what they were doing, and never wheedled any deeper than that.

"You want to know how it's done?" he asked. Wasn't that against the rules?

"Sure."

"It's in your eyes," he said. "No matter what, when you see your card, the pupils shift. They get bigger." Watching, that was it. That was the trick. Noticing and reading languages of the body that we can't control. It wasn't really magic at all. It was just looking closer than what anyone else ever bothered to do.

Months later, when I was living with a roommate in a rambling southeast house and coming oh, so close to moving to Los Angeles with my third one-night stand that had turned into a rheumy, abusive mess of a situation, Titan came to my going away house party. But never asked if he could bring anyone, and came with a murder of girls—at least six of them—and they were all simultaneously drunk and high. For five minutes, he found me on the porch while I forced down yet another cigarette. I didn't like the taste or effect anymore, and the smoke always wove its way deep into my hair so I'd find myself showering at three in the morning. But it gave my hands something to do, and I was just barely of the generation who still saw it as glamorous.

"So you're going to LA, huh?" he asked.

"That's the plan," I said. I never did make it, and maybe he saw that coming. Maybe my eyes told him.

"Running away," he said.

"From what?" He was right, I was, but by now he'd broken up with horse chiropractor in training and had moved onto a stream of girls that lined up one after the other. The whiter the better. Natural blondes and red heads that contrasted sharply against his own inky skin.

"I don't know from what," he said. "I'm just telling you what you already know anyway. You're not going to find anything there that's not here."

"At least it'll be different," I said, and he just shrugged.

For a year, he'd told me very little about himself. He didn't quite have the kind of Indian accent I was used to, but it wasn't American either. It was clipped, like his tongue moved too quickly to his teeth when he spoke. He was offended when I asked if his name was his birth name. I knew he was Catholic, that his dad was in the Indian military and they moved around the country often. I had seen a photo of his older sister and her one-year-old daughter, the most beautiful baby with kohl-rimmed eyes I'd ever seen. He'd told me, repeatedly, how ASU had one of the best engineering programs in the country at the doctoral level, and had even told me how much he made (just over six figures, though I didn't ask. I thought it would be more). He'd said how he saw that yellow Corvette and just knew, but I never told him his yearly changing of the vanity plate to relay messages like "Young Gun" by leaving out the vowels was childish and overtly vain. He'd angled himself to be so much above me that I'd just believed it all. Every time with him, every minute and every conversation, I felt myself being lowered a peg.

Maybe he was right. Maybe I was running, maybe my stomach was too fucked up for anyone to ever really want me, and maybe without a doctorate I had nothing to offer. Unlike many others, he found nothing profound or idealistic about my working for a non-profit. When I'd told him I'd started running, with far-off dreams of a marathon, he shook his head. "Runners are so self-involved. It's stupid," he said. "I'd much rather chase a ball around a field." He was on an intramural field hockey team and had slept with half the women on it, with their thick calves and makeup-free faces. After a month, I stopped running. I wouldn't start again for years later.

But once, once he'd said something kind that had nothing to do with how well I sucked his dick. We met at a happy hour bar across the street from one of my yoga studios. By then, I didn't care what I looked like around him. He found me wanting no matter what. "You look like that one girl, Hugh Hefner's girlfriend," he said. It didn't really matter which one, they were all so much lovelier than me.

"Why?" I asked. I really didn't know.

"Without the makeup. With the ponytail," he said. Apparently, that's what made me beautiful. Sweat and work and a lack of caring.

It was an excuse, the one I'd been waiting for. Not for him or for anyone else, but my permission to show my face to the world without carefully crafted armor covering it. Since I was eleven, when my mom took me to the Clinique makeup counter and they piled foundation, eyeliner, lip liner and everything else they could manage onto me, I'd never shown my face without it. How could I? I hadn't even started my period yet, and had been told exactly everything that was wrong with me. I was the only girl in sixth grade with a full face of makeup, concealer and all. Looking back at that year's school photo, side by side with all the others, I looked like a child prostitute.

In the end, I didn't go to LA and one of the drunk, thin by young metabolism only girls he'd brought with him stole all the full bottles of liquor and stowed them in her trunk. Another was so sure the keg needed to be moved into the bathtub with ice she attempted it herself and dropped the barrel right on the ledge. My roommate came barreling at me, drunk herself like always and demanding hundreds of dollars on the spot to fix it. "I'll give you money tomorrow!" I told her, and her boyfriend handed her a Costco-sized jar of vitamin gummy bears to distract and satiate her. The next morning, she asked, "Did you eat my whole jar of vitamins?"

"No ..." I said, rubbing my forehead to ward off the headache.

"You ate them," her almost-always silent boyfriend said.

"Oh. Well, you still owe me for the bathtub," she said. It hadn't even been my idea to have the party, but I handed over the four hundred dollars to shut her up. It didn't matter that her seventy-year-old house was falling apart, that the stairs were warped and the wallpaper peeling in every room.

I never saw Titan again, but followed his unfolding on Facebook. The engagement to the buck-toothed blonde. Their courthouse wedding and pedicab tour afterward with beers in hand. I wasn't jealous, not quite, but I just didn't get it. Why not me? Why not me.

xv. The Frog's Way to Love

It was equal, arranged marriages and love. But it's a time of transition, when a parent might not be able to handpick their child's spouse, but they have many decades of guilt-layering in their old hands. Learned years ago what moves would make their child swoon, what sharp words would hold them still. In this way, the Human girl's mother still held the reins tight. Her father, dead for a decade, rotted in peace below the earth.

"Why don't you just tell her you're marrying me?" Frog asked Girl. Like always, they were pressed close together on stolen time, the two hours in the evening where it was believable that she was with her friends.

"It's not that easy. You don't get it—you don't have parents like this."

"I don't have parents at all," said Frog.

"Don't play that card."

"Maybe I don't understand, but what's she going to do? Ignore you forever? You're her only kid, you know she'll come around."

"I know," said the girl. "It's just—it's easier, you know? Why don't we just wait? I still have one more year of college, and you—"

"Wait for what? There will always be more things happening, more excuses. It's been five years already."

"I know how long it's been," she said.

Maybe she didn't really want to marry him at all, he thought. "What, exactly, does she say? What are her reasons?" he asked. It had been years since he'd seen her mother, and only a handful of times then. He read the disgust in her face, the stiffness of her gestures, and was grateful when the girl said her mother never wanted to see him again.

"I've told you," she said. "It's the same old stuff. I need to be young, be single. How do I know there's not someone else I'd be happier with? Why don't I try—"

"So she never actually says it," said Frog, splitting a long blade of grass into the smallest of pieces.

"No. She doesn't say it." Neither did they, at least not often. Being different species, it wasn't so strange anymore, especially in the metros like this. Some elders looked and whispered, but for the most part the bigotry had died down. Now, apparently, it hid coiled deep inside. For Frog, there had never been any question of it. He'd loved her immediately, hard and fast. Without family, there were no strange bonds telling him what to do. What to feel. And he couldn't wait any longer.

Her mother was a superstitious old woman. She'd had a child at forty, and for that it seemed especially miraculous. Frog knew she tossed spilled salt over her shoulder even at fancy restaurants. About her vastly overpaying to fix a cheap broken mirror rather than buy a new one in an attempt to ward off the bad luck. How hard could it be to trick her?

Starting that night, he crept to the mother's window, her reading lamp lighting up the dead-end street like a target. "The faultfinder will die," he whispered. She'd never know his voice, probably hadn't even heard it over the roaring hatred in her ears when she'd met him. From behind the curtains, a rustling.

"The faultfinder will die," he said again, pressing his slick body against the cool brick of the house.

"Who is that?" she demanded, but her voice wavered.

"Faultfinders will die," he said again, and her heavy footsteps flew from the window to the hallway.

He didn't tell the girl, and the cheap ploy worked. Worked faster than he'd imagined it would.

"So, my mom?" the girl said a week later. "I don't know what happened, but she ... she says it's not up to her to find fault in anyone. Actually, she never really mentioned any faults she thought you had anyway. But she's given up. Says she doesn't care what I do."

"That's amazing!" said Frog, and he didn't even have to fake his joy. It *was* amazing, how quickly you could manipulate Humans. Their fear made them clench tight, but fears could be so easily overridden.

"Yeah," said the girl.

"So, when do you want to get married? I mean, I'll get you a ring first. Of course. We can go together and you can pick out the one you'd like—"

"I don't—I don't think that's a good idea," she said.

"Oh. Okay. Well, I can try to surprise you with one, but—"

"No. I mean, maybe we shouldn't get married. Maybe we should just, you know, call this whole thing off."

"What are you talking about? I thought you said your mom didn't mind anymore."

"I said she didn't care."

"Same thing."

"No, it isn't," she said. "Look, maybe she was right. You know? All along. I mean, maybe we were both so hell bent on this because she wouldn't allow it."

"And what? Now that the struggle's over and you've won, you're ready to just go on to the next battle?" He saw his words becoming solid in her deepest parts. He was narrating her moves, putting a score to what she's surely one day call a revolutionary moment.

"Kind of?" she said. "It sounds cheap, I know. And immature. And I've wasted so many years that I—I just don't want to waste any more."

"And what are you going to do when, the next thing you want, your mom just says okay? Just keep desperately running around looking for a way to piss her off?"

"That's not what this is about," she said.

"You have no idea what any of this is about."

Chapter Fifteen

I thought Sanjay was gay when I met him, and in that I found comfort. He was beautiful, certainly. The kind of beautiful where you wondered how others didn't fall at his feet when he walked past. The thick Indian name tacked onto an American-born boy whose family slowly inched their way here via the Fiji Islands gave him a kind of lost aura where he never quite fit in anywhere. I don't know why it was he locked onto me so tightly. Probably because he could tell there was no getting through the fog of my adoration for some other boy. Another man, another Indian. I met Sanjay a year after I'd fallen for Chakor—a Gujarati earmarked for an arranged marriage, whose name meant enamored with the moon.

Sanjay was the kind of distraction that came with no lumps or bumps. He wasn't Jimit, hunted by alcoholism and scared shitless that he'd die alone. Sanjay was six years younger than me and fully embraced by every club he sauntered into. Straight, gay, white, mixed, he didn't care. He told me while we sank into the suckling booths at the Alibi tiki karaoke slum that his longest relationship had been with a stripper. It was a common Portland sentiment, but he said it with no haunting of a brag, just a fact. Said he was never jealous, didn't care that she sometimes had customers stalking her from the backdoor to her car. I'm sure she was gorgeous, but I never asked for a picture. It was enough to try and measure up to the stripper I dreamed up in my head.

Really, I couldn't fathom what he saw in me. The second night we were together, he took me to his cousin's house in farout southeast Portland where his brother, sisters, and whole extended family gathered to keep drinking after the bars closed. The women all hated me, but I was used to it. Still, they didn't act like Sanjay did this all the time. It was a rarity. And their female friends whom he'd known forever shot me dirty looks as he draped his arm over me like it belonged there.

"Your sisters' friends don't like me," I said to him when they moved in one big gaggle from the living room to the kitchen.

"I don't really like them," he said.

"You act like you do."

"I can act like a lot of things," he said.

The skin-tight button ups, the distressed belts that perfectly ponied up against the designer shoes, the close lines in his hair that made you think he got trimmed daily, it was all one big lovely show. I was happy, when I needed a distraction, to bask in it.

And once, only once, did we fuck. It was cushioned on both ends by plenty of making out.

I did it because, even with all the affections, the kisses, the handholding and all, I didn't want even a pseudo-relationship with a gay man. I did it to prove something to me, to him, but it all came backfiring in one messy episode. Encouraging him to fuck me doggy style, so I wouldn't have to look too long at that too-perfect face, after less than a minute, he said, "Don't—" and of course I did. He came into the condom fast, and it was over, his long vampire fingers trailing along my hips. Would a gay man come that fast? I didn't know.

"I told you not to," he said, and I felt like I should apologize but I was getting too scarred over for that. I let Sanjay get added to my mental list, disappointed that a number should get tacked on for less than two minutes of effort. Still, I wasn't a cheater, not in that regard. I had to find some way, draw some lines, when it came to addition. The classic and ridiculous penis-in-vagina rule worked well enough, no matter the duration.

At the Cupcake club, the one that sounded like it should be a strip joint but wasn't, Sanjay introduced me to his friend Tim who worked at a newspaper in Vancouver. Tim was a classic white guy with a striped button-up that did him no favors and too much product in his hair. But he was nice enough. It wasn't until a year later, months after I'd stopped speaking to Sanjay, that I got a message from Sanjay saying, "You know Tim fell for you, right? We both did." I hadn't known either of that, and I never replied.

The idea of white men even finding me attractive was wildly foreign. To me, they weren't men, not really. That wasn't what I'd grown up seeing as a man, as a husband, as anything besides the little boys that ran around the schoolyards and called me a slut (usually) or fat (occasionally). To me, Tim was on the outskirts, a witness to my proof that yes, I could take someone as beautiful as Sanjay just like that. He wasn't supposed to horn in on our act.

When Sanjay got sick after that first month and had told me how much he loved the soup from a little Vietnamese diner, I bustled him a full quart on my lunch break. I don't know what I expected, gratitude maybe, but he looked more confused than anything. The "thanks" was riddled with fakery and I wish I'd spent that ten dollars on anything else. But still, he kept the rainbow lei from the night at the tiki bar wrapped around his windshield mirror. That had to count for something. If he was dating other girls, fucking other girls, other boys, I didn't know. Didn't really care. But surely they'd ask for the story behind that obnoxious lei dangling in his car. My presence permeated that old Volvo.

The sickness wasn't what broke us though, it was some foreign power play that I apparently played very well even though I didn't know the rules. Religiously, Sanjay would text me every Friday night. Every Saturday night. Usually close to midnight, but this wasn't a booty call. He'd be out, he'd know I was out, and ask to meet up. Demand to meet up. Require that I come to him, wherever that may be, regardless of where I was or who I was with. It was like being locked in my mother's house again, like curfew was calling.

"I'm with friends," I'd tell him. "I'm on the other side of town."

"I'm busy, you come here," he'd say. Like I was a dog, and he was doing me a favor by even offering up an excuse. I wouldn't answer. This went on for weeks, and I never did figure out the drive behind it. It was the only time he let a whisper of control leak out. I'd known abuse, lived it. This wasn't that kind of manipulative controlling. More like a begging to prove that he mattered even a bit to me, but he didn't.

Finally, after three months, he exploded. A raging text was sent declaring that, since I had consistently failed to jump on his commands, he never wanted to speak to me again. "I'm serious!" his text proclaimed, though I didn't know who he was arguing with. I hadn't replied all day. It was a good, clean excuse of a break for me, and I felt nothing. No sadness, no relief, not even a touch of regret that he'd wormed his way onto my numbered list. Just another check off the box, though I'd always consider him one of my loveliest.

Two months later, he messaged me like nothing had happened. "Hey, girl, what's up?" I didn't reply. Another year later and I'd get the message about Tim. Two years later, and I saw him on the sidewalk. He was anoretic, his bones showing through sheets of thin skin. I could barely make out all that beauty that had puffed up his cheeks before and rounded out his shoulders. The only way I recognized him was by the birthmark on his right cheek. And Sanjay, he didn't recognize me at all. I imagine ghosts usually don't.

"Hey," I said. It was an automatic response, like just what you do when you see the past meander by. Had he noticed me first, said something to me first, I probably would have plastered on a fake smile and willed the minutes to past faster. I didn't know if I was showing off my blasé-ness or what. Something in the deepest hollow of my throat commanded that I speak.

"Oh, hi!" he said. Less than a minute of pleasantries passed before the skeleton was addressed. "So, I lost some weight," he said. His smile looked to foreign now, teeth jutting out of the sickly brown earth of his skin.

"Yeah, I ... I noticed."

"Just, you know, low carb. Lots of working out."

"Okay," I said. I didn't know what else to say. I wish I hadn't spoken.

"You look good!" he said. Did I really? I was the same, the same size I'd always been. Just the blonde in my hair had grown out, been slowly cut off inch by inch as I let that chestnut reddish brown grown wild again. I'd stopped layering on the makeup, foregoing eye liner totally. Did we both really look so different? If I'd stayed, if I'd let him grab control every now and then, would I be a floating collection of bones along the sidewalk with him? Had he been a woman, he would have certainly been called full of grace and smashing. Shoulders like hangers and a rib cage that arched out in an attempt to contain his heart.

"Thanks." That's all I really could say.

"So, are you ... what's new? Are you seeing anyone?" he asked.

"Nothing much," I said. "You know, you know how it is. I'm at a new job, working at the hospital's philanthropy arm. That's about it." I wouldn't, couldn't ask him about himself. I didn't want to see his muscles strain at the masseter, or imagine what it must look like in his bleak, too-white apartment now.

"Yeah, nothing much with me either," he said. "The gym takes up a lot of time."

"I imagine. Well, it was going seeing you," I said. Those five words, I don't know how they became such common fodder. It wasn't good seeing him, it made me sick. Mostly with disgust, but with a twinge of jealousy that he'd started to disappear and I was still so present.

"Yeah, you too," he said. "And, just so you know. About that last message I sent you? I mean, I was just screwing around. If you want, you know, you should message Tim. Directly. About that."

"Oh, that," I said, as if I'd forgotten. "Yeah, no. I don't, I don't have any interest in that. I'd forgotten." At least part of that was true. Why he was trying, after all this time, to shove me onto his friend I couldn't understand. Tim hadn't been a sliver of what Sanjay was. He didn't have the face, the body, or even the job and prestige to compete. Was it just the fairness of his skin, the assumption that because we'd look like two white people together it must be meant to be? I was the same as Sanjay, and he never saw that. Just because my dad's Cherokee hadn't colored me like it should, that didn't mean I felt at home amidst the palest of the flock.

"Sure, sure," Sanjay said, and he walked away. I watched him for an absurd amount of time. How his hip bones shifted the pants back and forth, but it looked like there was nothing in those designer denim coverings. The way his head now looked too big for his body, even though he'd kept up with those insanely detailed haircuts. And how he never did look back, but I could feel the nerves bundling around his neck. He knew my eyes were on him, and it made him walk so stiffly that he could have easily taken flight in the wind.

There was something off about him, something that had kept me an arm's stretch away no matter how incredible he may have looked. No matter how kind he was, or how his eerie stabs at jealousy or control or whatever it was were reserved for the witching hour of nights. He was over thirty now, and still he wore the same uniform of the club kids. He'd never look old, unless the starvation finally kicked in and ran rivets through his face like it tended to do. That warm brown skin warded off the shallowest signs of aging, but I knew. I could see deep down to where he thrashed around, totally unaware as to what he'd been.

That night, I tried for the first time since I was nine to throw up my dinner. I never could do it, and I wasn't any better at it now. Easily, I could fit all four fingers to the deepest recesses of my throat and felt not even a tickle begin to give. Even at my worst, even in

South Korea when I got food poisoning from pig intestines and would have killed to have vomited, it just wasn't in me. My eyes never watered, my throat never bucked and made my teeth rake along my knuckles. None of it.

As a consolation prize, I skipped dinner for the next two nights and dared to look at the calories in my morning breakfast. It was five hundred, and I didn't know if that was good or bad. Didn't even know how much I should take to keep weight, lose weight, gain it, or anything else. What was I supposed to do with this number? Sanjay would know, certainly. He'd know how to carve it down and make it more manageable, how to close his lips and turn his head from food. But I couldn't ask him. How do you ask someone who's become a stranger to you the secrets to starving yourself?

That self-inflicted trial only lasted those few days before I gave up and blocked him on Facebook so I wouldn't be tempted to look at his photos again. The new ones, the recent ones, were all carefully cropped to only show his face. It had deeper lines when he smiled now, no fat to fill it out. Before, he'd been unabashed about showing his body, though it was never posed. Maybe he did know. Maybe he realized he was the only one who would find him good looking now. Now that his muscles had give up and his bones poked through everywhere. And me, though any attraction from him was long gone.

I was jealous now. I wanted his skinniness, his sallow skin. The way that last layer of fat didn't quite know how to cling to the bone.

xvi. How the Porcupine Lost His Fur

When the Gods dreamt up the porcupine, they didn't consider how far he'd roam. Like Humans, he was crafted naked, sure that the sun would be enough to bake warmth into him. And like Humans have always done, a trace of familiarity was seen in Porcupine and empathy poured from fingertips. As Porcupine began to head north into the cold, there was always Human to keep him warm. Blankets of rich furs, cultivated from other creatures and then groomed into luxury were draped over Porcupine in excess. Porcupine was gifted with the most beautiful fur of all, a rich and silky garment that made all others balk in awe as he walked along the trails. It was a cocktail of extravagance that Porcupine had grown used to.

"What kind of color combination is that?" Chipmunk would ask him. "All those reds and purples, you stand out like Peacock."

"Maybe I'm meant to," Porcupine would reply.

"You weren't born with that fur," Chipmunk would remind him, but Porcupine never cared. He'd swagger down the busiest of streets during lunch hour rushes, giving everyone a thrill as they gazed upon his fur's beauty.

"Why don't I see you at night anymore?" Raccoon once asked him as the two passed at dawn—Porcupine on his way to shimmy down the busy street hawking breakfast meats and coffee to the morning rush.

"Night!" laughed Porcupine, as if he hadn't been born with the ability to see in blackness. "What good would that do? My fur looks the most lovely in the sun." Raccoon would roll his eyes nestled deep in their bandit mask and continue on to his den. He didn't mind Porcupine going against nature and claiming daylight as his own. It meant more food and more fun for himself.

But the Gods, they were always watching. Measuring up who was breaching the natural laws, and they'd honed in on Porcupine for his wayward manners. The furs, they could understand. It happened with the humans after all, and it only made sense to combat nakedness with protective coatings. However, it was the influx of vanity that had them trailing Porcupine so closely. The shininess of that fur coat, the glaring colors, and his propensity to spend hours brushing and grooming instead of living was setting waves of wrongness into motion. The others, like Raccoon, were noticing. Even more were taking stock but not saying anything directly.

"What should we do?" asked one of the river Gods to another.

"Porcupine hasn't gone beyond what should be expected. And it was the Humans that bestowed that fur upon him anyway, he didn't seek it out."

"But still."

"Yes. But still."

Vanity is one of the sickest of diseases, and it harbors growth spurts. Porcupine might well live his full life not inching any deeper into that trap than he was, but the Gods knew better. They could, largely, foresee the path Porcupine was barreling down and the end results were almost completely disastrous.

"He must be punished for this indulgence," said an earth God.

"But what about the Humans who made him the coat?"

"Their foresight is lacking. It wasn't intentional," said a God of the air.

"What should we do? We can't just take it away, he'll freeze to death. Besides, he'd just find another one."

"True. How about this—a trade. Tonight, as he sleeps, we'll swap that fur for a permanent covering of quills."

"Quills, of course," said a sea God. "He'll be kept warm, but no softness can cover him again."

As the Gods wished it, the quills came to life while Porcupine was in the deadest of sleep. That night, his dreams raged and crashed against his membrane. Rarely did he remember his dreams, but the worst nightmares stuck with him. This one needled all the way to his bones. He was a child, so young he couldn't get the words, the feelings, to fly from his lips. And he didn't know where his mother was, though the surroundings were familiar. It was his childhood place, and grownups were raucous just a few feet away. They'd forgotten him, left by the food for comfort. Something deadly and dangerous circled at his feet, but he couldn't see as his mother had perched him on a tall stump.

Mom, mom, mom, mom, he screamed in his head, although his mouth felt wired shut. Far away, he heard her laugh. Below, he could sense a monster circling, an inky black with threads of green.

In a snap, the monster grabbed his legs and began dragging him. It had cold tentacle hands, and he was being raked through crunchy leaves with his face to the night sky. It was too fast, and wherever he was being taken, he knew it would be his last.

Porcupine woke with a snap, the heaviness of the nightmare still weighing him down. When he stretched, he felt it. Something was off. He moved awkwardly, forced to take bigger swoops with his arms and legs to work around some type of cage.

"What the ... what the hell is *this*?" he said. The glorious fur was gone. Vanished. In its place, heavy spikes protruded from the well of his body.

The price of vanity. The words drifted over him, not quite a voice but a kind of knowing. The price of vanity.

"I'm ugly!" he said, to no one. To them all.

"Oh, my God," said Chipmunk, scurrying past him to the tree with the good fruits. "Is that you? What happened? Where's your—"

"I don't *know*!" wailed Porcupine. "I don't know!"

"You should … damn. I've never seen anything like this," said Chipmunk before turning his striped back to Porcupine and racing up the tree.

Stiffly, Porcupine made his way to the lake just steps from his bed. It's where he'd spent countless hours admiring. Primping. Wondering at his own magnificence.

Now, the reflection staring back at him was a beast like he'd never seen before.

"I can't be seen like this," he said, slinking back to his den to wait out the hours 'til the sun retreated. He waited, shamed, to embrace the night.

Chapter 16

I met Jerome on a night I was with Titan, after spending two hours hearing about the latest dumb blonde thing to pose by his sun-bright yellow convertible. The Maintenance Room was a raucous karaoke bar in the pits of Chinatown, where there were never enough chairs for the sparse sprinkling of tables, but we'd gotten there early enough to claim a scratched up high table for ourselves. I was always, always, looking for an excuse to leave Titan behind, but he was the pilled security blanket I couldn't quite let go of completely. In between the brigades of poorly veiled insults, the occasional compliment that always appeared like magic would salve my wounds enough to keep me coming back.

I saw Jerome well before he approached me, all lithe body and dreadlocks to his waist. The knots laid across the green velvet every time he bent over the billiards table. He was slimmer and slightly shorter than what I normally gravitated towards, but there was something in the cacao of his eyes. The length of his hair. The wild foreignness of him that called me close. But not once did he look at me.

"She's terrible in bed," Titan was saying. I'd forgotten who he was talking about. "But, you know, maybe she'll learn. She's into the Blazers and actually knows what she's talking about with that, so that's a plus—" I was beginning to despise the way he talked about women, like we should all be lining up to turn ourselves into the idyllic robot for him.

"I have to go to the bathroom," I said. The bathrooms at the bar were notoriously long-lined and terrible, just a single toilet in a private room to share for all the women. The men's room also had one toilet, but a trio of urinals that had a number of women forcing their way in to lift their skirts and aim at the faded blue urinal cakes while the men railed about unfairness.

The bathrooms also forced you to walk right by the pool tables to get there.

"Aye," the long-haired man said as I squeezed by. He walked backward, taking up all the space in the long narrow hallway that harbored the two tiny bathrooms at the end. "Wat a gwan?"

"What?"

"That your boyfriend?" he asked. Shit.

"Oh! No, no," I said.

"Es good," he said. "I'm Jerome. Ya beautiful, ya know?"

"Thanks," I said. From the corner of my eyes, I watched Titan hone in on us. "You should get back to your friends," I said, pointing to the trio of white men who watched us with boredom.

"Dem ain't mi friends," he said. "Just met tonight, jus' playing a game."

"Well, either way."

"Can I get your number?" he asked.

"Sure, sure."

Before Jerome left, he ponied up to our table, shook hands and nodded with Titan, allowing just a sliver of attention to be directed from me. What would it be like, to have that kind of confidence? To gauge your surroundings, consider the obstacles, take a measured approach to get exactly what you want?

I could understand only a scraping of what he said, the Jamaican accent heady and too rheumy for me to wade into comfortably. It was exactly what I wanted. A lack of understanding shrouded in beautiful sounds.

"He asked if I was your boyfriend?" Titan asked as we headed to my car so I could drop him at home.

"Yeah."

"What'd you say?"

"I told him no ..."

What else would I have said?

Jerome texted, dutifully, three days later with no pretenses and no lead-ins that forced small talk. For once I was happy with a text. It ensured I understood him without my asking, "What? What?" over and over again.

"You want to meet up on Friday?" he asked. A Friday. He would give me that.

"Sure."

"You know Mt. Tabor?"

"Yeah ..."

"6 there? I'll bring rum." Rum. It was a caricature of what a Jamaican should be, and I was hungry for it. Maybe this was it, my airplane do-over, a full lifetime after the first one came crashing down.

"You got kids?" Jerome asked as we circled the carefully pruned, maintained asphalt of the southeast trails, the volcano rumbling somewhere far below our feet.

"No!" I said. I was twenty-nine, but still got a layer of defenses over me when I was asked. I'd had two cut out of me ten years ago, and somehow still felt too young for these assumptions.

"Ya should," said Jerome. "Getting' too old not to."

"Do you?" I asked.

"Ya. At least one. Back 'ome," he said. At least one.

"What about the mother?"

"What 'bout 'er?" he asked. It wasn't a challenge, it was genuine curiosity. He handed me the little flask of rum, sweetness that shot directly into my brain.

"What are you doing here then?" I asked.

He shrugged. "Won the visa lottery, thought affi give it a go."

"Did you work in a restaurant in Kingston?"

"Sometimes," he said. "Other times, nah." I imagined him as he was at Papa Higgins, the high-end patisserie where he was a sous chef. It wasn't something you happened into, crafting overpriced prix fixe dinners alongside the pink champagne cake. I didn't know much about the restaurant scene in Portland, but I knew it was fiercely competitive. I knew Papa Higgins wasn't a place where you just showed up with thick locks of black dreads and were granted a place alongside award-winning chefs. But Jerome's modesty was authentic, and that was something I couldn't figure out how to accept. "Why ya work with the black folks?" he asked.

"It was the first place that offered me a job when I got back from Korea," I said.

"Yah," he said. "In a desperate times, 'n all. Getting' dark. Wan go somewhere?"

I took him to Cult, an overstuffed club where I knew the bouncers and felt like home. There, in the bathrooms, the lighting was magical and made the forty-year-old women look like girls without even a smattering of alcohol necessary. "Got cover?" Jerome asked.

"Yeah."

"Aye," he said, shaking his head. It was a challenge, and he didn't even know he'd offered it up.

"I told some friends I'd see them there," I said. That wasn't true, but I wanted to see. See if he'd think me worth ten dollars.

"Aight, aight," he said, and he meant it. He paid the cash, bought the drinks, and when I thought he'd proven himself enough I took his hand and led him out.

"Hey! Hey!" A drunken white, blond boy yelled from the cab of a truck in the unlit parking lot. "You got some weed, man?"

"Nah," said Jerome, though I'd seen him thumb through pre-rolled joints to get to his ID an hour before.

"Dat ain't on dweet, mon!" bellowed the drunken boy, his attempt at a Jamaican accent overly ripe. Did that happen often, the sad assumptions of what it means to be black with dreadlocks? Did that boy think I'd met Jerome just now, that he'd sauntered into a club and picked up the girl with the snowiest of skin just to parade her through the streets like a prize?

The next time I saw Jerome, the task was simple. Mark a black man off my list. Call it whatever, but it was something that had to be done. Like getting in line for the big roller coaster even though you knew it would hurt your neck. His whole body was hard, sinewy and full of sharp angles. I didn't fit with him right, though I'd figured that out from the night at the club. From his lips, insanely puffy and soft compared to the sharp jawline and the mounds of his cheeks. I couldn't imagine what woman would mold against his, with those hip bones too pointed and the shoulder blades arching through his skin like wings. Really, I just wanted to get it over with.

Still. I'd never seen a man so expertly pull out a condom and undress it with his teeth. It was a movement that had to have been practiced a thousand times, as natural as taking a piss. There was comfort there, in the knowing and see that putting up a barrier between us—between him and whoever he entered—that put to ease any fears that he was carrying around something deadly.

Jerome inside me felt like a fire-hot spear gouging through my insides. It wasn't his size, though he was on the bigger end. Even so, I'd had bigger. It was something about the shape, the curve, the angle just being all wrong. He ground his cock into me hard but not fast, making every part of it burn. But still I wouldn't tell him to stop, even though I'd never had a searing like that so badly since my first time. There was no joy in it, and I willed myself not to bleed. *It's okay, it's okay, you're okay,* I breathed into myself over and over. Trying to make myself believe it.

It had been a lifetime, genuinely, since I'd let a man rip me apart before. Funny, how the body forgets pain. This time, there was no blood but the aches inside were the same. I don't remember what we talked about afterward, or how many times I asked him, "What?" because the accent was too drippy thick for me to make out the words. When it was done, I just wanted him gone. But I felt like he deserved a thicker, longer tick than the rest of them. I'd suffered harder for him.

For a week, the texts went on and I slowed down my replies. I've never been good at faking it, as being a hostess when I don't want to be. It's so obvious when I'm done. I didn't want to see him again, though he'd done nothing wrong. It wasn't his fault, not really. I don't think he even knew how much he'd hurt me. Maybe all women arched away from him, showed their teeth and squired away. Maybe to him, that was normal. That was sex.

"So, how was it?" That was the question I got from every white girl who'd never been with a black man before. They wanted to know, wanted to slip into my shoes and check out the feelings without having to do it themselves. How was it? I didn't want to disappoint.

"It was fine," I would say. "It was sex."

"I don't think I could do it." That was uttered more than once, and I just didn't get it. It wasn't like bungee jumping or facing that monster that's always been bumbling around in your closet.

"So I guess you don't wanna see me anymore." That was the last text I got from Jerome, complete with a period instead of a question mark. I could hear the lilt in his voice through the written words. He wasn't hurt, wasn't confused, just wanted some kind of validation. And I couldn't even give him that. I just deleted the message, deleted his number, and prayed that nothing would appear from him again.

It never did. Not until I saw him years later when I was pounds less and my hair two feet longer, so I knew he wouldn't recognize me. The anorexia was eating me alive by then, and I knew I didn't have the curves or the muscles that would make him look at me, so I was free to stare as I wished.

He was the same. The same long hair, the same sharp shoulder blades and the same flawless skin. If I didn't know, I'd probably try again. I'd walk to the bathroom too close to him, hold his gaze a little longer, let him come to me because I seemed like easy prey. But I did know, and the phantom ache in my pelvis told me to stay away. He wasn't with anyone, wasn't even looking for anyone. He'd never had that hunt in his eyes like all the other men had.

I wondered how many kids he really had, how many little brown feet like his were padding around the sands. If he was still pulling on that white hat in the evenings and making buttery amuse bouches for pompous asses like me. If he still had that worn down little flask in his jacket pocket, and what his liver looked like from the inside out. I rolled his last name over my taste buds, Ricardo. He was one of the few whose last names I'd learned and burned into my memory. Like Ricky Ricardo, like Desi Arnaz, my very first crush. Another man whose voice was too wildly different to make much sense to my ears.

I had nothing to say to him, and so I left. It wasn't good, revisiting the past, you'd just be disappointed either way. Maybe I should have let him have another go, maybe I should have numbed my insides with that imported rum he fed me in sips like a baby bird. Maybe that would have helped, would have made me so dangerously unaware that I would realize I was being ripped in two. Maybe I could have let him give me a delightful little baby, maybe it would have had good hair and my alabaster skin would have finally been broken down into something sun-glazed and lovely.

Jerome stayed perched on the bar like a hummingbird with feet too weak to walk, lapping up brown liquors and thumbing a right-hand ring. We're wild animals, all of us, constantly drawn to these watering holes like the drought just broke. Lions cozy up next to antelope and we all let the babies squeal and thrash in the water, an unspoken rule that in this safe spot we won't kill each other. We're careful still, of course, but the thirst overpowers everything else. Here, we're equals and all the hunting we do is narrowed down the most base of desires.

"Don't ever touch that." Young Moose could hear his mother's voice weaving through the pine trees. The "don'ts" were all around him, always would be. Telling him to be careful, to be patient, to not toe into a space where he couldn't be sure of the outcome. But why not? Why? She'd never answer those questions.

It was worst around a Human, the two-legged, hairless beasts who slouched through the forests with their big metal weapons and bright orange vests. For all his short life, he was warned about the death they brought. He could even smell it, that strange sharp note that leaked into the woods after a shot was taken. "You stay away from them," his mother said over and over. "You have no idea what they can do."

That was true, he didn't have any idea. She kept him locked up so tight, he couldn't even wander more than a breath from her big legs 'til his head reached the peak of her back. Now, though, she'd had no choice but to unclench her hold. Bitten by scared Snake, poison pulsed through her body and made her legs weak. Once the fear of her death gave way, once he saw she would come through, he allowed himself some joy. For once, he was free.

And now, "You shouldn't be smoking that" rang through his head. But he couldn't help it! It was sheer magic, that smoking pipe resting on the slender tree stump so perfectly it looked like it was floating. This smoke smelled like comfort, a big cushion of decaying leaves with the sweet rot. There were notes like flowers in it, and a dark earthy aroma that made his mouth water. When he first pulled the smoke into his lungs, it tickled and slightly burned, made him cough and hack. Then it soothed like a balm, and coated his insides with its magic. Twice, three times, he pulled the smoke in deep and imagined it ballooning up his lungs 'til he could take in no more. He held it as long as he could, then breathed it out. Through his soft, fuzzy lips. Out his nostrils.

"What are you doing?" It was an elder, one whose name he couldn't recall. One who had lived so long through the hunting seasons he'd learned how to move soundless through the trees.

"I—nothing," Moose said.

"Did you smoke that?" the elder asked. It was more a statement than a question, and Moose could see the knowledge in his eyes.

"No. I mean, not a lot. I wasn't the one to light it—" Moose began, the explanations and excuses piling up inside him and staggering around.

The elder shook his head sadly. "Do you know what this is?"

"Some kind of pipe. I don't know."

"It's from the Humans."

Well, yeah. I figured that. But those words Moose didn't say out loud.

"It's a trap," said the elder. "One of their oldest. Nobody knows exactly what it is, or how it works, but now they'll catch you. You understand me? They'll catch you and take you to slaughter."

"Are you trying to scare me?" asked Moose. Hoped Moose.

"I'm afraid not," said the elder, backing away like the curse would catch.

Moose didn't tell his mother that night, and she didn't ask why he smelled like wet grass. For hours, he rubbed and rolled in the strongest greenery he could find. Tried with all he had to get that smell off him. If she could sense the death on him, she didn't say anything. I probably wouldn't either, he thought.

When sunlight broke, he spent all morning waiting. Hiding. Sticking close to his mother, but the fear made him tired. The sunlight was like a drug, pulled and kept him close to the earth. When the human voices shook him awake and his eyelids crept open, his mother was gone and he was alone. She must have thought I was safe here, he thought.

There he is, said a child Human, half the size of the others.

A big, strong one! said another one.

Thank you for your sacrifice, said a third. *I don't ... I don't know if you can hear me? Understand me? But thank you for this gift. For that, we will treat your body with respect. You will live on in us.*

It sounded rather lovely, and suddenly death was nothing to fear. Moose didn't mind, and a jolt of joy shot through him with the bullet to the brain. He wanted to die, wanted to zoom through their strange Human bodies. To feed them, to provide nourishment. To find a million little homes in their round bellies and growing limbs.

Happiness waits for you in the afterlife. It was a marriage of voices, part mother, part collection from the Humans, and part elder. He'd never felt such freedom as this—the sprig of happiness he'd encountered when his mother became too weak to protest was nothing compared to this.

Moose, both amazing and strange, gave up his life, his youth, and became one with the Humans. They kept their promise and in his death, he watched them honor his body like he was a God looking down at the display. They lifted his old shell carefully, rubbed it with oils and massaged the flesh. With special tools, they pieced him apart and placed each part of him in thoughtful ways. His flesh was hearty and browned to something more perfect than he could ever have dreamt. His hide was lovingly curated and coaxed into warmth and luxury. The organs he'd already felt beginning to wilt from the day he was born were made into medicines or savored as luxuries by the revered Humans. Every last drop of him was adored, put to use, and went back into the earth.

In the preparation, he began to fade into a million particles that rained back down to the greenery. Peace when his flesh made its way into the permanent muscles of a young black-haired girl. Settling when his hooves were carved into tools that created shelter for a family. Relief when his fat was vetted and stored, flavoring nourishment for months to come and placed like something or worship on the good kitchen shelf. With every touch, with every labor, he became more vital to the living than he'd ever imagined.

In time, he forgot his mother. Forget the elder in the woods. Couldn't remember what it was he'd been called or how he'd come to be in his first form. All that mattered now was what he'd done and what he'd become. How he'd live forever.

Chapter Seventeen

"Is this seat taken?"

It was a stringing together of some of the four most common words ever uttered at a bar. I'd seen him coming from a block away, the type of man who collected gazes without even realizing. I had willed it, willed him. To cross the street, look through the big picture window, and choose this bar, this seat, and me.

"What's good here?" he asked. There was an authenticity to him, regardless of the perfectly lined fade. The diamond in his ear. His ability to wear a tailored suit in a city where CEOs and doctors got away with ratty All Stars and worn-down tee-shirts. Everything about him was flawless and thought out.

"I'm Derek," he said, before ordering a diet soda and honey drizzled cashews.

Derek didn't drink and had skin so black and buffed the light couldn't stop caressing it. Genetics had been good to him, shot him up well over six feet and gifted him with a shy little boy smile that showcased a child's type of white teeth. He told me about his years in the marines, I told him about the best times of London. He told me about growing up with his grandmother, and I pretended my own childhood could pass as normal. He talked about his latest founding of a company, the half a floor they had in one of Portland's most desirable of buildings, and I pretended to believe him.

"I don't do this often," he said, his big hands sucking the coolness from his glass. He spoke in clichés, but seasoned them with truth. He must not. Right? What kind of non-drinker prowls through bars before the sun has even gone down. Derek was so perfect, I wanted to like him. In another time, I may have.

"May I walk you to your car?" he asked after another hour, and I felt like a teacher granting permission to a third-grader.

Walking is all we did, he holding an umbrella over me when the gray skies got too pregnant to hold it anymore. He kept to the outside of the sidewalk, walked slow to pace me in my rickety heels, and asked politely for my phone number, too. Derek did everything he was supposed to, and still it wasn't enough.

A giant hole was stretching its perimeter in my chest, one that not even this giant of a man could fill.

But still, I could try. I could try.

The chaos of December kept phone calls—real, voice-laden, phone calls—sporadic and rushed. Derek's teenaged daughter was staying with her mother in Los Angeles, and both of us watched the holidays shy up to us like it knew it wasn't wanted. On Christmas

Eve, I asked if he wanted to go to my favorite karaoke bar. Bars, long havens for the misfits of Christmas, were the only beacons lighting up the winter skies.

"I'm okay with it if you are," he said.

"Why wouldn't I be?"

"Well, it's Christmas—"

"What does that matter?" I asked.

"It doesn't." Christmas has always been a minefield for me. Raised pseudo-Christian, my mother had me baptized "just in case," thought it was clear none of us believed in God. I was sent to Vacation Bible School for two years, until I refused to go again because one of the games required us to wash each other's feet just like Jesus did, and feet disgusted me. But most, mostly, Christmas marked the month when my dad would disappear for a week-long binge. He was always back by Christmas morning, but could take off any time between Thanksgiving and the week before the fake tree got its time in the limelight. For most of my childhood, I actually enjoyed that week. Saw it coming when he wasn't home by six, then seven, then it was midnight and my mom and I were eating toast and watching talk show reruns while she stared as the fluorescent clock.

Derek was already there when I sidled up to the table, and the bar was littered with the kinds of people who were alone for Christmas—the kinds of people that looked like all of us. An elderly wiry man sang "99 Luftballons" in flawless German, revealing a part of his heart I couldn't see at first blush.

"I can't believe how many people are here," Derek said, and neither could I. There was almost joy in the air.

"Sing something for me," I said. Test, test, test.

"What do you want me to sing?" he asked. "I sang in the choir in church, you know!" I didn't know, I knew nothing about him. But here he was, this stunning lumbering giant, happy to perform for me. The eleven-year-old girl tucked deep inside clamored for Jodeci, a song I hadn't heard since I woke up at four in the morning every school day to make my makeup and hair perfect for the boys who ignored me.

Derek pulled off "Come and Talk to Me" like he'd been practicing it. Waiting for it. Knowing that the day was almost here when some quiet girl would request that he serenade her to a childhood fascination.

That night, he took my hand and led me to the high floor of the building where he worked, the one where a top-ranked restaurant called the top floor home. He hadn't been lying. He knew the security guards, had the keys, and showed me room after room. His office with the floor to ceiling windows, the game room with the luxury bean bag chairs and gaming systems.

"I thought you were lying," I told him as we both stood against the windows watching the flickering lights below.

"Why would I lie?" he asked.

"I don't know."

That's when he first kissed me, thick lips engulfing mine. But it was like having surgery, an out of body experience. I watched us from somewhere above, couldn't really feel the happening. I noticed my perfectly tailored pea coat and the way his tie complemented the silk square in his suit pocket. Everything aligned like it should, and I couldn't stay there. Couldn't let the moment wrap me up.

"You know what I like about you?" he asked, pulling away.

"What's that?"

"You're fun sized."

"What? I'm five-seven," I said. I'd been in between regular and long pant lengths ever since I can remember.

He laughed, throwing his head back like a teenager. "That's nothing," he said. "My ex in LA is six feet tall." I could picture her, a baby giraffe of a woman with long, natural hair. "She was a model," he explained, as if he needed to. Suddenly, the competition got stronger. What was he doing with me? She must have been all long legs and angular jaw. Nothing like me, nothing.

"So, who is this guy?" I'd been living with Sue-Ann for four months, a former sorority sister I'd never spent a single conversation with alone. We were thrown together during a summer BBQ, and when she came into my little basement of a studio to help me pull out dusty bottles of liquor, she couldn't believe where I lived. "It's so tiny!" she'd said, as if I took up more room than that. She demanded I move in with her, into her sprawling six-bedroom house in far southeast that was falling apart. "We're flipping it," she said and her boyfriend of six years just grunted in reply.

I'd told her it was a mistake. Told her it wouldn't end well. Demanded a written agreement and made sure she called the shots. She was adamant that she wanted company, that was all, but already it was like she was doing me a favor. Like I was the one who'd begged to be let in. "Can I claim you as a dependent on my taxes?" she'd asked as soon as the new year rolled over. "Can I have a few hundred extra in rent this month? I spent too much on shoes on my trip to San Francisco." I was plotting my escape, but had nowhere else to invite Derek. And I wanted to show him off, upstage Sue-Ann's Neanderthal boyfriend who spent all day watching hentai and happily settling into his minimum wage job.

"Where'd I meet him? Where do you think?" I asked her. She shrugged, she knew. Sue-Ann was a raging, blackout alcoholic who couldn't fathom anything of interest happening outside of a bar. My finding Derek at a stretch of a sticky bar made perfect sense to her.

"What's he bringing?" she asked.

"Popeyes." That had been my idea, and I'd never had it before, and it was low carb if I got it grilled instead of fried. Derek had been shocked that such a staple wasn't part of my diet, and claimed that it wasn't "exactly good fried chicken, but it was famous for a reason." That worked for me.

The moment he arrived, he did his best to pretend Sue-Ann's hellish dog's jumping and hair flying didn't bother him. For once, he wasn't in a suit, but in perfectly designed denim and a tee-shirt that cost more than my shoes. She took one look at his overwhelming size and put him to work, holding the microwave up so she could screw it into place. Moving the furniture into a better location. Her boyfriend could have managed, but tearing him away from porn and video games wasn't worth the effort.

Sue-Ann flirted with everybody, but her squat little Chinese body made her look like a toy next to Derek. She chewed with her mouth open, the sole hangover from her early childhood in Shanghai that she held onto. "So, wait, your company is in *that* building?" she asked as she drilled him about work. "Do you get deals at the Grill?" Non-stop happy hour prices began to flash across her face, the alcoholic in her salivating.

I never slept with Derek, I just couldn't. I'd like to think it was because it just wasn't right (it wasn't), but it was more than that. Since forever, I'd been drawn to browner men. Growing up, my Cherokee father with his black hair reaching for his belt, that's what I thought men were. I didn't even realize he wasn't white until I was a teenager, no matter how many years my pale skin had been juxtaposed against his. My mother had put something on hold at Radio Shack for my father to pick up, and I went with him grateful for a reprise from her screeching and swearing. I was thirteen.

"My wife put something on hold," my dad said as the young clerk sized him up. They thought he was Mexican, they always did.

"Is *this* your wife?" the clerk asked in disgust, nodding towards me.

"That's ... my daughter." I'd never heard my dad so quiet, so beaten down. It was his prison voice, I was sure of it. I refused to go anywhere alone with him again until years later, after I'd lived in a car and he was close to his cancer diagnosis.

And with Jerome? That was different. His dreadlocks gave him away well before that song in his voice did. He wasn't *black* black. He was Jamaican, and for so many people that made it okay. He was exotic, and at an average height he wasn't intimidating.

Derek was none of this. He carried himself like a southern black gentleman with a purple heart tucked away at home. I'd never seen, never noticed, so many eyes on us before. When Derek took my hand to cross the street, older white couples murmured and showed the whites of their eyes. When we shared plates at restaurants, the bleached blonde waitresses plastered on fake smiles and wondered what he was like in bed. Wondered if it was solely my whiteness that drew him close to me. I'd never been so aware before, never so beneath a microscope.

After that Popeyes night when Sue-Ann treated him like hired help, I just stopped. Stopped taking his calls, stopped returning his calls, stopped wondering if he was who I was waiting for.

"I want to get married again one day," he'd told me, just like that. Like it wasn't something to be ashamed about.

"Oh," I'd said. Maybe I did, too, but not to him. Not to him.

"My ex and I, we were young," he said by way of explanation. "We just grew apart because we weren't done growing when we met. She's a wonderful woman, a great mother, but it wasn't right," he said. So he knew what wasn't right felt like. Wasn't he feeling it now?

Two years later, I saw him again at a luxe restaurant. I was with Edee, a whitewashed black girl with glowing honey eyes. I didn't even know it was Derek, but again his form grabbed my eyes and wouldn't let go. He came straight for Edee, ordered a diet coke and said, "You have great hair." Did she? I didn't know.

It was then that he recognized me. The pleasantries were lightly sweetened and naturally salty. *I could have had you.*

"He's corny," Edee said, sipping on her cocktail. Her and I were just starting to test out a friendship born at work. She'd invited me to her bible study, and when I told her I wasn't Christian she said, "That's okay! I just didn't want you to feel left out."

Derek slipped away into the crowds, and I wanted to tell him he wasn't a fetish. The fact that he happened upon me with Edee didn't mean that I went out of my way to surround myself by people so different than me. I didn't even know what I looked like, didn't know what race I fell into.

Before my father died, but after that long black hair snaked all the way down the shower drains, he took out his tribal card. Full-blooded Cherokee, it said. "Bet you wish yours said that," he said meanly. Did I? I didn't know. All I'd ever known was my tribal card to say ½ Cherokee. But who wanted to be half of something? Whole was so much better. What's good in a half—those half-baked ideas never blossomed into anything. The half-hearted tries turned ugly for years 'til we put our whole everything into it. Half-assed, half-witted, half-breed, half-dead. Let's argue about glasses half-full, tumblers half-empty and how it's all in your head. So fill me up with something, I'm sick of explaining my Cherokee half. I'll take anything, just swell me with wholeness even once, even in passing, even at the gamble of spilling it all over the goddamned hideous floor.

But the worst part is that I just kept throwing everything away. I'd pick up something shiny, spin it around, and get lost in the glitter until it became too heavy to hold. Was it that I looked so white, but there was something dark lurking below the surface, that had these men shotgunning towards me?

xviii. Owl vs. Rabbit

In the beginning, it was mostly nighttime, and nighttime was when the magic happened. When Owl could scrape his wings across the sky and take in the world below. Dawns and dusks, sometimes he'd perch warily on a big post and try to lure his parliament to meet him. But they were scared and the light burned their eyes—he understood. The sun rays blinded him, too. But it was those early hours when he'd see Rabbit racing from bush to bush, snapping up dewy leaves.

"Stop watching me," Rabbit would tell him as he nuzzled greens into his maw.

"Why?" asked Owl. "I'm not going to eat you."

"I know that," said Rabbit. Neither of them knew that for sure, but Rabbit was semi-confident that he'd grown too big and too fat to tempt Owl. "It's annoying. The sun's up, shouldn't you go to bed?"

"The sun's not totally up yet," said Owl. "Besides, it's not required that I leave when it's light. I've seen you at night before, too."

"God. I wish it was daylight all the time so I wouldn't have to feel your bulbous eyes on me at breakfast."

"You wish it was daylight all the time?" asked Owl. "I pray for night."

"Why don't we will it then?" asked Rabbit. He'd heard of a place that had done that before, somewhere way up north where his far-off cousins grew thicker hair and denser layers of fat to ward off the cold. Still, word had traveled that for many months out of the year, it was daylight all the time. The tradeoff was a few months of constant night, but that he could manage. Rabbit preferred the light, but understood the delicacy of nightlife. In the blackness, it was easier to hide from those who hunted him.

"Will it?" asked Owl. "And how do you suppose we do that?"

Rabbit shrugged, snapping off a groomed rose from the old Human woman garden. He didn't understand why she tried to battle the rose test garden a block away for the loveliest of roses, but he didn't complain. She didn't deadhead as quickly as the official garden trimmers and kept a small vegetable plot in a raised bed with inky black soil. Hers was always his first stop in the mornings. "You can encourage the Gods to do a lot of things," he said. "You think I'm this fast by chance?"

"I don't know," said Owl. Wasn't there something wrong about playing with the normality of the world? Would the Gods even listen, and what if Rabbit won? What then? "There needs to be some kind of rules."

"Of course there would be rules," Rabbit said. "But, really, the trick is simplicity. It's not like we can meet with them or anything. I think it's best if we each just chant what we want. Day and night, over and over. If we can get a crowd, the Gods will be more likely to listen."

"Then what?" asked Owl. Rabbit seemed to know what he was talking about, like he'd done it before.

"Easy," said Rabbit. "Whoever messes up first, like if you say day instead of night, loses."

"That seems fair," said Owl. Something wasn't quite right about all this, but he couldn't figure it out. He was tired, the light was getting too bright, and his low eyelid was creeping up. "Next Monday, then," he said as he shook his wings for flight. "We'll do it next Monday."

Rabbit had an incredible gift of gathering. In just one week, word had spread that the two were going to compete to change the earth. Everyone came out, gathering at the fountain near the playground that sounded like church bells when the water rang off it. And everybody had an opinion, siding with Rabbit or Owl depending on if lightness or darkness better suited them. Opossum rallied behind Owl while Squirrel stuck close by Rabbit. Amidst it all was a generous layer of fear and wonder. Were the Gods listening? How quickly would the winner get their wish? The contest was held at the earliest of dawn so that both Owl and Rabbit had a fair playing ground.

"Ready?" asked Rabbit, and the two sucked in their breath to begin.

Night, night, night, night. Day, day, day, day. Owl tried to close his ears to drown out Rabbit's incessant chanting. Rabbit did the same, stomping on his long lop ears to muffle the sounds around him. They appointed Cat to referee if need be, since she enjoyed day and night equally. She stretched and yawned as the chanting began, languidly looking around and flexing her pointed toes to remind the onlookers to keep silent.

It went on for hours, 'til Owl and Rabbit both got cotton mouth. *This isn't fair*, Owl thought to himself as he began baking in the morning light. But it was too late now. He was getting tired, didn't want to be doing this anymore. And Rabbit's maddening voice was digging a worm into his brain. His mouth begged to form any word but "night."

As noon creeped forward, Owl's determination waned and he couldn't help himself. "Day," he whispered. It was the saddest of defeats.

"Day! He said day!" Chipmunk squealed, and Rabbit dropped to the grass in exhaustion. The change was immediate, the sun somehow getting even brighter and driving the nocturnal to seek shade.

It wasn't right, Rabbit knew that. It had just started as a game, a joke. A way to piss off Owl.

"Hold on," Rabbit said. "Hold on." Raising his head to the sky, he pleaded with the Gods he could only imagine. "No," he said. "As the winner, I want a different prize. A lesser prize. Split it into two, half day, half night, so that we might all enjoy the world."

As the sunlight dampened a little and they all felt the pull of night a few hours away, the crowd dispersed to eat or sleep, run or hunker down in nests and dens.

"You didn't have to do that," said Owl.

"But I did," said Rabbit. "I did."

Chapter 18

"You don't talk a lot," said Nikhil. I hated that phrase, but it was better than, "Why are you so quiet?"

"So I've been told," I said.

"You should talk more." *You should.* I'd been sitting across from him for less than five minutes and already he'd come up with one flaw he'd like to change. I hated how men did this. Women, too. Sized you up, figured out what was wrong with you, what they'd like to change, then start making and sharing a list as if you've been waiting for them to come alone and list your faults.

Nikhil was one of my first forays into the mess of an online dating world, and almost attractive. Almost. He was insanely tall for an Indian, well over six feet, with a dense mess of hair, striking eyes and full lips. But there was something about him, something off. He slouched and hunched as if his height were a burden. His scowl wasn't good enough to substitute for a smile, and yet his smile seemed forced even though he had good, white teeth. He was constantly missing the mark, but hit close enough to make me put up with his wish list of what I should be.

"You smoke?" he asked.

"Smoke what?" It was the return question that let everyone instantly know that, yes, you imbibed. I'd never been a stoner, never managed to smoke more than once a week even in college, but it was a distinction that demanded exploration.

"Anything," he said.

"Cigarettes only when I'm drinking. Marijuana, not so much anymore."

"Why not?" He seemed truly fascinated, perplexed that anyone who did smoke would choose not to.

"A lot of reasons. Mostly because it makes me groggy and I can feel it in my body for days afterward."

"You're not smoking the right stuff then," he said. It was the first time his eyes lit up. Talking about his work at a bank's headquarters, grad school in the US, his "very minor stint" in modeling on a catwalk (which reeked of bullshit) all kept his eyes dull like a snake ready to shed. But this, this woke him right up.

"I'm from here," I said. "Oregonians know how to smoke."

"No, no—" he began, and I could see him mentally making another note of yet another item to fix on me. "I have these friends? They grow, legally, for the state, and ..."

How many of those tatchos would he eat? I'd asked to meet here, at Whitebottom, because it was walking distance from my house and I knew I could order the mezza platter and not worry about carbs. But Nikhil had ordered the tater tot nachos, fried and breaded and full of potatoes. I couldn't imagine what his mouth might taste like.

"You'll see," he said. "Their stuff doesn't give you a hangover at all. They make a lot of edibles, too. Cookies, that sort of thing."

"I didn't say it gave me a hangover," I said. "And, still, I don't eat carbs."

"Yeah, but these are so good you will." He was so sure of himself.

"That's not really how it works."

I don't know why I saw him again. Boredom, fear of spending another two consecutive weekend nights hunting the same grounds, or maybe I thought he'd blossom just like he wished it of me. Either way, Nikhil and I fell into some kind of half-time relationship. Neither of us wanted to be alone. For the most part, Nikhil was vapid and the marijuana was eating away at his manner at a fast clip. Maybe this is what happened when you found yourself in a liberal-rich state after a lifetime in India. Did he think us as foreign as he seemed at times?

"Tell me about your first job in India," I said over a heaping scramble at the Bel Air Café. A baby blue and white restored model of the namesake was parked beside us, reflecting the stacks of pancakes and oozing hollandaise sauce off its glass.

"It was actually pretty interesting," he said, guzzling from the glass of orange juice and leaving a pulp streak down the side. "It was what I guess you'd call a summer job. I grew up in the north, in a city but not far from the jungle. I had a job for a few months counting tigers."

"Counting tigers?" I could see him, neatly checking the wild things into pre-determined boxes. *This one has a crooked tail, this one has a limp.*

"Yeah, for a research company. I had to hide in the trees so they'd come by as naturally as they could. Then I'd just count them. It was for about ten hours a day, but those hours aren't very extreme for India."

I couldn't imagine him, all gangly legs and need to change everything, sitting patiently and watching the tigers stroll by below.

"Much more interesting than mine," I said.

"What was yours?"

"Well. The first one I kept, legally, for more than a couple of weeks was at a store in the mall. But I worked at the concession stand of a racetrack when I was a kid."

"Have you ever thought about dying your hair blue?" he asked.

"What? No, why?" He had no ability to segue or transition. It kept me loopy, like I was half drunk.

"Just wondering. You should. I love women with blue hair." Well. That was something I'd never heard before.

I'd just started, six months prior, the arduous process of growing out all the blonde and learning to enjoy my natural color before it turned gray. It hung between my shoulder blades and had streaks of organic, neon red in the right sunlight. "It looks trashy," I said, and I could hear my mom in my voice. Trashy. White trash. Two of her favorite insults.

"Don't you ever like to do anything different than the norm?" he asked. It was the fifth time we'd had a proper date, and the constant accusations were starting to wear against my teeth. He knew nothing about me, I'd made sure of that. Not the homeless years, how I knew the best ways to maximize a timed shower in a truck stop, or how quickly I could move when a man's knee was crushing my windpipe.

"If you want a girl with blue hair," I said slowly, "they're everywhere. You live in Portland now." It was true—one glance around the restaurant showcased two girls immediately with faded Manic Panic colors. Or maybe Manic Panic wasn't a thing anymore, I didn't know.

"You know what else I always thought would be cool?" he asked, the far-off look in his eyes telling me he'd moved on, for now, from a fascination with hair that looked like it had been soaked in a chlorine pool. "Having kids before getting married. Or, you know, without getting married at all."

"You think it would be 'cool' to plan to have kids single?" I asked. He was like a child, a junior high kid hell bent on pissing off his parents, be damned whoever else he dragged into his mess.

"Yeah, kind of," he said. "I mean, who says you have to be married to have kids anyway?"

"It like you want to be a hippie," I said, pushing the toast around my plate. They hadn't substituted berries for it like I'd asked, so now I would drown the carbs instead.

"Hippies, they know how to live," he said.

You don't even know what a hippie is. But I said nothing, there was no point in arguing with him. He propped me up like a Mrs. Potato Head, put on some parts and took off others at a whim. I could have been anyone, any woman, sitting across from him.

I couldn't say that every move I made was corrected by him. That would make it too easy to predict. Maybe one quarter of the moves one day. Half the next. Occasionally almost all of them. And they came at random, a spray of shots so I couldn't get a hold on the predictions. "You shouldn't do that," he said once as I dropped Visine into my eyes. It was after a disastrous pollen attack, my eyelids threatening to stick closed for good.

"I kind of have no choice right now," I said.

"It's bad for your eyes."

A lot of things were "bad for me," but never marijuana or scotch. "You've dated an Indian before?" he asked. I couldn't recall how it had been brought up. An off-handed remark on a name, perhaps. Or my seemingly oddly accurate knowledge of Indian food.

"Sure," I said.

"That's disappointing."

"Why's that?"

"I prefer, the girls I date, that I be the only Indian they've ever dated."

"What, so you can be some kind of novelty?"

"So I won't be a fetish."

"It's Portland. There's Intel. Good luck finding someone who likes darker looks and an education but who hasn't dated an Indian."

The sex was the worst—thank God I was drunk the first time. Not that he was bad, not really, but he felt wrong. Immediately, every time, I would forget what his cock looked like. That meant it must have been perfectly normal and forgettable. But his chest hair was as thick as blackberry bushes and just as brambly. He trimmed it religiously, and I wasn't sure if I should be grateful or not. It left him with sharp thorns exploding from his collarbone to his bellybutton and scratched my torso up like I practiced flagellation.

And he had to be high. Every time. Only once did I let him smoke me out, too, hoping that maybe this time would be different.

I hated being touched when I was high. Hated even being around people, especially if they weren't on the same level as me. Those partiers who smoke a joint then go to clubs, it had never been for me. I just wanted to be home, preferably alone, rubbing my face along the furry purple blanket that demanded dry-clean only. With Nikhil, stoned sex seemed to last even longer. I was hyper-aware of his hairs raking across my body. Of the taste of his mouth and the faint lingering of weed.

"What's the matter with you?" he asked after we'd had yet another tussle of words. I didn't know. What was wrong with him? What was so wrong with me that he constantly had to keep growing his list of complaints?

"It just seems very clear that you're not exactly thrilled with anything about me, so what's the matter with *you*?" I asked. We were in the living room of the townhouse he proudly owned, right on the outskirts of a close-in southeast district that had almost turned hipster. We were en route to Las Vegas, a shitstorm of a trip that I'd hoped would alleviate some of the pressure.

We missed our flight in San Francisco, and all others were booked until the next day. It was a sign, a glaring one, but I still wanted to make the most of it. A rented car, a cheap hotel room, and a hot walk along the piers. We took obligatory pictures on the trolley and blurry photos of the sunbathing sea lions.

It left us with just one day in Vegas, and that was more than enough. Nikhil was a gambler, which he'd hinted at but I hadn't understood in all its wantonness. For hours, he disappeared to private tables and games, letting his eyes grow and even thicker glaze on them. I lounged by the pool where I felt old and kept having to re-apply sunscreen with every wayward cannonball. Drinking in the heat gave me an instant, headache-filled hangover, skipping over the drunken part altogether.

There was one shining moment. At night, at a steak restaurant where the chunks of meat melted on tongues. Afterward, at a tiny sliver of a club where Nikhil looked truly handsome in the light and we made out in a corner booth. In the photos, we looked happy.

A murderous hangover grabbed me the next day, and we had seven hours from the hotel check-out 'til our flight. I'd like to think we both knew it was the end, and I wanted him to remember me. Not as the girl who had so many things wrong with her, but as the crazy one who at least got freaky like he'd never known.

Like it was kismet, hours after check-in our hotel keycard still worked. There was someone else's suitcases stacked on the dresser, but no other sign of life. It was the fastest blow job of my life, and I got no thrills from the thought of being caught—but he did. "This is insane! I can't believe this!" he kept saying, and I figured it was worth it. Blow jobs were easy, didn't even make my throat sore anymore. And it was a parting gift that, for some reason, I felt I owed him.

Surprisingly, Nikhil was easy to fade away from. It was nearly mutual, though we never really talked about it. His last words were, "I was really starting to fall for you" and they made my stomach twist up. He couldn't possibly believe that. Is that what he thought love should feel like? Then it was blocked emails, blocked Facebook, and he disappeared into what I could only imagine was a smoke-filled haven.

Two years later, he messaged me from a new email address. Asked what I was doing. By then, I was moving to Costa Rica. Had started my own business. Had some semblance of what I wanted to be doing.

"That's the girl I wish I'd met!" he replied when I gave him the short version of "what I was doing." I never did reply, and took my own turn at blocking his email.

But yet. Since then. Occasionally I look him up, now that he's taken down all those walls. Not for regrets or because I feel any pang of remorse, but just sheer curiosity. It seems like he's been with the same girl, a pale redhead with a big nose, for many months. Is he her first Indian? Does she get a pass from dying her hair blue because redheads are so notoriously tough to color? She looks so fucking normal. Maybe she smokes, maybe she doesn't, but she certainly doesn't look the type. Seemingly free of tattoos, and likely a job at a desk where her chances for promotions are slim at best.

And I don't know if they look happy. If he does. But she smiles at me from a photo a stranger probably took like she's won the best of prizes.

xix. The Groundhog's Escape

Not all who burrow into the earth are dead. It's what Groundhog's mother always told him, her words branded into his mind's eye. She shouldn't have bothered—he never minded the earth. Loved the smell of the aliveness when it was all around him. When he was young, she'd taught him how to dig quickly and efficiently, milling out smooth cave walls that hugged him close. No wonder the hibernation always felt like he was floating between this world and death. Maybe he was, as the worms tickled his sides and the farmers seeped fertilizer into the soil.

Unlike the others he saw, Chipmunk and Squirrel darting up trees, his safety was securely in the earth. Sure, he'd heard the stories. The ones about Humans who bolstered one of his own up like a blue ribbon prize, made a show of some far-off kin who could predict the seasons. A part of that fame, if it were even true, trickled down to him. Something about fear and shadows, he wasn't quite certain. Regardless, if he were ever asked if he could talk to the weather, he'd surely be able to bluff himself something marvelous.

Always be watching. That was something else his mother had told him. It proved handy when he built his grandest of burrows, the one that was over sixty feet deep. There were squatters and cheap shooters everywhere. Snake that tried to slip in when he wasn't looking, and the ugly Mole that was too lazy to build his own home proper. Coyote, angry Dog, and Wolf who watched him close. The Wolves. They were the worst.

The hardest part? It was the beginning of a new burrow. Once he got down deep, at least a few feet, he could build in relative peace, the darkness cloaking him. But those early days, the ones where he was partially exposed but had to keep his face planted in the earth, that's when the fear ran strong. Once, he was nipped by Dog, a rabid-looking thing with knots in his fur and yellow teeth. Not even enough to break the skin, but enough to remind him. Here, on this sprawling farmland, he could never let down his guard.

And then the pack happened.

The Wolf who travels in a pack, knitted close and able to read each other's' minds, those are the deadliest of all. It happened just like it ought to, during a dusk that was easy to forget. For once, just this once, Groundhog had traveled farther than usual for dinner. Past the barn with the peeling white paint, beyond the barb-wired fence that kept only the biggest, dumbest animals controlled. The land was dry, barren, and the berries had dried up early. The special caging the farmer had put around his wilting vegetable garden was strong enough, for now, to keep Groundhog at bay. He'd heard the stories about the long guns, too, and the bullets hungry for Groundhog.

His raging stomach made him scramble to a far-off piece of the land he'd never known before. That's when they found him.

"What are you doing so far from your hole?" Wolf was a towering white beast with cacao eyes and silver threaded throughout his coat.

"So far from home," echoed another, this one female and so lanky her body begged for meat to stick to the bones.

"I, uh—just getting some berries," said Groundhog, already backing away. His heart exploded in his chest, and he willed them not to hear it.

"Ain't no berries here," said the smallest of the lot, awkwardly slender and face like a teenager.

"Yeah, I, I didn't know," said Groundhog. He calculated the distance to his burrow. It was way too far, he'd never make it. He hadn't ever tested it, but he was sure the pack could overtake him in seconds.

"Seems you don't know a lot of things," said what he could only guess was the alpha. There were seven in total, lucky number seven.

"I guess not."

"You guess not. Let me ask you—are you ready to die tonight?" It wasn't a threat, it was fact. Just as the sky was big and the clay soil so hard.

"I don't ... I don't want to die," said Groundhog quietly.

"That's good! That's good," said the alpha. "Nobody wants to die—unless they're ill, of course. And if they're ill, we don't want them." Groundhog hadn't noticed how it had begun, but he saw it now. The pack circled him slowly, inching closer. There wasn't even the faintest window that he could race through even if he could outpace them.

"Listen," said Groundhog. "Listen, listen. I'm not even going to try. To run. You know? I'm going to die with dignity."

"That's surprising—for a groundhog," said the black female.

"Just let me give you something first," said Groundhog.

"Give us something? You're already giving us quite a lot. What a generous little beast you are!" said the alpha.

"Seriously," said Groundhog. "I never ... I never had kits. Okay? I never got to, you know, pass anything on."

"I am *not* fucking a groundhog!" said a nasty female with yellow eyes.

"Nobody asked you to," said the teenager.

"No! Not that," said Groundhog. "There's a dance. A special dance that only we know. It makes the earth within a foot of you crumble, just like dead leaves. It's how we make those burrows so deep." The lies rolled off his tongue like they'd been waiting there, greasy for years to drip out.

"Really," said the alpha. It wasn't a question.

"Really," said Groundhog, unsure where the resolve in his voice came from.

"And you want to teach us this? Why?"

"Why not? I mean, it's not like it'll be that useful to you, but still. It's something no other Wolf will know."

"Okay. Okay," said alpha. "I'm intrigued. How do you do it? We're not letting you out of the circle."

"That's fine!" said Groundhog. "Here, just let me show you, okay? I don't need to move much." With everything in him, all the way to the coppery marrow, he began a frenzy of a dance that moved him swift as churned butter in the center. All his ancestors must have lit him up like a firecracker, moving that round body like a dervish. Groundhog could hear some of the wolves whooping and howling, amazed at the quickness and grace of the one who lurks in the ground.

"Faster! Faster!" a teenager's voice screamed, and he delivered. He delivered, and all the while he dug a deep, deep burrow well beyond the nose of any wolf and covered it up lightly with debris just a smoothly.

"My God, that Groundhog can move!" said the alpha. From the corner of his eyes, he saw some of the wolves unclench their jaws. Lessen the stiffness in their legs, their readiness to pounce. One even, he swore, dropped to their back haunches and let their tongue loll out in delight.

"Show us, show us!" squealed a child's voice. And that's when he knew he had them.

"Okay! Alright," said Groundhog. "Now I'll teach you how to do it, but you have to be fully committed. Don't worry about how you look. And the real key is the spin. Got it? It's the spin that gives you momentum."

"Like this?" asked the teenager, hopping with no grace at all.

"Not quite," said Groundhog. "Build up some speed perhaps, and use your whole body to spin."

The circle of wolves spun faster and faster, even the large alpha became a whirling cloud. "That's it! That's it!" said Groundhog as he toed the earth, feeling out the outline of his burrow.

"I'm going to be sick," said a female voice, and the black one began to slow and shake.

Not all who burrow in the earth are dead. Groundhog dove into the makeshift burrow, the pack disappearing above.

"Hey!" cried the female. "Hey!" A sharpness jolted through his tail, a warm spurt running down his leg. The pain was muted, but he was alive. He was alive.

"He's gone, he's—what the hell, there's a hole here. But I got his tail! I got his tail!"

"You tricked us!" said the teenage voice, now sounding miles away.

Groundhog waited 'til dawn, long after the pack left before he dared spring across the farm to his home. For hours, he licked the bloodied stump where his tail once sprouted and thanked the Gods, thanked his mother, that only a small part of him became a Wolf.

Chapter 19

"Do you know how to empty the storage?"

"What?"

The little bar was shoved full of people during that peak hour when midnight was crawling closer. I'd noticed him when he'd arrived, though not for the usual reasons. Nobody would call him handsome, but his aura had heavy magnets. Bald and pudgy with deep dimples and perfect teeth, he was identical to Ian Gomez. Larry Miller. I didn't know what was wrong with me.

"We have the same phone," he said, gesturing. So we did.

"I'm Luis," he said. "These are my friends." He waved behind him, but they all blended together.

"Justine," I said.

"You're striking, you know that?" he said. "I mean, I don't say things like that often, but ..."

"Thank you." I still couldn't place it. Was this what people meant when they said inner beauty? Is that what I was seeing? The blackness of his eyes were hungry as suckling pigs. I didn't care that you could see the terrible male pattern baldness poking out from the smooth skull he must shave daily. The beer gut didn't matter. He was just so fucking sure of himself.

"Well, we—my friends and I—we're actually heading to a party now. But can I get your number?"

"Sure." Maybe he was a nice one, a good one. One that I could keep pace with. "Here, give me your phone, I'll enter it," I said.

"No, no, it's okay," he said. "I'll remember it."

"You'll remember it?"

"Yeah, I'm good with numbers."

"Okay ..." If it was some kind of game, I didn't see how I could lose at it. What's the worst that could happen?

He texted two days later, using flawlessly strung together sentences and full punctuation. It looked odd, no abbreviations and words with more than four letters splaying across my screen. "Do you want to go to dinner?" he asked.

"Sounds good. When/where?" I asked.

"Causa?" he asked. The upscale Peruvian tapas place folded into the guts of the Pearl. I knew the price point and how it was always better to sit in the bar even when you did have reservations. "It's Peruvian, I'm Puerto Rican, there has to be some kind of common thread there," he said.

Puerto Rican. That was different.

I didn't let him pick me up, but that didn't stop him from doing everything he should. The opening of doors, the offering of an elbow, the wearing of a suit jacket with new-smelling denim. But I felt it as soon as we walked through the doors. Some floors are greased like the flagpoles at Costa Rican rodeos, traps for women in slender heels. It was like walking on ice. Maybe, surely, I could at least make it the thirty feet from the hostess stand to the table, but no. For the first time in my sober adult life, the floor was pulled out from under me and the hostess looked like she saw a beheading. The tight purple dress, the ankle-tied shoes, the men who whistled at me on my way from the car to the restaurant, all of it disappeared. I was a pathetic adolescent all over again. Any power I thought I had over Luis was spilled and lost along that overly mopped floor, too.

After the "Are you okays?" from him, the hostess, from everyone, he couldn't stop laughing. I faked it, because what else do you do? "You know, in Puerto Rican culture? Nobody would ever let you live that down," he said. At least some dignity had been salvaged. The dress had miraculously stayed no higher than my thighs even as I had spread across the floor.

I hated eating in front of men. Unless it was handpicked bite-sized pieces that were designed to mimic sex, you couldn't do it without looking like a bumbling animal. But it was all about food, all the time, the social lubricant everybody agreed upon. But at least you could get a preview of how men were in bed. They fuck like they eat, all of them.

Luis was one of the types of engineers with a PhD for show who wore bunny suits in the lab. A recent transplant from his doctoral program at Penn State, he was the type who picked up friends and those who adored him without even trying.

We tried for three months—gave it a real shot. He met my friends without complaint, took me to soccer games and let me meet his already close-knit brood of heavy drinking buddies. Once, he told me with sorrow about the Jewish girl he left behind. I took him to Sauvie Island where we watched the naked people and shivered with a blanket on the hood of his car. And the sex? It was good, it was easy, and I felt like I didn't need to constantly pose or suck in my stomach. Even though the first time, he grabbed a half-used bottle of lube from his bedside table and I couldn't bring myself to ask. Was it all for masturbation, or did he bring home so many women he needed a 12-ounce bottle at the ready?

Then the blackouts started. I'm good at those. There was the time we were together at Horseshoe Bar, and a strange man snuck up beside me and said, "You could do better." I told him "Don't!" and was so proud of myself for sticking up for Luis without ever even telling him about it. There was the time I was driving him and my two girlfriends through Chinatown looking for parking on a Friday night. Luis claimed he saw a friend, and asked to be let out to meet us there. It was pouring, that Oregon kind of shower. So wet I dropped my friends off and had to walk seven blocks by myself. Luis showed up two hours later. I tried to push it aside, but it lingered just like that tacky bottle of lubricant.

I was losing him.

And then Japan. He went there on a business trip for a week, and I thought nothing of it. The photos he posted were innocent enough. Two days after he returned, he asked me to come over. "I miss my friend!" he said. I should never have gone. He tried to go down on me, but I pushed him away.

"Japan was intense," he said, raising up like he'd bent down to retrieve a dropped napkin. "There was this girl I met in some hole in the wall place? Gorgeous! Truly. She bought me a drink, and then ... that's all I remember. I, uh, I think she roofied me."

I didn't know what to say to this. I'm sorry? You deserve it? Why the hell are you telling me this?

"Why do you think that?" It's all I could come up with.

"I woke up in some motel room without my wallet," he said. "But at least I still had my liver."

When he walked me to my car, I knew it was the last time. And I wished I'd told him about the Horseshoe man, but now it would reek of pettiness.

xx. Bear Feeds Raven

Bear watched Raven for a good ten minutes, grounded on a mossy branch during a torrential Northwest downpour. When the sky raged, it never bothered Bear. Actually, it shook up some of his favorite hunting grounds, the added wetness making the fish jerk and twist. He'd never much cared for fowl—whether eating them or talking to them. But something about Raven made him stop. There was no telling how long the rains would come down, or how long it had been since Raven had eaten. Bear was feeling generous, his own belly full and swimming with rich fare. Counting the stock he had back in his den, he tried to determine out which would be kind to Raven's stomach and which would make it lurch.

"Hey!" he called up to the black, glistening bird. "Are you hungry?"

"Are you talking to me?" asked Raven.

"Yeah. Are you hungry?"

"Why does it matter to you?"

"I don't know," said Bear, and he realized it was true. "I just … if you are? I have some food at home. Vegetarian food. I'm going back there now if you want to come."

"What is this?" said Raven. "We've never spoken before."

"It's just an offer," said Bear. "I have a lot more than I need."

Raven didn't want to trust Bear, knew the dangers that popped up when two should-be enemies got too close. Still, his stomach was screaming and it shook the hollowness of his bones. The rains had been coming down non-stop for days, flooding the streets and halting the electric trains. Any stray grains, seeds or chunks of bread that might have been close enough to walk were so thoroughly soaked they'd disintegrated or been swallowed back up by the earth.

"How far is it?" asked Raven. He couldn't fly well in such heavy rains.

"Not far," said Bear. "You can ride on my shoulder if you want." Bear saw the fear in Raven's eyes. "Don't worry," he said. "My mouth can't reach my shoulder or upper back. Besides, I just ate more than I needed. See?" he asked, nodding to his swollen middle.

"Well. Okay," said Raven, climbing down the tree and jumping onto Bear's back. "Thanks," he said.

He'd never noticed Bear's den before, the ivy covering the narrow opening so perfectly he'd always assumed it was a big, knotted tree trunk. Built on a hill's swell, it tucked perfectly into the earth. Blackberry bushes flanked either side, providing Bear with both ready-made berries in the spring and an added layer of protection with the sharp barbs. Raven's stomach gurgled louder at the sight of all the berries.

"I have more berries inside," Bear said, poking around in Raven's mind. "The ripest ones."

"It's … cozier. Than I imagined," said Raven, looking around as they entered. The den was small but homey, yet he felt more like a guest than an intruder. In the corner was a makeshift kitchen, piled high with food. In the center, a well-crafted bed of dry leaves and grass so perfectly tended it made even Raven want to nose in and sleep. The smell was a mixture of, somehow, baked goods and warmth.

"You have to have cozy for hibernation," said Bear. "Sit where you like, and I'll make some food."

"Make?" asked Raven.

"Sure," said Bear. "Give me a few minutes, and I can make something. If you're really hungry, there are some nuts and berries that I've sweetened and seasoned in that tin over there."

Raven did his best not to gorge himself on the fare, drizzled with honey that still had flecks of honeycomb in it. "What are you making?" he asked, watching Bear's hurried back bend and twist over a variety of fare.

"It's a kind of granola, I guess," said Bear. "Better than what the Humans have, though. You just heat it for a few minutes, and it makes it all come together."

"You can have flames? In here?" asked Bird. He'd known of some animals who could control fire, but he'd never tried it himself. Had never actually known someone who did.

"Sure!" said Bear.

The granola, or whatever it was, was warm and gooey and felt like home. Raven hadn't experienced anything like it since he was a chick and his mother would bring him sunny goodness home in her mouth.

It had been a year. The two had experienced a kind of coming together, a connection, that's only possible in the worst of circumstances. But Raven never forgot Bear and looked for him constantly. He never dared go back to the den, though sometimes he flew over it hoping to see the staggering beast.

On the first day of spring, it happened. "Hey! Hi," said Raven. "Remember me?"

"Of course!" said Bear. "How have you been?"

"Been well," said Raven. "I never really thanked you for what you did, and wanted to see if I could return the favor."

"Well, I'm not exactly starving …" said Bear, who had indeed put on even more weight since last year.

"You know what I mean!" said Raven. "You should come by tonight. The big cherry tree by the golf course. I'll make you something this time."

"Well, alright. That sounds good," said Bear.

Raven had been practicing with fire, and although it still scared him, he was getting used to it. The little pit had been burning bright for an hour when Bear arrived, and Raven was dashing from dish to dish making sure all the ingredients were ready.

"You're here!" he said. "Just a few more minutes—" His nerves rocked him hard. Made him dizzy. He wanted to impress Bear, thank him, show him that he could work magic with food, too. In his rush, he tripped over the big shell of grains and stumbled right into the flames. The heat burst through his body like a blossom.

"Oh my God! Are you okay? Are you okay?" Bear's voice rang from somewhere far off and Raven's feet. His feet. They were blackened and scalded something terrible.

"I just ... I just wanted to make you something special," he said.

Chapter Twenty

"I have someone I want you to meet!" said Sue-Ann.

"Who's that?"

"His name's Naveen, he's a contractor at my work."

"Why do you want me to meet him? Because he's Indian?"

"Well. Yeah," she said.

"Uh, yeah, it takes more than that. But what do you have in mind?"

"Just come to my work's happy hour on Friday at the Maraca. There's a bunch of us, and people bring friends all the time."

It was about time to start widening my circle. Faces at the bar all became familiar, and I knew too many names.

"Okay," I said. "Just don't say anything to him about me."

"What do you think?" Sue-Ann drunk-whispered to me over the screeches and screams in the cavernous happy hour space.

"About the guy? I think he's awkward," I said. I hadn't been lying. "Being Indian" wasn't the only pre-requisite for me to have an interest. It wasn't even one of the requirements. It was clear Sue-Ann had said something to Naveen, but for once I was grateful I didn't suffer from the common womanly problem of feeling obligated to be nice to everyone. Barely polite enough worked for me.

"He's nice!" she said.

"I didn't say he wasn't nice."

"Oi, what are you talking about?" Daniel asked, brushing his leg against mine, a weighty Manchester accent seeping through dark Italian lips.

"*Nothing!*" Sue-Ann said. "You're so nosy!"

I'd never heard about Daniel before, and why should I? Solidly in his fifties, he was one of the VPs of Sue-Ann's company, heading up a Fortune 500 operation even as he channeled George Clooney. But more slender. And with a much more delectable accent.

"I like a woman who knows how to drink," he said to me, gesturing to the whiskey with a hand that held a wedding ring.

"Does your wife know how to drink?" I asked.

"My wife? Oh!" he said. "She did, yeah. Maybe too much. Or maybe I'm the one with the too much. Regardless, it certainly played some kind of role in the divorce."

"If you're divorced, why are you wearing a ring?" I asked.

"You noticed." It wasn't a question.

"You've been tapping it against your glass for the past hour."

"Habit, I guess," he said. The silver whiskers reaching out from his face looked harsh as a scouring pad. "We're not divorced yet, but legally separated. She just moved into her own house two months ago. But, the kid, you know—"

"I don't know."

"I guess not," he agreed. "You look a bit like her."

"Nobody looks like me." It wasn't a gloat or a challenge, just a fact. I'd never seen anyone who looked like me.

"Oh, hey! Hey!" Sue-Ann said. "Justine's looking for a new job. Daniel, you should see her resume. Master's in writing."

"Oh, yeah?" he asked. "Here, take my number," he said, grabbing my phone like he had a right and punching in a number.

"Daniel asked about you," Sue-Ann said on Monday. My heart jumped. It had been awhile since it made that kind of sideways move.

"What about?"

"Kind of about the job thing, but ... then kind of general. Like if you were seeing anybody."

"Really?"

"Oh, my God, do you like him? What about Naveen?"

"What about Naveen?" I asked.

"Daniel is, like, twenty-five years older than you!"

"Twenty-seven. And what does it matter? It's not like I want to marry him. He isn't even divorced yet!"

"You know, I was trying to set you up with a nice guy. You should give Naveen a chance."

"I'm not interested in Naveen. At all." I hated this, the cornering to people did to get everyone to squeeze into a suitable box.

"You'd better not do anything about Daniel. Seriously! That could mess up my job."

"How could it mess up your job?"

"I don't know! If things go bad, he might take it out on me."

"I'm pretty sure that a VP isn't going to try to exact revenge over a fling."

"Just be careful."

It was another week before I had enough alcohol to muster up the nerve to text Daniel. I wasn't drunk, but buzzed enough. "Sue-Ann thinks I shouldn't message you," I texted him. "What do you think?"

The reply was immediate. "Can I call you?"

I forgot the conversation as it unfolded, lost in that British accent that took me back to grad school. To walking High Street and stumbling around the Apple Peddler with my fellow interns. But I remember this: "Do you want to meet for coffee?"

"When?" I asked.

"Thursday? I can walk over during the lunch break."

"Okay."

It was the kind of established pre-cursor to a date or a hookup or something where both parties knew what was happening, knew the rules, and so the construct was maddening. Daniel looked different, in running shorts and a Man United jersey. "I run at least five miles at lunch every day. It's the only way to squeeze in marathon and triathlon training." God. He was well old enough to be my father and in better shape than me.

"So I take it you're not having any liquor in your coffee, then?" I'd chosen the place, my favorite coffee house hidden inside an old Victorian on northwest 23rd. They were known for their crepes and propensity for turning any favorite coffee drink into a cocktail the minute they opened at sunrise.

"I'm British, love. I can drink and run."

We talked through the bullshit and the Mexican Coffee I downed did its job on an empty stomach. I got nervy when the liquor was in me and the sun was still up. "How old is your wife?" I asked.

"Thirty-five," he said. I don't know if I was surprised or not.

"Show me a picture," I said.

"Alright. Or …" he began, scrolling through his phone, "you can just meet her if you want. We're going to Erin's Saturday for St. Patrick's Day. A group from work and some of her friends."

"You want me to meet your wife?"

He shrugged. "I don't see why not. Sue-Ann might be coming."

"She didn't say anything."

"Here," he said, handing me his phone. His wife was lovely, prettier than I thought she'd be and thick in all the right places. She didn't look like me, not quite. She looked like me blended with Jennifer Aniston.

"She's pretty," I said.

"I know."

"You're seriously going there?" said Sue-Ann.

"Yeah. I mean, his wife's going to be there. And other people. Other people from your work. Why don't you come?"

"God. Okay. I might as well watch this shitshow unfold."

Sue-Ann could be a hyper happy drunk, or a hyper mean one. I drove, but she immediately went for the Irish car bombs and I lost her in the roped-in back patio near the boxing ring and beyond the bagpipes. But Daniel, he'd secured a corner booth with a hodge podge group of people. Some looked vaguely familiar. And his wife looked just as she did in the photos.

"Hi!" she said. The only open seat was next to her, with Daniel positioned directly across from us. "Thank God. It's nice to have a woman who isn't either twenty or fifty come out!" And she was nice, too. She drank her scotch straight and could dress for her body. In another life, we could have been friends. I felt Daniel watching us from across the booth.

There were brown outs that night. Suddenly I was outside, and Daniel was holding my arm. I didn't know where his wife was. "Where's your wife?" I asked.

"She took a cab home. Doesn't like to get home after midnight when Mark's with the sitter. She liked you."

"I could have her, you know," I said.

"What?" It sounded like "wot."

"I could have her."

"No. She's not like that."

"We're all like that."

"Not her."

"I'll prove it to you," I said.

"How?"

"She gave me her number."

I had no idea what I was trying to prove, or to whom. She *had* given me her number, after I promised to take her on a tour of the best gay clubs in town. Sue-Ann swore that maybe they were some kind of swingers or into polyamory, not really getting divorced, but I didn't get that feeling from them. Plus, with women, you don't have to play hard to get. We're easy with each other like that.

The next weekend, I met up with the wife, who had told Daniel to stay home with their son. She held a vivid life deep in her center, so bright it glowed bright as a Chinese lantern. "Dance with me!" she said, and we did, the gay boys in their glowing white underwear swarming around us. I didn't particularly want to kiss her, but wasn't against it. It was just kind of there, like the last piece of cake. You're not hungry for it, but you're not stuffed, so you just eat it to get it all done with. She tasted like cheap liquor and peppermint gum, a combination that strangely came together with a perfect rhythm. We made out for hours, until I asked why they were getting divorced.

"We're just too different," she said.

"How so?"

"The age thing—you think it doesn't matter. If you love someone. But it does. It does. The little things start to add up." That admission cracked my heart, but not deep enough to keep from bragging to Daniel.

"You shouldn't have done that," Daniel said days later at happy hour. It was just the two of us, hunkered over ceviche and cocktails at an Italian eatery.

"Why not? I told you I would." Between kissing his wife and now, I'd asked for a nude photo and got it. For evidence of his marathons and was met with snapshots of bibs and medals. Everything went fast, fast, fast. Maybe that's what happened when time wasn't so sluggish for you anymore.

"She's my wife."

"Was."

"Is."

"But not for long."

"Sure," he said. "You should come to Arizona next week. I still have the house there, pool and everything."

"What are you doing in Arizona?" I needed to buy time. It was terrifying, the thought of truly being alone with him. No buffers like waiters hovering over us or the gaggle of colleagues that often met with us in the later hours.

"Work meeting," he said.

"Maybe, I don't know. I have work."

"I thought you were looking for work."

"I am, but I'm still at the interim job." It was partially true. After the recession hit hard, I'd been laid off from the stifling non-profit job I'd had and fell right into another, temporary one. The departments were shutting down quickly, and it was my job to put in that last stab wound. The kill. Really, I could leave whenever. What could they do about it?

Daniel got too close and scared me. Or maybe it was his wife's words that lingered in my head. Once, at dinner, the waitress called him my father and I couldn't tell who was most embarrassed. Or maybe he was used to it and the redness I thought I saw spreading over his face was actually the bright glow from me. He'd make cultural references I didn't know, and I'd do the same. It was clear, had always been clear, that he was hungry for a string of flings, and that was fine with me. But did I want to be the first? I didn't know. But I was fairly certain I'd be the best, if only for my youth.

The first time he kissed me, long after I'd kissed his wife, it was in his car as he was dropping me at mine. It was aggressive, and the stubble hurt even more than I imagined. His lips were too thin and his slight, muscly body provided no comfort. I didn't feel safe there. And I knew I couldn't ride on the virtue of my youth forever.

I felt fat next to him. Soft. Wanting.

"You can't just do that," I told him on the phone.

"Do what?"

"Whatever you want," I said. What I wanted to say was, "I'm a person, but I'm sure you think I'm stupid with inexperience." I'd once asked Jimit, who consistently railed about how young I was (him being twelve years older) if he was so wise, to tell me something I'd know at his age. "You don't know what you think you do." That had been the only wisdom nugget he'd ever offered up.

The annoyance in Daniel's voice was palpable. "I don't know what you mean," he said, and I hung up.

I hated myself for this, but my reply was in a text. I'd never been able to say what I mean with a voice, had always taken to writing things down. On a blank sheet, I could fill it in with shapes and dark scratches that came directly from my middle. For some reason, it flowed from my fingertips so much easier than my mouth.

"I want to be courted," I said. "I want romance, all of that."

"Are you being serious?" Daniel replied, and I could almost hear the shock in his voice. Right then, I knew it was over. Was it so wrong? To accept a casual relationship and still want to be treated like a woman? Like a person worth trying for?

I never responded, and Sue-Ann never asked for details. Although she did still say that he asked about me for weeks to come.

"You should have gone with Naveen," she said.

xxi. The Owl and the Hunter

What does he do? the girl's mother asked.

He a guard, works the graveyard shift. She knew as soon as she said it that her mother would never agree.

You need to marry a hunter, she said, shaking her head. *A man should be able to live off the land if necessary. Fix things. A man should either be able to use his hands, or have enough money to hire someone who can.*

It was the same story the girl had heard for decades. Find a man like her father—maybe her mom was right. After all, it's not like she was in love with any of the men she'd dated. Not really. Not that heart-throbbing, gut clenching feeling some of her friends had described.

And besides, she was thirty-five now. That was old. Like, really, truly old. Old in the way that if she wanted to have kids, and she did, she had to hustle.

Owl had been watching the girl since she was five years old. They grew up together, but she didn't really know it. A handful of times, he was sure she'd spotted him perched on the mossy apple tree in the backyard, the one that shaded her window. Eyes had locked, he was certain, but that was all it had been. Two lanterns catching her notice in the night.

He'd been listening to her and her mother having that same conversation for years, too. Had seen the boys, then men, come and go. Their cars got a little better and their hair thinner, but for the most part it was the same. Chemistry was so lacking he never felt more than a twinge of jealousy.

Now it was his time. He'd been practicing and could hold the mirage of a man for a full day.

And, of course, he knew how to hunt.

"This is Tsigili," said the girl. Owl stood, in his human form, before the old woman with crepe paper for skin and threads of silver in her hair. He'd watched her, too. Saw the sadness envelope her for keeps when her husband died. Watched as she went from the peak of ripeness to the falling apart before him.

"Sight-jee-lee?" she asked. "What kind of name is that?"

"It's—" he began.

"*Mother.* Don't be rude," she said.

"You don't look foreign," the old woman said, sizing him up. That part he'd carefully constructed. The mirage looked just a touch like her late husband, but not enough to draw suspicions. But, perhaps, enough to make the girl fall for him instantly, even if she couldn't be certain why. He'd picked up the human social cues over the years. How to be a gentleman, but still play hard to get. Humans were easy to mimic. The love part, though, the reason he felt such things for this girl, that was still beyond his grasp.

Six months later, he asked the old woman if he could marry her daughter. She agreed before she could even finish chewing the half-burned cookie she'd made for his visit.

"Where are you going?" the girl asked him the morning after the wedding. A carefully constructed lie had squeezed him into living in their home, and he knew her mother required proof for him to stay.

"Hunting," he said.

It proved harder than he'd imagined to catch big game. Or even mid-sized game. His human form wasn't as agile as his natural one.

That was okay. Instead, he sprouted his wings as soon as he was out of sight and caught the biggest of fish. Hunting, fishing, it was the same family. Right?

"What's *this*?" her mother asked when he returned.

"I decided to fish instead," he said.

"We don't eat much fish," she said. "But these are quite big ..."

"They are very good," he said. "Trust me."

Something was off with her husband. The girl knew it even during the little wedding ceremony in the back yard. Maybe she'd always known it. She couldn't quite figure it out, and he did all the right things. Said all the right things. But it just didn't settle into place like it should.

After two weeks of him bringing fish, fish, fish for dinner, her mother was beginning to complain. First just to her, but then passively loudly enough for him to hear. It wasn't that the girl minded the fish—actually, it was welcome after the years of red meat and oil-soaked chicken her mother preferred. But why wasn't he doing the kind of hunting that would make her mother happy? How difficult could that be?

When he left the next morning, she locked herself in the powder room with the water running so he'd think she was busy. Quietly, carefully, she trailed after him into the light. He walked both reckless and full of grace, with a gait she'd never seen before. It had been one of the first things she'd noticed about him. That walk. And those eyes, a nearly yellowish type of honey that seemed to drip from a place she'd never known.

She wasn't sure what to expect, if anything at all. How exciting could fishing be? But as he crested the hill that led to the valley floor, he picked up pace. Faster. She began to run to even keep up, praying that he didn't turn or hear her crushing the leaves behind him. Yards ahead of her, he shrugged off his coat, paused just a moment to drop out of his pants, and in a whirl went from man to one of the biggest owls she'd ever seen.

He was easy to spot from the hilltop, swooping down to the lake below. Somehow, none of this seemed strange. It fit together perfectly.

"I knew it!" her mother screamed. "I knew it! There was always something odd about him!"

"I think you are an owl." When the two women confronted him as soon as he got home, fish clenched in a bag, no words appeared for him. What could he say? And the girl, she'd loved him. She must have. But now, standing before him, he saw a monster reflected in her eyes.

Owl grieved for the girl, pined for her, and keened into the night. He wore away to nothing, his feathers dropping into the dry grass. Still, he wouldn't die. Not when his bones cracked and the wind whipped them to slivers. Always, his great head remained. Eyes big and watchful, beak strong as steel. He just couldn't stop watching the girl through her bedroom window as she brushed her hair. Folded her clothes. Stared at the wrinkles that were creeping like spiders at her eyes' corners.

Chapter 21

"I'm going to fuck the hottest guy here," I told Sue-Ann as she suckled on a plastic straw like it was her lifeline.

I was. It had been decided. I needed a distraction, an ego boost, and something to take up my time for the next few hours. In the echoing concert hall with the floating floors that bounced, a half-Irish, half-Indian band was scattered across the stage, largely drawing an Indian crowd with a seasoning of hipster-leaning pale Portlanders.

It wasn't that I was particularly drawn to anyone here, but in any crowd of over one hundred people, you could narrow down your selection to something you wouldn't totally mind. I wasn't in the mood for games or flirtations, furtive glances across dingy rooms. I just wanted to take whatever looked best and go home.

Maybe I chose him because of the care he'd taken with his hair, the lightest dusting of salt in the sideburns and the way the thick black locks stood shock-straight up. Maybe it was that, by Indian standards, he was one of the tallest in the room without being awkwardly lanky. Most likely, it was that he was alone, surveying the crowd like a shark. It's always an added thrill to take down a fellow predator.

"Can I buy you a drink?" I asked him, direct. Well aware that I was far too overdressed for this venue, for this place. Also the blondest, the bleach always easily lifting that auburn right out of my strands.

"Sure," he said. As if he'd been expecting my arrival.

It's hard to talk over blaring guitars and drums, just the way I like it. Over numerous shouts, I learned his name (Raj). What he did (managed a perfume store). Where he was from (Marathi Indian by way of Los Angeles).

Then I got so drunk I only have flashes of taking him home. Sue-Ann driving, Raj following with the occasional headlights flashing. The sex itself was total darkness, as if it never happened.

This I remember: It must have been around four, five in the morning. He made an excuse to leave, and I was so goddamned grateful. Work, I think. All I wanted was to wake up alone, reassured by an empty condom wrapper and the fading smell of strangeness on my pillow.

"Jessie, its Raj. U free for dinner?" The text came at noon, my head still pounding from the bottom shelf liquor the night before. What the hell was he doing? Why had I even given him my number? Then I remembered, it was a safety net. Just in case he lost us on the way back to the house.

My whole gut screamed at me to ignore the call. Block it if necessary. Any other time I would have, but there was something enraging about him not even knowing my name.

"My name's Justine," I said.

"Sorry! Sorry!," came the reply in seconds. "It was hard to hear over the music last night."

I mean, I guess the excuse made sense. Maybe? It was loud. But was there really an excuse for forgetting the name of the person you're fucking? Or never knowing it at all? Especially if you were going to have the nerve to make contact after the fact. Ours was something that was supposed to be swept under rugs.

"Why do you want to get dinner?" I asked. And suddenly realized I didn't really remember what he looked like. I'd been largely sober when I first saw him, but the dimness of the place was generous with shadows. I couldn't summon the exact color of his eyes or the shape of his lips. In my mind, he'd been good looking enough, but what if I was wrong? Did I really want to take that gamble?

"Just thought to try another first meeting," he said. This was strange, but I was bored. Bored and not totally against some wound lickings after last night.

It's a bitch to pull yourself together through the drumming of a hangover. I chose the place, an upscale Indian spot in the alphabet district. Jeans and a tight tee-shirt. Thank God when I arrived, he was the only person there. I may not have recognized him otherwise, especially since the customers are usually Indian and Pakistani.

I hadn't made a mistake. Drunk Justine had done alright selecting based on aesthetics. Raj was good looking enough, with just a hint of a soft jawline and designer clothes. He was the type who would have any woman with a brown-skinned fetish looking. But I had no idea what he wanted.

And, honestly, I just didn't care about anything he had to say. His need to build himself up and flank himself in excuses before I even had time to pass judgment. Why he only had a bachelor's degree, why he was working in retail (management!), how he came to the US. He asked me almost nothing about myself, his interest only piqued when he drilled me about the men in my life and tried to skirt around questions to figure out if I was as big of a whore as I seemed.

Something impressed him, intrigued him. Maybe that I was more educated, more well-traveled, more well-read, I don't know. But he wanted to prove himself to me, and he knew just how to do that.

"You know, I knew," he said. "Last night, I knew you weren't really that kind of girl." I hated being called a girl.

"What kind of girl is that?" I asked.

"You know."

"No, I don't."

He sighed, irritated as if a child were squirming in his lap. "The kind of girl who does one-night stands."

"Well, clearly, you wouldn't let me have a one-night stand."

I'd meant it to be condescending, but he took it like a compliment. And I was too tired to correct him.

I'd never been bullied into a relationship before. Boys had tried, as teenagers, but they weren't as persistent as Raj. For a month he flooded me with gifts, expensive dinners, cash I didn't ask for—all until he revealed he was now broke, but wasn't "too small a man to admit such things." Then he asked for me to pay, and stupidly I did. I thought it would shame him, but it's like he didn't even know enough to be embarrassed.

"I've never seen snow," he told me, and I thought that was so incredibly sad. I wanted to be the first, the first to show him something so spectacular. That would be so much better than taking anyone's virginity. Wouldn't seeing your first snow trump that?

November had arrived, and I bought chains for my car to whisk him away to the base of Mt. Hood where you could rent black rubber tubes and slide down bunny hills. We'd done all the requisite autumn couple activities already, ticking them off like a grocery checklist. Hay rides, pumpkin carving, matching Halloween costumes. He was addicted to Indian dance nights, dragging me relentlessly every Friday and Saturday. And the words were started to actually sting and stick, like a bee's sting that I couldn't dig out.

It started little, as they always do. "You look *almost thin* in that shirt," he said. For the first time since I'd lost all that college weight, I began to question. Was I getting fat? Already fat?

When I saw a skinny girl with a mermaid's name and hair to her ass sidle up beside him like she knew him, knew him, on an Indian night, that woman's instinct kicked in. I don't even recall my exact words, but he lapped up that suspicion with a great thirst. "*Nothing's* ever happened between us," he said. The words sounded like they were supposed to reassure, but I could read the gloating in his eyes. "You know what your problem is? You don't trust me. I think I should take her out, on a real date. You need to trust that if I do, nothing would happen."

But then he'd make my Skype with his mother and sister back in India, and everything seemed to be moving forward. He gave me two thousand dollars to put in my savings account since, as it turns out, he was in the states illegally and for whatever reason it was better to keep money outside of his accounts. He'd let his holiday visa expire a year ago. Worked in retail because he'd happened upon an Indian small business owner who was more than happy to figure out an under the table gig for him.

By the time we actually set off for Mt. Hood, I felt up to my thighs in quicksand. It was easier to just keep moving forward than to cut him off. I could tell, already, that he'd be up for some hellish type of fight I'd never known before. It had been just a few weeks, seven at most. Already he was talking about my working for him. Moving to LA. Getting married because he knew *I'd* know "it wasn't about a green card."

Something was off, even more than usual, as I crept the car through the increasingly slick and frozen streets.

"Just don't talk," he said. "I have a headache." I hadn't said a word.

"What are you talking about?" I asked, my hands aching from gripping the steering wheel too tight.

"Did you hear me?" he asked, the meanness in his voice spilling out. "I said don't talk. Can't you even follow those instructions? You can speak again when I tell you you can."

I felt like a dog, a dirty bitch, but I sucked and chewed on my cheeks to keep the words in. This must be how it feels to be a pitbull suddenly dumped into a dog fighting master's backyard. Stupidly unsure of the rules, but knowing intuitively that you'd better figure out how to follow them. You'd never been in a fight before, but the wildest parts of you knew about them somehow. You knew you had to conserve your energy if you were going to win.

Once we got to a point where snow piled up along the banks, looking like cookies and cream ice cream, Raj's mood lifted. He'd been toying with his phone, turning it away from me at certain points though I could see his text screen reflected in the window. I was his chauffeur and he was, I'm sure of it, setting up plans with a myriad of other women even as he'd just talked about marriage a few hours before.

Parked at the snowtube site, I tried to push the drive up out of my mind. My throat was dry and my voice was hoarse from lack of talking.

"Don't be such a downer!" he said, laughing as he ran through the snow. There were two people in him, that was clear to see. And I'd never know which one was going to show up.

It was there, in the freezing gusts of Oregon, that I knew I had to leave him. But I knew I couldn't until he'd had his fill of me. We were getting closer, that was evident. The fights lasted longer, his words more brutal, but he wasn't done with me yet. I'd have to push him over, make him think he was leaving me.

As it turns out, such an opportunity presented itself spread eagle like a gift. He was making concrete plans to move back to Los Angeles, and the stories about his ex there— the one with the sixteen-year-old daughter—were replaying from his mouth more often. About how she was some big shot movie producer, Indian but American born. How he'd caught her sexting with his former best friend, and what a puppy dog of a victim he was.

He'd demanded a going away party at my house, at Sue-Ann's house, and that I gather all my friends to ship me away to the place where palm trees took the place of pines.

The day before the party, it happened. He'd borrowed my laptop and made the ridiculous mistake of not logging out of his email. It was college all over again. A girl, Dipali, from India was all over his messages. Asking "How's Justine?" and his asking, "How are the kids?" before they both dove deep into such graphic description of sex it's like he was someone else. We'd fallen into a pattern of him blaming me for his inability to get it up. The only way he could be remotely excited is if we acted out a rape scene. In the end, that was fine with me—I wouldn't have to pretend I wanted him.

He told her to sit on his dick and spin around. She said, "Whoohee!"

There were the emails from his ex in Los Angeles, her begging him to take her back and him saying he still loved her. With her emails, her photo popped up each time. Her with a thick waist and drooping boobs hanging out of a too-deep V-neck. And then there was me. The one who he said dressed like a slut and should only wear turtlenecks and long-sleeved tees.

I waited until the night of the party for my attack. Partly because the atmosphere might intensify the battle. Partly because having so many people around might give me some protection.

"I can't believe you went through my email!" he roared when I told him what I'd uncovered.

"*I* didn't go through it! You left it up on *my* computer," I said.

"That doesn't matter! You should have logged out as soon as you realized that."

"Don't tell me what I should and shouldn't do."

"You're pathetic, you know that? I was trying to help you! But now, now you've just fucked yourself over. I'm done. You can just stay up here for all I care," he said.

Thank you. Thank God.

"Fine," I said. "Fine."

We'd rolled with the argument upstairs and into my bedroom. Below, I could hear the rattling of music, the drunken shrieks and chantings. We were in darkness and now, now ... the party seemed a world away.

He had to walk past me to get out, the narrow little passageway not allowing nearly enough room for all this fear and hatred.

As he barreled by, he grabbed both my wrists. They felt hollow as bird bones in his meaty grasp. "You stupid bitch," he muttered, slamming my hands and forearms into the wall behind me. I heard a crack, but he was already through the doorway and heading downstairs.

It wasn't my wrist bones that broke, but he'd pushed my hand so hard and so far that it went clear through the wall, splitting the switch plate right in two.

xxii. How the Deer Got His Antlers

The Gods made a crown just for a mortal to wear, and it was glorious. All arches and points, a covering of velvet and if it were lost—if it got too heavy—a new crown would grow again from the forehead of the one who deserved it.

"Antlers." The name of the mortal crown spread through the valleys, shot over hills, and soon enough nearly everyone was vying for it. It was simple enough, in the beginning, to figure out who it would belong to. There were a handful who didn't want the burden. Smaller beasts, of course the insects, and some who thought they already had a gorgeous enough adornment like the peacock. A series of tamer competitions were held that vetted out even more. In the end, only two remained: The Rabbit and the Deer.

"How will the winner be decided?" they all asked. Deer was too demure to recommend a challenge, and didn't have a particular one in mind anyway. Actually, he wasn't even sure about the crown. Was it a trick? Would it slow him down through the woods? Make him easier for the hunters to catch, get tangled in the low-hanging limbs?

Rabbit had no such reservations and salivated every time he thought about the prize. With antlers, he'd be unstoppable. From time to time, he thought about the added challenges. He'd have to dig holes deeper, make dens larger to fit his new accoutrement, but it would be well worth it.

"A race," suggested Moose. In this instance, everyone listened to him. He already had a kind of crown, and there were some who thought the Gods modeled the antlers after Moose's own headpieces. But Moose's were rounder and without sharpness. Like a dull mess of spades that no longer served a purpose.

"Yes! A race!" many echoed, and neither Rabbit nor Deer argued. After all, they were both fast. The differences in their legs were evened out with Rabbit's muscled flanks. It was the fairest judgment either of them could imagine.

But the night before the race, Rabbit couldn't sleep. What if Deer was faster? What if those long legs proved to be a bigger advantage than he thought?

The insomnia gave him a jolt of energy, and Rabbit snuck to the trails that had been mapped out earlier with little red flags. Carefully, he cut a clearing so that it blended in with the rest of the forest. He left his own marks behind, little cairns, so he would know exactly where the shortcuts were. By the time pastel streaks painted the sky, his teeth ached from all the cutting and he could feel the tired spreading through his body. But that was okay. He estimated his shortcuts cut his race in half.

He was right. But first, he had to sprint far ahead of Deer so he wouldn't get caught taking that first shortcut. His long ears gave him powerful hearing, and he could tell where Deer was along most of the trail. Once, he even stopped, caught his breath, so he wouldn't finish so freakishly fast as to draw attention.

When he did leap across that finish line, Deer was a full ten minutes behind him. The cheers didn't sound so sweet and he didn't have the gush of glory that he'd felt when he'd won contests before, but the antlers would make up for it. He waited, impatient, listening to the sound of Deer's light stampede through the wood chipped trail.

"I'm surprised!" said Hummingbird. "I thought for sure Deer would win."

"I hope you didn't lose any money on it," said Rabbit.

When Deer finally arrived, his eyes were big but he didn't seem disappointed. It was like he'd already known.

"Congratulations," he offered to Rabbit, who ducked his head and looked away.

From the back of the crowds, chattering gave way to full-blown wails. "Are you serious?" asked a voice. "Are you sure?"

Moose emerged from the crowd, a cloak of Hummingbirds around his head. They were all blending together, flashing their camouflage colors. "Uh, Rabbit? Can I have—would you be quiet?" he said to the birds. "There's been murmurings that you, uh, took a shortcut? Is there any truth to that?"

"A shortcut?" Rabbit asked, as if he'd never heard the word. "Not that I ... not that I know of ... I mean, I think I was on the trail ..."

The Hummingbirds railed, voices blending together. "I'm hearing," said Moose, "that there was a shortcut trail made. With markings, too."

"I don't—I mean, I'm not sure ..."

"Tell me this," said Moose. "If I go to the trail, which I will if I need to, will I find a shortcut? And a clearing with fallen branches that match your teeth marks?"

"Maybe." That was the closest to an admission that Rabbit could get himself to come.

"I see," said Moose. "Look, there's no crime here, okay? Not really. All we can do is, well, we're going to give the antlers to Deer. By default."

The whispers in the crowd grew to a stadium-level roar. Deer looked lost, confused, but even Rabbit had to admit: When the antlers sprouted like magic from Deer's head, he looked regal. They fit him. It was like they were meant to be.

"Are they heavy?" asked a young Skunk.

"A little," said Deer.

Rabbit could say nothing. He could only limp away, sucking at his bleeding gums and wishing painfully for that crown.

Chapter 22

"Is he gay?" I asked Olivia.

"Felipe? No!" she said.

I wished she'd lower her voice—we only had a few seconds. I didn't know Olivia well. It was one of those friend of a friend of an acquaintance type of situations and we were both clearly trying to force it. The only thing we had in common is that we were both single when everyone else was paired up. American-born Chinese, she called herself "skinny fat" and tried furiously to do all the things 20-somethings are supposed to do. Like host Thanksgiving in July parties, making us (her guests) drive all over town looking for cranberries and crunchy onions to put on the dishes we brought to her skinny townhome.

I'd come alone. I didn't know anyone but her. And I felt terribly awkward in a sea of very Portland, very white people with beer bellies. The men sported beards and the women makeup-free faces with the kind of confidence I could never muster.

Felipe was different. He'd brought his dog, Bagel, a half-beagle, half basset mix that could jump four feet on stumpy legs just to get to his lap. He looked immediately other, perhaps like how people saw me. Black, thick hair, eyes the color of good soil, and a V-shaped build that whispered of youth and gym-formed muscles. He was too perfect to be straight, though Olivia swore he was.

He was also five years younger than me, as we she. They'd met in college when she had a crush on him but he had a long-distance girlfriend. By the time she found out they'd broken up, her crush had faded to solid friendship.

Or at least that's what she said.

And when he brought up running, and his attempt to start, at the long stretch of a table, Olivia was quick to play wingwoman. "Justine's starting to run!" she said.

"Really?" he asked, and I felt cornered and like I had to make an admission. Make it clear that I wasn't a runner at all, but at least I was trying. I told the truth. Said I just woke up a few weeks ago and decided to run three miles to prove to myself I could. I didn't know that wasn't normal, and certainly that it wasn't considered healthy. Bad for the knees, the table agreed, but Felipe said nothing.

I timed it perfectly, making my way down the narrow bannister to the landing at the same time as him.

"If you ever want to go running, you should let me know," he said.

"Sure. I go most mornings."

"Cool. O has my number, just let me know."

It was as simple as that. Funny, how relationships start.

I knew nothing about him, gave myself three days before using the number I got from Olivia. "He's the nicest guy ever," she swore to me, but she didn't need to. I could read that in his eyes. Niceness, authenticity, it always scared me. She told me he was Costa Rican, how he studied chemistry in college. How he was getting ready to apply to med school now to be a surgeon.

"Why didn't you tell me the hot Latin guy was going to be a doctor?" I demanded. Suddenly he seemed even more perfect. And she just laughed.

"Would it have mattered?"

It would have mattered a great deal.

The first time I texted him, asking about a run on the waterfront, I could feel the hesitation in the words. I got it. I ran at five or six in the morning. To me that was normal, especially in a Portland summer. It was before the heat, before the birds, when the coolness of night wrapped itself around you. Plus, it got it over with for the day. But he agreed. He agreed. We scheduled a run at dawn starting below the Burnside Bridge.

He was late and I left my phone in the car. I hated to run with any kind of technology, though I'd brought my iPod as a buffer. When he did show up, fifteen minutes late and panting, he pointed to the bridges. All of them were raised, steeples from boats forcing the entire city to shut down. "Why'd you park on the east side?" I asked.

"I didn't realize," he said.

That's how I came to know. He was sweetly stupid, socially stupid, and brilliant at science. It was like showing an alien around, though he'd moved back from Costa Rica at thirteen. He knew nothing of the city, stuck to the Tigard suburbs instead. Barely drank, but when he did (in college) it led to blackouts and stomach pumping in the ER. I wasn't sure if I was up for this. It was like adopting a puppy.

In big rushes, he exposed all of himself to me. About how he and his three brothers were all adopted, and how every girl he'd ever liked or dated—and there weren't many— always ended up falling for his eldest brother. The one who couldn't drive because of so many DUIs and, sporadically, worked at jewelry stores in the mall. About his family back in Costa Rica and how he didn't miss them at all. About how all he ever wanted was to be a surgeon. "That will always be my first priority," he told me at the end of our run. I was the one who cut it short. He was so much faster than me. "Before any relationship or anything." It felt like a warning I could read as a challenge.

I hated that. How easy it was for a stranger to make you want them more than anything.

I forced myself onto Felipe because I'd already strung my heart to another. For the past four years, I'd offered my heart up, seasoned and peeled, to Chakor—who'd told me on the first date that he was earmarked for an arranged marriage. That he'd never been in a relationship and never would, not until his family had selected a woman for him. Through all the ups and downs, my heart was tired and Felipe seemed like an excellent way out.

We'd just so happened to meet at that fake Thanksgiving on a day when Chakor had drastically pissed me off with his moodiness, and I just wanted to move on. Move on. Move on.

"What are you waiting for?" I asked Felipe that afternoon, after he'd so effortlessly asked me to pie (pie!) at a suburban restaurant where his family knew the owners.

"For medical school? I don't know," he said. "I applied to a couple of schools but didn't get in. But really, that's not uncommon."

"What about Costa Rica? You don't want to go to school there?"

"I've thought about it. I have dual citizenship, and it's definitely cheaper there."

"When does the academic year start there?" I asked. I was already calculating.

"January."

"Huh."

I really needed to speed this whole relationship along, and it wasn't hard. He was beautiful, he was kind, and for some strange reason he seemed totally smitten with me. Four days after the run, I invited him to one of Sue-Ann's happy hours that I knew Daniel wouldn't be attending. Felipe came, played ping pong with the guys from her team, and we all ended up at the same karaoke bar where I'd had Jodeci sang to me all those years ago. It was crowded, everyone else was drunk, and I couldn't tell if Felipe actually liked me or not. Was he gay, and Olivia just didn't know it? I couldn't tell. He hadn't made a single move besides shaking his head, his long eyelashes lowered, when I'd offered to split the tab when we got pie.

The brick of the karaoke bar's exterior clung to my dress as I leaned against it.

"Look," I told Felipe, "I have enough friends." That's what made him kiss me for the first time. I guess we all rise to the occasion.

When I asked him to come to my car to make out, he agreed like a dutiful pet, but later told me he didn't know what making out was. If it was sex, or what. I didn't get it.

How could you live in this country and not know the commonest of phrases?

I overlooked a lot. His immaturity, his innocence—even his porn addiction. He was quickly forthcoming with it, and I didn't mind. Not really. And then he told me he thought it de-sensitized him to the real thing. The sex was okay, mediocre, but after the first time he said he didn't like going down on girls. It was bargaining time, and I gave him an ultimatum. Taught him how to do it.

I felt like he'd never be able to protect me.

Two months in, and he delivered a messy gift. "I just want you to know," he said, "when I was thirteen? Me and a bunch of my guy friends, back in CR, we were hanging out after school. And just, you know, decided to have sex."

"What?" I was in too deep now, too deep. I'd met his family, had brushed away his brother's advances until he called me an ugly bitch online. Had met Felipe's best friend from high school, a plain girl named Sara who was obviously in love with him. I couldn't back out now.

"I just didn't want to keep anything from you," he said.

"So, how ...? I mean. Like, giving? Receiving ..."

"Both," he said. Thirteen. I remembered being thirteen. I was obsessed with boys, of course, but I couldn't fathom getting together with a bunch of my girlfriends and kickstarting an orgy. Kids didn't do that. Did they? "I realized I didn't like it, so that was that."

I didn't say, "Wouldn't you realize really fast whether you liked it or not? How long did this go on? Why don't you consider thirteen the age you lost your virginity instead of eighteen?" It was best to just be quiet. Be quiet. Still, I felt like he was waiting for something in return. So I told him I was date raped, though I've never been certain if that was really true. That night, just a few years ago, was blurry. I'd said no, but I'd been the one to initiate communication afterwards. So I just let it sit there like a festering wound I knew better than to poke at.

Three months later, he got into medical school in Costa Rica and I clung to him as we went, together, into a place I'd never been and what everyone called paradise. Chakor texted me two days before I left after months of no communication. "Why didn't you just slap me?" he asked, but I was in waist-deep now and couldn't turn back.

I told him he could write to me in Costa Rica, but that I was going. I was going. I'd wasted too much time on him already. I left Portland with two suitcases and the bulk of my heart back in the rainy city.

Costa Rica showed itself like I imagined it would. Naked with dry palm trees and barely a whisper of civilization. Granted, we flew into Liberia—not San Jose—to spend a week with Felipe's family in his grandfather's home that was now shared amongst the generations. His cousin, Maya, picked us up and once she'd exhausted my limited Spanish, she said, "Solo ingles?" and Felipe replied for me. "I'm only going to speak Spanish to you from now on," she said. "So you learn." She clung true to her word, only breaking it once. When she called Felipe an asshole, along with a smattering of Spanish words, throwing the milk at his head after two days of staying in her closet (her literal closet) in San Jose as we searched for a house.

"We're leaving now," he said. But not before giving her a handful of colones to replace the milk.

It got bad, bad, bad and none of it was his fault. I hated the city, hated the country, from the machismo to the strange sense of entitlement that everyone seemed to have. "Where you from?" vendors would ask us, fanning out their palmito cheeses and metal jewelry. I could understand more Spanish than I could speak. "She's from America, I'm from here," he would say in that sing-song Tico Spanish.

"Bullshit," they would reply. *Mierda.* "All you gringos wish you could be us."

"I wish I was lying," he'd tell them, taking my hand and leading me away.

We did find a house, a little green casita in Moravia with a carniceria two blocks away and two Labradors, one white and one black, next door. They'd nuzzle us with their cold noses when we came home while their owners yelled their strangely English names from inside. "Michael! Evelyn!" and the dogs would tuck their tails and slump inside.

I was dying here. Folding in on myself. After a particularly trying time at Wal-Mart, the Tico idea of luxury, when there were no prices on the furniture and six different sales associates shrugged and said, "Pura vida," I broke down crying in the parking lot. It had been one month. I just couldn't take it anymore.

"I know, I know," Felipe said. And he did, maybe a little. But he didn't know what it was like to be so white here. To only understand a fistful of what was being said to you. About you.

When he started school, it got worse. I worked from home, writing travel blogs about being *en paraiso* and trying to make all the beaches and hotels sound like magic. That was easy, telling foreigners what they wanted to hear. Men would ring the bell, wielding their machetes, and try to negotiate with me to cut the grass. Beggars would clang on the metal gates at the sidewalk—every house was caged in from the street all the way around—and yell "*Upe!*" so I'd hide behind the couch until they left. I had nothing for them.

I began the online, emotional affair with Chakor almost immediately after I arrived. It was New Year's Eve, the night Felipe lit firecrackers by his grandfather's pool and fed me tortas that were perfectly burned from the *soda* shop across from the big white church.

I planned to leave him in the least painful way possible. There were plots and plans. But first, first, I got crazy about the cheap plastic surgery in Costa Rica. I went impulse buying. Tummy tuck, thigh lift, breast lift, upper arm lift, and various liposuctions to even it all out. Pay cash, and it was even cheaper. I did it all for twelve thousand dollars in nine long hours. Felipe had school, so I took the bus. "Respirar, respirar," said the anesthesiologist, and as I drifted out of consciousness I was terrified. I couldn't see his face.

"You need to breathe!" a woman screamed into my face, but I was groggy. I couldn't move my arms. I wanted her to leave me alone, I was so tired. "There you go, there you go," she said. Lazy lungs. Later I was told I was refusing to breathe on my own when they brought me out.

I looked like Frankenstein, felt worse, but told myself, "You did this to yourself. No use in complaining now."

Still, just one week later I climbed to the summit of a volcano with Felipe following closely behind. He must have sensed the ending. When the stitched yawned and blood blossomed on my stomach like a heliconia, I said, "It's kind of beautiful, isn't it?"

My plans went to shit. I'd picked up a gig travel writing for no pay, but plenty of comped perks. Five-star hotel rooms, ziplining, catamaran tours, and food vouchers to the best restaurants. It was all on the house. And it was Manuel Antonio, miles away and far after the car broke down on the bumpy dirty roads, where I did it. We were on a boat tour, both of us getting woozy and seasick. The words were worse than the vomit collecting in my throat, and I just couldn't hold them in anymore. It had been six weeks since surgery, and I'd already begged off sex with the best of excuse all that time.

"I'm going home," I told him.

"I know." That's all he said.

An Indian couple beside us, clearly on their honeymoon, asked us to take their picture and I let Felipe do the dirty work. He managed to snap one photo before both of us raced to the starboard and threw all our dirty innards to the salty waters.

xxiii.

By the time the two of them pulled into the dusty parking lot, through the wooden archway with the peeling paint, the girl was tired. When she'd agreed to this whole wolf sanctuary trip with her grandfather, she hadn't realized it would take four hours to get there. She was hot (his air conditioning wasn't nearly as good as her mother's), she had to pee, and he hadn't let her get what she wanted when they stopped for gas and a snack.

I think they're closed, she told him wishfully.

They're not closed, it's just not busy, he said. *That's a good thing.*

Was it?

There was a part of her, the little girl part of her which she was slowly burying, who knew she should be kind to her grandfather. But he annoyed her, and she just couldn't help it. They rolled out of his chortling green sedan and into the little gift shop where you could buy tickets and overpriced wolf stuffed animals.

One child, one senior? the teenage boy asked, and she blushed. Was it so obvious what her age was? How old her grandfather was? *You're just in time,* the clerk said. *Our resident tour guide is here.*

The first stop was a big wolf that looked and acted like a huskie. She wasn't scared of him at all—and she shouldn't have been. *This one you can pet,* said the guide, but the big wolf-dog knocked her down and began sniffing at her pants. Her face turned bright red, but neither the middle-aged guide or her grandfather seemed to realize it's because she was on her period. It was only her third. *Sorry about that! He's not usually like that,* said the guide and she averted her eyes. Pretended to be busy brushing off the dirt.

Some of the wolves, it was obvious why they were here. There was the fox-colored one with missing eyes. They thought he'd perhaps been caught and tortured since the vet said the wounds seemed to be made with a tool instead of the fangs of another animal. There was the black one with three legs and bright orange eyes. *This one's wild-wild,* said the guide, an Indian with a black braid to his waist. *Stay away from him. He's killed two wolves in the sanctuary already—he's in solitary confinement now.* She didn't have to be told. She could see the ferality in his eyes. He watched her like she was a pot roast.

But the wolf in the cage one over—that one. He was snowy white with big brown eyes that should have belonged in a Labrador. *What about this one?* she asked.

Ah, he's sweet! said the guide. *But he was raised since he was a pup as a pet. Can't make it in the wild on his own now.*

Her heart broke a little for him. She knew exactly how he felt. *You want to pet him?* the guide asked. *There were little girls where he grew up. He's used to you.*

"Little girl" hurt some, but not enough for her to say no. She nodded, and the guide began to untangle the complicated locks to get into the white wolf's cage. Inches away, the night-colored wild one waited. Watched. His pupils never changed, stayed just as pinpoint-thin as ever.

She wanted to tell the guide to watch out. To not turn his back against the mean-looking one. But the words stuck in her throat like peanut butter.

Hey, I don't think— began her grandfather, but it was too late.

It wasn't the guide the black wolf was looking at. It was the other wolf. He was half the size of most wolves and slipped through the loose wires between the gates in a snap, knocking the guide back and barreling straight for the sweet white wolf.

Get back! Get back! the guide yelled, quickly stringing the gate to the world back up and locking the two wolves in together.

She wanted to look down, away, anywhere but at the wolves but she couldn't. As her grandfather dragged her away, bright blossoms of blood were blooming on the white wolf's coat. But then again, blood on the black wolf wouldn't show itself.

Which one is going to win? she asked her grandfather as they settled back into the car for the hours-long trip home. She couldn't bring herself to ask which one was going to die.

He shrugged. *The strongest one,* he said. *The one they feed the best.*

Chapter 23

For four years we toiled, tried to summon growth out of the hard clay soil. I met Chakor like I met them all—on a night when I was flirting between buzzed and drunk. Both our wrists were stained with stamps and his first words to me, "You wear a wicked grin," are forever burned into my limbic system. He told me over our first formal drinks that he was meant for an arranged marriage, but he didn't even want that. But it's why he chased the older women with the dyed red hair through the night. Dated strippers and girls who stole his credit cards from his wallet.

I didn't choose him. It just was, and we just needed to hold on.

I did hold on, through all those stubborn years. How many of these men were peppered in between our meeting and trying to define the difference between monogamy and exclusivity? Sometimes I'm not certain. They all blend together, wild, animals.

I ran away to Costa Rica with Felipe to try and forget him. The Puerto Rican was supposed to be my getaway, but he turned into an anchor. Titan delighted over my misery. I looked for Chakor in all of them, sought that black-black mole and those over-ripened lips in every person I took to bed. But they could only wear his mask for a little while.

There was the boy who asked, *How do I know it's mine?* before I had the mistake vacuumed out. The one I left on impulse after seven nothing years—who, when I asked years later why he didn't fight for me, said, *I realized you weren't worth fighting for.* Remember the one who looked so damned good at the bar in that across the room second—the alcoholic I traded cries with, crumpled in his medical scrubs? Then there was the man whose dreadlocks whipped my arms raw, lucked in with a visa lottery who fed me sips of rum on our first date. His accent was lovely, heady and congealed but still, he wasn't him. Chakor usurped them all, needled deep into my meat, the organs, into the weight of my bones, the everything of all I had to give.

And I waited, I did. For the infatuation to ease and for him to stop taking up every little space in my thoughts. It never stopped. Distractions aren't meant to be permanent.

Chakor smelled like bread in the mornings, something I want to curl into. All rising yeast and cardamom notes. It's in the early hours when it's sweetest, unable to open both eyes and black ribbons of hair break free from yesterday's oil. His heat bakes into the blankets like an oven—that's why I come back after my tea, after the lemon squeezes, after the first writings pour from my fingertips. In tangled sheets and waves of duvets I ride the surf into the morning sun with him, tucked safe as a child in those arms.

It was a place, a space, I just couldn't leave.

There were ugly fights, hideous cries, and after six years finally—finally—he took me to India and told his family. I'd never seen him so nervous, knee bouncing like a shaky rickshaw while his mother beamed before me. His father, arms crossed and petulant, looked just like him when he was angry. Was I supposed to be intimidated? It took my all not to laugh.

And still, we sleep like dogs, backs pressed flush against each other. Pack animals, he'll guard the door while I keep watch of the closet—who knows what monsters may appear, which drunk neighbors might rattle down the hall. His body's musk slips moist fingers over my hips, sticks my skin to his while we curl in for the night. Bony knees and thick thighs reach outward like stars in our cry, our little litter, our mute in the duvet wilds.

And when we married ... when we married ... I was to be blanketed in a Paneter saree with threads of gold and his mother's heavy bridal jewelry—all tikka headpiece and freshly pierced nose. For me, I was playing dress up. The seven walks around the fire, the hiding of the shoes, it meant nothing to me, just like the Christmas trees were lost on him. That's why I bought a turquoise garter, peacocked with feathers, jewels and beads to slip like something naughty beneath the heavy silk folds. Nobody but us would know of it, the Americana abreast my hennaed legs like a wedding topper too foreign and foolishly superstitious to admit.

From him I learned the art of waiting, the art of patience. I thought I knew quiet, drenched myself in it as a child, wore it like a puffy coat well into adulthood—when quiet breaks down, you can bury yourself in layers of fat and bad skin. But when that sloughed off I was left with nothing. No quiet, no buffer, nothing to keep me safe from the shark-like assaults of the world. He showed me what it means to wait. To not speak just to soften awkwardness, not demand answers when they're as undeveloped as the embryos I flushed from my body, never regretted remnants from the lost years.

He taught me the beauty of closed lips, the power of reticence and how to command, thundering like a lion with my eyes.

Let Me Go Quietly

I don't want anyone saying they knew me
should I die ahead of others or when I'm gone
before the whispers. I don't want women
I can't stand, who despise me pound for pound,
muttering niceties over raw earth or prettying up
memories alongside casseroles. I don't want
men sniffing around, saying how lovely
I was when they used to comment on my bones,
the propensity of my skin to mar. I want you

to be the only one to say my name like it mattered.
The body of my pieces I wrote for you, the meat
of my words thickened from our story and the heat
from what we bore isn't for the gawkers
or forced, awkward acquaintances. Let them forget me,
feel satisfied that their bodies wore out last,
store up those social graces like pinching shoes
they'll never wear. You're the witness
to my entirety, attestant of my every,
the only I want following
my loping footsteps into the deep.

Forthcoming Titles
For a full list of books available soon from Musehick Publications
please check out http://www.musehickpublications.com

Made in the USA
Middletown, DE
13 September 2019